Soon After

Soon After

Sherryle Kiser Jackson

www.urbanchristianonline.net

Urban Books, LLC
78 East Industry Court
Deer Park, NY 11729

ISBN 13: 978-1-60162-867-1
ISBN 10: 1-60162-867-6

First Printing September 2010
Printed in the United States of America

10 9 8 7 6 5 4 3 2 1

Distributed by Kensington Corp.
Submit Wholesale Orders to:
Kensington Publishing Corp.
C/O Penguin Group (USA) Inc.
Attention: Order Processing
405 Murray Hill Parkway
East Rutherford, NJ 07073-2316
Phone: 1-800-526-0275
Fax: 1-800-227-9604

SOON AFTER

Dedication

To LB Kiser, my dad and Delores B. Kiser; your parenting was the perfect blend between bravery and vulnerability, traditional rigidity and flexibility. The epitome of compassion, you let me and Monique see the dents in your armor and let us learn from them. Next to Christ, you are my heroes.

Acknowledgements

I never wanted to write a sequel, let alone, a mystery of sorts. I am a Christian fiction writer with heaven, not the hell of crime scenes and jail in my view. But I went there. It was indeed a journey that started in January '09 when my executive editor, Joylynn Jossel, advised that I neither put anymore time nor another book between my debut novel, *Soon and Very Soon*, and its sequel. So thanks, Joylynn, for that.

I wanted to be a career writer, so this was the test. I had to turn this around in nine months. I knew it could be done. All good writers, Cleage, Briscoe, Dickey, and the dynamite Christian fiction authors, Kimberla Lawson Roby, Victoria Christopher Murray and all the Urban Christian authors write on a schedule, right? They show me the tireless effort of writers that create, edit, market, and promote all inside of a year. I met some great people and learned some invaluable lessons at the '09 Faith and Fiction retreat, as well as the '09 National Book Club Conference. What an amazing job and undertaking of authors, Tiffany L. Warren and Curtis Bunn respectively, to bring together readers and writers on such a grand scale.

I think it was Victoria Christopher Murray, who many affectionately dub as the godmother of modern Christian fiction, that talked about her recurring character, Jasmine as a franchise character in one of her interviews. I thought about that when bringing back Willie and Vanessa Green. Whole

Acknowledgments

NBA teams are built around a franchise player, and the Greens as a newlywed couple that live between ministry and insanity had not finished telling their stories to me. What do you know? There might be a part three. Lord willin' and the creek don't rise.

Thanks to all that dispensed legal advice, Christine Northern, Crystal Evans, and Tonia Fergueson. It's convoluted to me. Did I interpret that right? To Lisa A. Herb at ATF and Joy Copeland who pointed me in the direction of a series of books to begin my fire investigations research, I appreciate the help.

Ms. Ella Curry, your manifold blessing is on the way for helping me and the world of Black literature as a whole. I know no one who works as hard as you.

To all my friends, family, saints, sorors, boosters, and road dogs, thanks for taking the ride with me to the brink of insanity.

Sherryle Kiser Jackson

Prologue

Alexis Montgomery, the local assignment reporter, didn't hear her Channel 7 production assistant re-enter the editing room. She was listening to old voice tracks from the Harvest Baptist Church fire story she broke nearly a week previous on Easter Sunday and a subsequent report recorded earlier. Martie Hamilton plopped down beside her and began unpacking his dinner.

"It's dying, Martie," Alexis said, dropping her face to the desktop. "My piece is dying right before my eyes."

"What happened? You were so adamant at this morning's production meeting that this was a story with legs—good enough for the *Inside 7* segment. Everyone was saying, the new girl has got spunk. She's already figured out how to work the system and get resume-worthy air time. I thought you were going out to do another remote after that speed camera's piece you covered this afternoon. Sunset is catching up with you, kiddo."

"No one has any free time. I can't pay a crew to go out, and what's the use? It's the same charred and crumbled mess. I must have been high off of Frappuccino this morning. I've been so concerned finding the right story to get me more air time and beat those jerks on assignment at the other station to the anchor chair, that I'm stuck. I thought I'd get clearance to walk inside by now, detail the damage, you know, or to at least get a fire official to shoot some footage for us. That's it. The building's taped off, and I'm waiting for the magic word."

"So much for passing out Starbucks gift cards to the Bureau secretaries and other informants around town," he said with a smirk. "You're playing anchor on assignment. There is a long road to the anchor chair, darling. Very few find that golden story, become the golden guy or gal of the station, and have their profiles framed out every night on nightly news, especially in this area. It's too much going on. Sorry to put it to you this way, but you've got the community beat, not politics, not sports nor high-crime. You're the low man on the totem pole. By the way, Stan told me to give you the heads up. The Marc train derailment that happened mid day will have two remotes tomorrow, Greenbelt and New Carrolton. You'll be splitting yourself in half tomorrow. But if anyone can do it, it's you, Milky."

Alexis winced at the nickname she has tried hard to shake. She garnered that nickname back home in the small town of Kannapolis, North Carolina where she started out, also on assignment. She was known to do anything for a story, kiss babies, handle animals, and demonstrate stunts. While reporting on the county fair she stepped in to demonstrate how to milk a cow. The oversized cow doused her with more than a fair share of milk. Because she was reporting live, she continued her interview with the dairy farmer, unknowingly giving the tri-state area an eye full of her ample bosom through her white blouse. The film made it to a national blooper show when the pig of a camera man who couldn't manage to shoot the frame from eye level sent a copy of it in. It ran repeatedly.

Needless to say, she got a lot of unwanted attention. It was like the beauty queen turned weather girl. Alexis was offered the most bizarre assignments. Any opportunity to get sweaty or dirty for the good of the story was given directly to her. She was quite popular, but for all the wrong reasons. She was a journalist. She wanted to be taken seriously. So she left the station choosing not to be pigeon-holed into the role of media eye candy.

Alexis watched Martie open a bag of chips and shook a few on his Reuben stacker before pressing the rye bread with the flat of his hand until the chips snapped like twigs and the thousand island dressing seeped out the sides like sap. She didn't want him to see her sulk, so she took possession of his half-empty bag of chips as she thought about her story. She certainly didn't spend time setting this story up just to start another assignment. That would give another available reporter, or worse, an anchor the chance to revive the story when the truth was uncovered. She didn't know why, but she had faith in this story as an investigative piece. *She should have gone out to do more leg work in her spare time—spoke to some more people in the community.*

"The big boys agreed to run the follow up. It can't be that bad." Martie noticed her pained expression and offered her the other half of his sandwich with a nod of his head.

"It's like day old carryout," Alexis whined.

"It's not like we've never warmed up leftovers on network news before. Let's hear it."

Alexis pushed the PLAY on the machine that timed her new voice recording-over to the week-old footage of the burnt and hydrant soaked church building.

This is Alexis Montgomery for Channel 7 news. You might remember on Easter Sunday we brought you our first report of a fire at a local church. What was unusual was the praise vigil that brought previous members back to this edifice in memorial to their former church home. As we've been reporting, the Harvest Baptist Church located in the 8900 block of Lincoln Avenue in Capitol Heights, Maryland remains taped off from everyone but authorities as an ongoing investigation of the Easter morning inferno continues. Sources tell us officials from both the PG County Fire Department and the

local sheriff's department have ruled out electrical failure, but are
guarded as to the actual cause of the blaze. What we do know is that
early estimates of $400,000 dollars in damages have been increased
to a little over a half a million. The question remains—was this fire a
random act or intentionally set? This last but important detail has to
be determined before plans of rebuilding can begin.

"It ran at five and six. Didn't even make the recap at seven
before the World Report. I can kiss the *Inside* segment goodbye." Alexis spoke of the local weekly news magazine that was
similar to *60 Minutes*, which was the closest a newbie like her
got to anchoring if the story was right. She had seen some assignment reporters have the great fortune of covering a wind-
fall of a story that garnered those recurring weeks with the
host, Lizzy London, at the anchor's desk.

"Might run at eleven, but won't have a chance without a
fresh remote and a fresh angle. Six A.M., New Carrolton Metro station—interview commuters inconvenienced by the Marc
train situation," Martie said.

She would be there. She had to if she wanted to keep her job, but
she wasn't interested in any derailment story. The Harvest Baptist
Church story fascinated her. The building reminded her of
her church home and of her grandfather who was the pastor
there. She didn't see too many of these small congregations
thriving in the midst of the mega ministries in the DC Metropolitan area. Even some of the most historic ministries had
upgraded or had a face-lift or two. The people she saw that
Easter Sunday decked out in their Easter apparel were rooted
in faith and the traditions of the church.

Alexis missed her old church that was the center of her
rural community. Maybe that's why she hadn't been able to
find a church home that suited her after moving to the metropolitan area and breaking into broadcast journalism. Her
grandfather had been concerned that she'd lose her soul chas-

ing her dreams to the big city. In addition to leaving the sexist station, she was trying her best to outrun the ghost of shame she had tried to leave behind in Kannapolis.

"There's something there. There is more. I'm going out on my free time tomorrow to find it." New determination was in her eyes.

"What is it about this story? I don't get it. This is not like that string of church fires in Alabama. This is one isolated case—an act of God. Isn't the mark of a good journalist to know when to move on? I'm afraid you're going to lose your objectivity going after your perception of truth.

"For one thing, this church has got a cast of characters a mile long. I've kept a list from my initial report," she said, consulting a notebook full of notes. There is the former pastor who conveniently moved on after a nasty split from his members a few months before the suspicious fire, a deacon who sparked the whole rift, a new pastor who stands to get a new building depending on the insurance figures, and a homeless guy who is like a renegade that found Christ and now is hungry for a pulpit and a willing ear."

"There's your stories right there. Pitch them to the *Inside* 7 producers." Martie put his hands up in a revelatory gesture.

"I'm tracking down a few, but I don't want to work a tabloid piece, Martie. I'm a serious journalist. Besides, if this thing swings the way I think it will, the aforementioned better have good lawyers lined up. Mark my words: that church didn't burn down by itself." She indicated to him that he had a glob of Thousand Island dressing left in the corner of his mouth, which he promptly took a napkin to.

"Many reporters on assignment have built a successful career on tabloid-ish, or what I like to call human interest stories. The really great ones know how to mix both. Go after your stories. I'll back you at the next production meeting."

"Thanks, Martie."

Just then her Blackberry vibrated. A text from her source at the fire department who she met after the first story was telling her to check her email. She remembered extending him a generous fifty dollar coffee tab for allegiance. Alexis strained her eyes to make out the miniature scanned report that was on its way to the office of the Prince Georges County Fire Marshal and Maryland State Fire Department marked with the magic word–arson. She didn't need Martie's backing. All of a sudden her story had sprouted legs and was walking.

Chapter 1
No Rest for The Weary

Willie Green strolled leisurely from the front entrance of the Pleasant Harvest Baptist Church to the office suite. He was keenly aware that his feet were confined to his dress shoes and his neck was noosed by his tie. As busy as his year had been combining churches with his wife, the couple decided to take an early vacation, a free frolicking Spring Break, like college students take. It started Easter Monday and lasted one blissful, congregation-free week. After seven days and six nights of sleeping in, walking along the Jersey shoreline, and dinning out at the quaint restaurants of Cape May, it was official. He had to go back to work.

He spotted Luella, their administrative assistant, on the telephone as he cleared the corner. He could tell by the tilt of her head and the coil of telephone cord around her finger that she had been conversing for a while and that the call was a personal one. Their absence had not offered her time off, but rather had offered a more relaxed work schedule. He cleared his throat to announce his arrival.

"Goodness, Pastor. You scared me," Luella said, pausing to say goodbye to someone who had enough sense to quickly relinquish the call. She stood up. "Sorry."

With a wave of his hand, Willie assured her that she hadn't committed any cardinal sin. "Next time I'll announce myself with a chorus of 'Sign me up for the Christian Jubilee'."

The joke was lost on her. She was a young woman with an old name. She couldn't be any older than thirty. Good home and business school training, but a bit too staunch for his taste. Give him personable over professional any day, like his old church clerk and mother-figure, Mae Richardson, who had passed away right before their churches combined. Willie and Luella hadn't quite bonded, but Willie could understand why she and Vanessa meshed so well. His wife was all business, all the time. She would give Luella an itemized list of things to do with a timeline, then lock herself away for hours working on a project. Willie was always stir crazy locked in his office too long and craved social interaction by noon.

"I figured since it was after eleven that you and Sister Pastor were taking another day off. Where is Sister Pastor, by the way?"

"She's taking another day. Like you said, sometimes you need a vacation after your vacation." He covered his mouth with his hand as if to let her in on a secret. "I think she just wanted a Willie-free day."

Willie had thought certain that Vanessa would be ready to return to the church operations as well. He had always known her to quickly move on to the next thing. She had outlined at least four sermons while they were away that he knew she wanted to cross reference with the catalog of sermons she kept on her office computer. Plus she was involved in the planning of both the upcoming Trinity Conference and the Church's 50th Anniversary.

He gave her a lecture about being present, enjoying the moment, and not taking too much work with them on their vacation. Once she got the idea, he figured it was taking her awhile to switch back out of relax mode. Willie nudged her at 8 A.M. and then again at nine thirty when he finally got up to eat and get dressed. She rattled off some excuse from their four poster bed as if he were her employee and she was calling in sick.

"Well, I certainly have missed you two, and so have the fifty or so people who've called or left messages for you all," Luella said in her chipper cadence.

As if on cue, her desk telephone rang at that moment. Willie listened as she acknowledged the caller with a perky and polite Pleasant Harvest greeting. "As a matter of fact, he's right here," Luella said, banking the call before he could object.

"So much for getting situated," Willie murmured as he looked for a place to rest his briefcase.

"She's on line two."

"She?" Willie asked. His finger was poised on the receiver.

"Alexis Montgomery, a reporter for Channel 7." She referenced a pad on her desk. "Called twice while you were away and once this morning. That would put her at the top of your call back list."

Willie put up a finger to halt further explanation as he tried to figure out for a moment the possible nature of the call. "Hello, this is Pastor Willie Green."

"Pastor Green, this is Alexis Montgomery. I am the assignment reporter that did the remote interview with you at the site of the Harvest Baptist Church on Easter Sunday."

"Yes, I remember," Willie said.

"I was wondering if I can set up an appointment to sit down with you to discuss a story idea I'm working on that would go into your affiliation with that church," Alexis said.

Willie shook his head as he thought of the four months it had taken him to let go of his affiliation to Harvest Baptist Church, where he had served as a pastor for the past ten years. His mini vacation had helped to further remove himself from the recent calamity at his former church and its ramifications on the now homeless members.

Willie let out a puff of air. He felt a headache coming on. "Ms. Montgomery, I literally just got in the office. Let me get situated and get back to you as soon as I can."

"Please, Pastor Green, this meeting, like everything in journalism, is time sensitive," she pleaded.

"Ms. Montgomery," Willie said, cutting off her hard sale with a diplomatic voice. "I am passing the phone to our secretary to get your call back information. Talk to you soon. Be blessed."

Willie heard Luella ask the reporter to hold before banking the call again.

"I'm an administrative assistant," Luella said.

"Huh?"

"You called me a secretary. 'I am handing the phone off to my secretary.' My title is administrative assistant."

Her tone was serious, but not sassy, so Willie looked at the young woman standing on the other side of the desk briefly to see if he had hurt her feelings, "Sorry."

She reached across the desk and handed him a stack of mail and papers secured in folders and bound with a rubber band. "I guess I should debrief you. Wanna go in Sister Pastor's office or the study?"

Willie thought about it. "No, I'm going down the hall to my office. Give me a minute, you know, let me get acclimated to being at work again before coming down."

Willie approached the door of the office that he used to seclude himself. The door was freshly stained after removing the lettering that read: FIRST LADY'S LOUNGE. This had been the space where his mother-in-law kept his now wife and her sister out of their dad's hair when they were little and where they entertained the companions of traveling ministers. It was down the hall from Daddy Morton's personal study and the adjoining office that was now Vanessa's spacious headquarters.

His wife was rooted here, and being in a space that was once her father's had to have special meaning for her, Willie thought.

Although he had pondered remodeling the office suites to suit them both, he didn't want to have that debate with Vanessa. It would be like negotiating more closet space at home. It wasn't worth the breath. He didn't know why it bothered him so much. Maybe because he was the co-pastor to a congregation of nearly 500 whose office was in a lounge. It was a modest size office minus the gingham covered couches and doily-covered coffee table. In fact, with the addition of his old office furniture and desk set, it was eerily like his office at Harvest Baptist Church. Maybe he was being a stereotypical man, but size did matter.

The pile Luella gave him got tossed in the center of his desk along with his keys. From his briefcase, he extracted a souvenir photo of him and Vanessa on a dinner cruise. The empty case got placed by the door for the return trip home after placing the photo in a prominent position. He took great satisfaction in booting up his office computer. According to technicians, his computer rendered the only stable connection to the outside world when they had come to work on the church's system. They had no immediate solution to getting Vanessa's computer online or maintaining Luella's connection. He welcomed Vanessa and Luella who had no choice but to come-a-knockin' every so often on Willie's door when they needed to reach out to resources beyond the Pleasant Harvest network.

Willie was trying to figure out the password to the guest-book feature that allowed people to reach out to their ministry online for prayer requests when Luella buzzed to say she would be coming down. He unraveled the bundle he was given earlier so he could be prepared. Contracts for conference space and spreadsheets of allocated funds for the Trinity Conference followed by a few preacher profiles cluttered his desk. There were checks made out with a financial secretary report that needed Vanessa's authorizing signature. Underneath all that was a call back list of people he didn't know and drafts of ministry lessons he didn't create.

Luella entered after a short rap on the door. She extended more papers for him to grasp. "I accidentally gave you Sister Pastor's pile."

Although he was still gathering Vanessa's bundle back together, he noticed Vanessa's pile was considerably thicker.

"So what do you have for me?" Willie asked.

"Membership roles, invitations, a couple of messages, and a few commercial Bible study aides to review."

"Is that it? " Willie said.

"Yep," she assured.

Willie looked up at her from her tailor-made suit to her tailor-made smile. He wondered if she could be stashing his work in File 13. He looked through Vanessa's pile again. Although he and Vanessa had informally designated the membership needs to him and the business end of the ministry to her, who was to say he couldn't handle both in her absence?

"Why don't you sit down, Luella?" Willie said, noticing how she anxiously stomped the heel of her right shoe into the carpet. "How did things really go while we were away? Tell me about Sunday."

He watched her sit down hesitantly in the small leather upright chair across from his desk and tilt her legs to the side before crossing them at the ankles. She used Vanessa's inbox pile that he had given back to her to cover her lap. Willie pushed back in his chair as if he were about to unload his burdens to a therapist.

"Well, Sunday was interesting. Minister Morton preached.

No, it was more like she taught a lesson on Faithfulness. Although she kind of lost people, trying to relate the text to her personal stories about her engagement and wedding planning. It was like Star Jones on *The View* before her wedding to Al Reynolds." Luella chuckled, allowing herself to fall back into the pad of the chair. She caught herself and brought back the professional polish with a fake cough. She stood. "It was good though."

Keisha Morton was Vanessa's sister and the current minister to the singles at Pleasant Harvest. She surprised everyone when she informally announced her engagement to Willie's mentee, Paul Grant, on Easter Sunday.

"Oh, and tell Sister Pastor that I'd like to personally thank you both for not informing her sister and your sister-in-law that you were going out of town when you asked her to preach." Her perturbed expression revealed the sarcasm.

This time Willie chuckled. "She worried you to death, didn't she?"

"She called for a moratorium on scheduling things on the church calendars until she decided on a date for the wedding. How dare you go out of town before she officially declared the date for the wedding of the century? Dra-ma," Luella sang.

They both shared a good laugh before Willie said, "All I can say is pray for Paul."

"Pray for us all," Luella responded, doing an about face for the door.

"Wait a minute," Willie said, halting her retreat. "What about my members?"

"We had to use the Ministry Tree you came up with. I know Sister Pastor thought it wouldn't work for a congregation this size, but the chain of command really worked well. We alerted all ministry heads that you were out of town. Plus put a note on our website. Then Theodora Marshall was rushed to the hospital on Wednesday."

"And?" Willie said, cutting her off. This is what he had been waiting for. This was the kind of stuff that got his blood pumping.

"We started at the bottom and worked up. She is a part of the Prayer Partners Ministry. We called the ministry leader, who in turn kept her watchcare deacon and ministry members updated. I even went to see her myself on Thursday after work. Another member was about to be evicted, but that got resolved. I made you a report that I will email you later."

Willie didn't want a report. He wanted Luella to sit down and describe for him how Sister Marshall looked. Was she rail-thin or did she look about ready for a chicken dinner, as Mae would have categorized it? He wanted to know details about the sacrifices people made to help her and others in need. He wanted to hear how the saints rallied around her and prayed for her strength.

"Like I said, the Ministry Tree worked well and should alleviate some of the personal responsibility that falls on you and Sister Pastor," Luella said, practically from the doorway.

Work so well they won't need me, Willie thought. "Wait, why do you keeping rushing off?"

Luella's voice was anxious. "I forgot that I have to complete some important business for Sister Pastor."

"What about the people I asked you about for the Young People's initiative?"

"That's what the membership roles are for, Brother Pastor." Luella backtracked to his desk. She flipped back the cover and pointed, "See here, I printed a spreadsheet of all our members with children ages eleven to eighteen for the Young Missionaries Program and those who have boys ages six and up for the Scouts. This was based on the combined church census we conducted right after Unification. It should adequately represent our membership. I need to show you how you can sort the database for whatever category you want. Then you can play around with it while you are at work."

Vanessa had important business; he had time to play, Willie thought. This church had more children than he had members at Harvest Baptist, with not many church structured activities to promote growth and fellowship. The Young Missionaries program could offer the right young people from their congregation the opportunity to train locally and travel across the nation helping others. Far be it for their *administrative assistant,* who was also a member, to help recommend some people for the program. A perfectly formatted document did not tell Willie who to approach to help start a scouting program at church.

What am I complaining for, he thought, *she had done her job.*

Luella stood at his desk as if she awaited a hall pass. He motioned for her to sit down again. Vanessa was at home, and her assistant would just have to help him with his pressing business.

"So, what do we know about this reporter who called?" Willie said, once again pushing back in his chair, this time to cross his legs.

"She called a couple of times—sounded real anxious to get in touch with you. Then on Thursday people started calling the church after the noon broadcast because they were talking about the fire at your old church again on the news."

"I wonder what she wants to talk to me about," Willie said more to himself than to her.

"I don't know," Luella replied.

"I guess if I don't call her back in a timely fashion, she will have to find someone else for her interview." He began clicking his ink pen to a rhythm to help him think. "What do you think?"

"I think you should call Sister Pastor. She always knows what to do."

"Thanks, Luella," he said abruptly. She stood for a third time and headed for the door. He didn't know what he was hesitant for, or why he needed anyone to justify his actions. It was time for him to take charge. "Get me that reporter's number."

"I gave it to you with your other messages, Brother Pastor. It's number one on your call back list," she called to him from the hallway.

He consulted his watch before picking up the phone to dial. It was only one o'clock. It felt as if he had worked a whole day already and it was barely lunch time. He was determined to plow through his membership roles and make some decisions on the Young People's initiative, then get out to see Sister Marshall at the hospital before heading home.

There were two numbers listed for Alexis Montgomery. He chose the latter that appeared to be a cell phone number in hopes of connecting the call directly. She picked up on the third ring.

"This is Alexis."

"Ms. Montgomery, this is Pastor Willie Green returning your call."

"Great, I'm glad you got back with me so fast. Like I said I want to move on this story quickly. I'm looking to do a series of angles on this story to propose at the next production meeting in hopes of stretching the story to its fullest potential."

"I guess you need to help me understand. There was a fire. It made the news. I guess I don't see what is left to report." He used his first two fingers of his right hand to gesture.

"I don't know if you're familiar with the *Inside* 7 segment, but it is our weekly News Magazine where we bring a more in depth coverage on local stories of interest. We get so bogged down with D.C. area politics that this show is devoted to the people of the D.C. Metro area. When I broke the story

I knew it had potential, but recent reports and support from our viewers makes us here at Channel 7 believe that this is a story that's worth investigating further."

"I see," Willie said although he did not completely see his role in the whole thing.

"I interviewed several people, but you're the only one I could get in contact with again because I had written down the name of your new church. The initial report sparked quite a bit of mail bag response. Many want to reach out to the members of your former church. I'm sure you've been thinking about that to."

"My wife and I pastor another church," Willie responded absentmindedly as a surge of guilt took over him. He had not thought about the people, many of which he used to pastor. He had not thought about the community he loved to service. He had not thought about Charley Thompson, the deacon that was so adamant about staying at Harvest that he rallied members behind his back to sign a petition to stop the move to no avail.

"Do you think we can get together this afternoon so we can discuss this further?" Alexis asked.

"I don't know," Willie said. Indecisiveness once again was taking hold.

"Please, Pastor, you are my only solid lead. I went back to the neighborhood today and everyone talked so highly of the church when it was under your pastorate."

Willie thought about it. "My afternoon is booked. I have to visit a member in the hospital before heading home this afternoon."

"I could meet you at your home. The initial interview won't take long. I could even bring something to eat." Willie could hear the desperation in her voice.

"No," Willie said, thinking about Vanessa's reaction if a

strange woman brought food into their house. "That won't be necessary."

"Maybe you need to call your wife first and get back to me."

It was an innocent statement that was said by someone he was sure didn't mean anything by it. "That won't be necessary either. You can meet me at my home around 6:30 this evening. I live at 442 Barney Lane in Temple Hills."

She thanked him as if she had been waiting all day for that answer. He emptied his lungs out in a puff of air as he replaced the receiver.

After nearly forty-five minutes of staring down at the membership document Luella had prepared for him, he folded the cover back over. He would be taking work home tonight. He prepared himself to leave for the hospital. He looked at their dinner cruise picture and said, 'Honey, guess who's coming to dinner?"

Chapter 2

Battin' Down the Hatches

Vanessa found herself temporarily caught up in the lives of those appearing in front of the judge on *The People's Court*. One episode in particular pit a mother against her own daughter. It was the case of the college refund. The mother was suing the daughter for the amount of her college tuition after the daughter went off to school in her third year and eloped with someone of a different race. The mother, who was obviously hurt and seeking revenge, claimed she didn't send her daughter to school for marriage, therefore their agreement was broken. *So much for forgiveness*, Vanessa thought. She found herself calling out to the television, "You need to get your butt out of court and heal your family before the Lord comes back and passes down real judgment for your tail."

When she looked at her bedside clock, she realized it was 1:00 P.M. She expected Willie to call her when he reached the office to let her know what tasks lay in store for her upon her return, but she was glad he didn't. She hadn't bothered to call him either or check in with Luella. She hadn't realized how hard she had been working until she woke up this morning immobilized.

Vanessa had a gift of discernment. Sometimes it wasn't always a privilege to perceive things beyond what the natural eye could see. Something felt wrong or out of place. Since she could not put her finger on the likely source or severity of the problem, she did nothing. She decided to pray it away. In her relationship with God, she knew Him to be a guide that would send a word in and out of season. Something she would likely preach next week might be the very sustenance for someone's life next month. She thought about her meditations with the Lord, some that led to sermon topics. Wasn't it she that just recently preached, "Battin' down the Hatches," about the Apostle Paul's shipwreck on the island of Malta?

She had told her congregation that being a prisoner, Paul could hardly persuade his captors that the favorable weather they chose to sail in would soon turn deadly. Just like Paul predicted, there was a change of winds and tides, and a powerful storm arose. Before it was all said and done, they had to band the ship with ropes and throw cargo off, eventually crashing off the coast of the island.

Oh Lord not again, Vanessa thought. She had spent the better part of the morning watching foolishness when she should have been praying. It wasn't that she couldn't handle what the devil threw her way. Paul had received assurance from the Lord that although it appeared the ship may go down, there would be no loss of life—all would be saved; Vanessa didn't feel so sure. Ironically, she remembered using that point in her sermon to get everyone happy when she proclaimed, "Go through the storm. It might seem rough. You may even feel like you're in isolation, shipwrecked with your problem, marooned on an island with despair. *But* your promise is on the other side of the storm. There is a rescue team led by God looking for you." She had even gotten happy herself.

She didn't want to go through another tumultuous storm. She was tired. The thought made her yawn.

Vanessa set off for the kitchen to scrounge around for something to eat. She picked a few grapes from the fruit bowl to help freshen her mouth from the bag of Doritos she had demolished earlier bedside. She had not thawed anything that could be an entrée for the night's meal. Willie would be home soon and not having something prepped and underway was a cardinal sin in their household, especially since she was home all day.

She wasn't a great cook, but she had gotten a lot better at it with the help of her sister, Keisha, and television cooking shows. She had to take up the art of cooking after marrying Willie last year and deciding she didn't want the women of the congregation cooking for her husband like they did when he was a single man. Call it a peeve, but it is what motivated her from being Pastor Carry-out Queen to Co-Pastor Domestic Diva-in-training. One of her worst fears was that a sexy siren like the Italian celebrity chef, Giada Laurentiis, would steal her man away with her robustly flavorful meals. So she frequently turned on *The Food Network* for ideas and recipes to sample.

Most times Vanessa's dishes didn't even remotely resemble the ones seen on those cooking shows, but she could garnish a plate to look nice. That was her specialty, garnish and ground beef dishes. She had perfected spaghetti meat sauce, meatballs, meatloaf, and hamburgers. She thanked God that Willie wasn't a picky man.

The thought of ground beef sparked her desire for chili, and just like that, dinner plans were made. She unwrapped a block of frozen ground round in the center of a skillet and waited for it to start to sizzle before prying the meat away from the frozen pack as it browned.

From a distance, Vanessa noticed the light blinking on their answering machine that was sitting at the far counter. She remembered from the night before that Willie was too eager to check messages on his office line downstairs after their return. Vanessa had been eager to hit the sack, leaving their personal messages on hold. Figuring that she couldn't escape the present any longer, Vanessa pushed the button to replay her messages after adding water to her pan to speed up her meat's thawing process.

The first message was from Keisha. At first her sister's playful scorn admonishing her for leaving town as if she were the big sister, was misleading. But there was something else in her voice. It was a sadness that Vanessa detected as Keisha ended the message with, "Call me as soon as you get back."

Something is wrong, Vanessa thought. She had done more than her share of rescuing her sister in the past and could tell. She hesitated before dialing her sister's work number. Her greeting was chipper enough, but just like a baby who takes a tumble and cries only after realizing that Mommy was there to witness it, Keisha poured on the emotion.

"What's wrong with you?" Vanessa said, taking the phone into the adjoining dining room to take a seat.

"It's Paul," Keisha said. "Hold on a minute."

Vanessa's thoughts entertained everything from Paul being gravely ill to the unthinkable. "What's wrong with Paul? Did he have a change of heart?" Vanessa asked as soon as Keisha came back.

"No, Vanessa, why would you ask something like that?" Keisha whined. "Wait, have you talked to him?"

"I've been on vacation. Of course, I haven't spoken to him. It's just that you're so upset. Girl, I could hear the sadness in your voice even on the message. What's wrong?"

"Paul is highly allergic to everything; grass, ragweed, tree pollen, not to mention all his food allergies."

"So?" Vanessa said in a tone that demanded she serve up the bad news soon. She rubbed her temple and braced herself.

"I can't get married outside. Paul said his allergies are so bad that he'd be miserable the whole time~ even into late fall. Now, I am miserable. I always wanted to get married at the Garden Gazebo." Again she whined.

Vanessa swallowed relief before getting flustered all over again. "Wait a minute, why aren't you planning on getting married in your daddy's church?"

"You didn't even get married there," Keisha was quick to point out.

"That was different. Willie had his own church at the time, and I was honoring my husband by getting married at Harvest."

"Yeah right, Vanessa," Keisha said doubtful.

"I surely would like to know why you'd think I'd lie about something like this."

"You didn't press Willie to get married at Mt. Pleasant because just like me you have an issue with our church not having a center aisle."

Vanessa wanted to end the call right then and there. She never thought the construction of the church would be a deal breaker. She knew trying to convince her sister otherwise was futile.

"Here I am thinking you're having a real issue. As far as I'm concerned you've got three options. You can rent a foreign church with money that could be better served elsewhere so you can have your precious center aisle, or shoot your groom up with so much Benedryl that he can't stand straight so you can get married outside anyway. Option three is get married at Pleasant Harvest if you want your big sister to officiate the wedding."

There was silence. The babe was back. Vanessa could imagine her sister's pouty mouth and eyes ready to spout tears. This was a big deal to her. Even before the prospect of planning her own wedding, Keisha took over orchestrating Vanessa and Willie's wedding for them. Vanessa wondered how many more months she would have to take of this melodrama.

"When is the wedding?"

"That's just it, Vanessa," Keisha snipped, "I can't decide whether it should be sooner, like the end of this year, or later. Since an outside wedding is not an option, I was leaning toward—"

Vanessa heard the key in the front door and looked at her watch as her sister droned on about the endless variables that prevented her from picking a wedding date. She pointed to the phone when Willie appeared in the door frame as if he would immediately know who it was. He backed away and began poking around the kitchen.

"Do you love Paul?" Vanessa asked once given a chance.

"Of course I do," Keisha assured. "What kind of question is that? You sure you haven't spoken to him? Willie either?"

"I know this might sound crazy, but why don't you ask your fiancée where and when he wants to get married," Vanessa said, hoping not to germinate the seed of doubt she already rooted in her sister's mind. "Listen to me. I bet if I had talked to him he'd say he'd get married anytime and anywhere as long as he was marrying you."

"Awwww," Keisha said. Her smile beamed through the phone.

"Well, look; Willie's here, so I'm going to go finish dinner. I'll talk to you later this week," Vanessa said, hoping her sister would not call her with daily wedding planning updates.

Willie lifted the lid on the ground beef before asking, "Hamburger Helper again?"

"Hello to you too," Vanessa answered before taking the lid from her husband in one hand. With the other, she began breaking apart the tender meat that had begun to brown for the second time after the half a cup of water boiled out.

Willie stepped behind her and planted a kiss on her cheek. "Spaghetti?"

"Chili," she said to the tune of yummy.

"What else are we eating with that?"

"Why are you so concerned? Didn't you eat lunch?" Vanessa said, searching for their colander to drain the fat. "Chili is a stand alone meal. It's got kidney beans in it, but if that's not good enough for you, then I'm sure we got some salad in there or something. Now get out of my kitchen. It'll be about another half an hour. I'll call you when I'm done."

Willie did as he was told. "I invited someone over," he threw over his shoulder as he departed.

"Wait," she shouted. "Come again; someone?"

"A young lady," he added, noticing her eyebrows forming question marks. His smile was as big and as devious as a Cheshire cat's when he returned. "Well, I've been following that polygamy case on the news, and I figure since I am a man of the cloth, and it wasn't unheard of to have multiple wives in biblical days, that I'd invite Alexis over and see if the two of you get along before I ask her to join our family."

"Don't play with me, Willie Green," Vanessa said, realizing that his sense of humor was what she loved about him, but also what had come to frustrate her about him lately. She was not in the mood for wisecracks or guests.

"For real, why are you so tense lately?" Willie rubbed her shoulders. " You rested today, right?"

Instead of shrugging his hands off her shoulders like she wanted to, she moved out of his grasp to open the can of beans with the electric can opener. *Was she tense? Did it show that much?* "Is someone coming over or not?"

"Alexis Montgomery, she's a reporter for Channel 7 news. She is the one who interviewed me that day of the fire. They want to do a follow-up story. I don't know exactly, but I guess, the story will be like the history of Harvest."

Vanessa hurriedly added the rest of the ingredients to a small Dutch oven so that it could slow cook. She took a seat on a nearby barstool. She felt she needed a break. "Gosh, I'm so over Harvest. Every time we try to pull away from that place, someone or something draws *you* right back to it."

"It's ironic, I know. They say irony is God's intervention, and in some cases His comedy. I figure it can't hurt to talk to the woman," Willie said, still standing from when he had returned.

Vanessa felt a chill that reminded her of stormy seas. She had to be the voice of reason. "This is not a good idea. Why are we memorializing a burnt building?"

"How about it's the place where I preached my initial sermon as pastor and saved a good many of souls. It's also the place where we got married." His voice was charged with emotion although he appeared to remain calm.

"Well, it just seems like a tragic waste of time."

"That's 'cause it wasn't Mt. Pleasant that caught on fire," Willie said so quickly that Vanessa almost missed it. "Look, I don't want to talk about it anymore. I've made up my mind. The woman is coming over and I'm going to talk to her."

He was dismissive, putting his foot down right on her ego.

"Lord forbid, if I share my reservations with my husband. Reporters have been known to put a provocative spin on the most basic of stories. It's what they do," Vanessa said, preparing to grate cheese and chop onions to top off her chili. "But I'll keep my comments to myself. Where should I serve you and your new wife? Will the dining room do, or would you prefer somewhere more intimate like the kitchen nook?"

"Now, you know I was joking. I'm not even remotely interested in this woman," Willie said with an incredulous look.

"I'm joking also. Ha-ha," Vanessa said in her blandest of tones.

Vanessa ignored his questioning gaze. His look was asking everything she didn't have an answer for. She bore down on the block of cheese with her right hand as she grated to take the edge off her frustration.

"If I had of known we were having company, I would have made something else. Something more complete like Giada would have made."

"Who?"

"The Italian chef," She looked up to see his confused expression. "Oh, never mind."

"Is that what this is all about? Chili is fine and you will be fine too, after you freshen up. You've got a serious case of bed head."

"Thank you for the tip, but I've got to complete the meal first." She used her forearm to wipe away fresh tears that began to well up catching her completely off guard. He was only playing, but his criticism of her meal and now her appearance was a little too much to bear. "If you tell me your guest will be here in the next ten minutes or so, I will absolutely kill you."

"My, aren't we violent," Willie chided. "She'll be here at six. You have plenty of time."

Vanessa watched him exit the kitchen, giving her enough breathing space to hatch a counter argument.

Chapter 3

Like Doubting Thomas

Vanessa wore her favorite lavender sweat suit and her hair hanging down past her shoulders, the way her husband liked it. Three helpings of chili were ready to be served in the two-handled soup bowls they received from William and Sonoma as a wedding gift. They were topped with a dollop of sour cream, cheddar cheese, chives, and onions in small ramekins.

Vanessa sized up their dinner guest as she took the woman's coat and led her into the dinning room. Alexis hugged both of them as if they were her parents and she had just come home from college. She was a slender woman of average height with a smooth youthful complexion that apparently had never been the battlefield for pimples in her youth. Her eyes told a different story. They were surprisingly mature. Vanessa wondered how old she really was and suspected she was closer to thirty than her counterparts at the TV station probably realized.

Willie blessed the food from the head of the table, leaving Vanessa across from Alexis. She seemed to prefer the corn chips Vanessa had also put out. She was moving the kidney beans around to the opposite side of the bowl before taking bites of the chili. Vanessa was almost halfway through her portion, and was wondering, like Willie, what else there was to eat.

Willie covered the pleasantries while they ate, discussing with Alexis everything from the unusually warm spring weather they were experiencing to ride in Alexis'. Apparently she had gotten lost although their house was a direct shot from the Capitol beltway. Vanessa remained silent, with ample smiles to pass around the table at the mention of their recent trip. She didn't dare breach the topic of the hour first.

She was waiting for Alexis to sprout two heads even though she found the girl charmingly clumsy, not at all like her on-air persona. Halfway through dinner, Alexis scrounged through her purse to find a ringing cell phone, dropping her keys in the process. Both she and Willie watched as Alexis absent-mindedly reached for the item with an open purse, losing even more of its contents. Willie tried to get up and help, and narrowly escaped bumping heads with Alexis who wasn't so lucky with the edge of the table. She left the dining area to step into a nearby room while rubbing her head with her left hand and using the right to retrieve her phone's call back list.

Willie and Vanessa looked at one another with a mixture of amusement and amazement until his eyes warned her to contain herself before their guest came back. He took this opportunity to get more chili while Vanessa settled on more corn chips.

Maybe there wasn't a storm brewing after all, Vanessa thought. She thought about how she had jumped the gun earlier with Keisha. It was time to start taking people at face value. This girl needed more help than anything.

"Are you all right?" Willie asked when Alexis reentered the room.

"Yeah, that's the hazard in this job. You're always on the go and sometimes your body is moving before your mind has had a chance to think," she said to a chorus of her own contagious chuckles. "I've had more spills and falls than I care to mention."

"So you got stuck with reporting on the old church fire, huh?" Willie said.

"I chose this story actually," Alexis said.

"Why?" Vanessa couldn't resist.

Alexis cleared her throat. "Or shall I say it chose me. I did the initial story, and I don't know really. There is something about Harvest that's familiar."

Vanessa could detect a southern upbringing sprouting up in Alexis's speech. It was an accent that Vanessa was sure Alexis tried to smooth over with either plenty of practice or formal voice training.

"Familiar?" Vanessa questioned.

Alexis volleyed glances between the two of them before settling on Vanessa. "I grew up in a small, tight-knit church much like Harvest Baptist Church."

"Well, Harvest is no more," Vanessa pushed out through a yawn in an attempt to stop the train from traveling down memory lane with her husband aboard.

"Yes, ma'am, but what about the people that were going there?" Alexis asked.

They should have moved over to Pleasant Harvest with the rest of the church, she thought.

"So, tell us more about home," Willie jumped in, letting everyone know he was the conductor. He had pushed back his plate as if he were ready for a lengthy conversation. "And how were you drawn to this story?"

"Like I said, I grew up in a small town in Kannapolis, North Carolina. My grandfather, C. Paul Montgomery, who raised me, was and still is the bishop and pastor of Greater Hope Baptist Church. It was the only African American Baptist church in the whole area for a long while. I graduated high school early and went on to North Carolina Central University. Worked at WAKN—the local station there—could have easily been an anchor by now, but home wasn't where the big stories were," Alexis said.

Vanessa noticed she had elected to give them the bulleted version and wondered what fell in the gaps. "And this Harvest story is a big story?" She almost laughed.

"The game is played differently here. DC is a major market. I'm not just handed air time because I am Bishop Montgomery's granddaughter. If nepotism is alive, it's apparent I don't know the right people," Alexis said, a drawl punctuating her sentences. "You work from the bottom and move up on merit. You have to prove yourself daily. Prove that you can sense a good story. When I arrived on that fire scene and witnessed the invincible spirit of the people there, dancing and praising God in front of that edifice, I knew there was more to the story. Growing up in church I learned that great praise comes from a great testimony. You carry on like that to express gratitude to God or to taunt the devil one; get him off your track. So, Reverend, which one was it? Why did you leave, and what made you come back that Sunday morning?"

"Is this off the record?" Vanessa questioned.

"I guess this is as good a time as any to begin," Alexis said in her on-air voice as she took out her voice recorder. "The initial interview that we do today helps me develop angles for the story or stories. Then we arrange a date for you to meet with the camera crew."

The switch Vanessa noticed in Alexis's speech and demeanor that subtly put Vanessa on the defensive again. "Until we are sure what angle you are going to take, we will have a Public Relations-slash-Media Ministry at our church to handle our public persona with the press."

"We have a Public Relations Ministry?" Willie asked.

"Yes, we do, honey," Vanessa said as if to jar his memory. Her look demanded he keep up or at least pretend to. "It's

headed by Brother Mike Pearson who was some sort of entertainment lawyer turned PR person."

"As you can see, my wife's a little skeptical," Willie announced as if it weren't apparent.

"I sure am. I saw how the news sensationalized a story just
last week about Pastor Kennedy's church. Someone fell out
during service, now they are calling to question the certifica-
tion of the Nurses' Unit."

"I can assure you, Pastor Vanessa, that's not my aim. It's my
hope to get a substantial amount of history on the church before the fire. Many in the community say the church was like
a beacon when your husband was pastor. Maybe follow-up on
what Pastor Willie is doing in Ministry now, and of course,
you're a big part of that too."

"See, Vanessa, a simple history," Willie said. "Satisfied?"

Willie's head was obviously growing. He was being pleasant and patronizing at the same time. She hoped that wasn't
his signal for her to leave well enough alone because she
couldn't. She remembered her mother knew that signal. She
would slave in the kitchen to prepare a five course meal for
her daddy and visitors he would invite over to dinner, only
to abruptly uproot herself and the children into the cramped
kitchen when the conversation had turned inappropriate or
business needed to be conducted. She never remembered
her father asking them to leave; her mom just knew. Vanessa
wasn't built with that kind of navigation system.

Lord, I promised you I would not show out, Vanessa thought.

"Unless you're planning on taping and showing a service in
its entirety, I don't want any cameras in *our* church," Vanessa
said to them both.

"I'm sorry to hear that, because I think it's important to
show Pastor Willie in that context. In a world of sound bites,
staging is just as important," Alexis said.

"How's this for sound bites and staging? In Pastor Kennedy's church they zeroed in on the 'Jesus Saves' sign, and then led into the story by saying something like, it was too bad there was no one to save the lady who had a medical emergency there."

"That's awful," was all Willie could say.

Even Alexis was speechless for a while. "That was irresponsible and unethical journalism," she finally said.

"You bet it was," Vanessa agreed.

"If I may, I think you're being a little hasty in your decision about the story that I am working on based on what you've seen." Alexis leaned in toward Vanessa to make her plea.

"And, I think you're not telling us everything. I'm sorry, but I don't believe for a minute that you haven't thought about how you'd like to cover this story."

"Vanessa," Willie pleaded.

"It's okay. She's right. I do have an angle in mind." Alexis paused as if she were thinking about which one to pitch. "I want to find out who has an interest in Harvest Baptist Church and who has an impact on its future."

"You've got the wrong people." Vanessa was quick to reply. She looked to her husband and wondered why he wasn't jumping in. "Neither of those applies to us. I believe in staying in my lane, Ms. Montgomery. Our lane exits at the Pleasant Harvest Baptist Church. Shoot, this sounds like a straight up suitcase, like Daddy used to call it—lawsuits and court cases. Are you working in conjunction with the police on this?"

"Journalistic Code of Ethics requires that we act independently to bring the truth. My only obligation is to my Channel 7 viewing audience."

"Uh-huh," Vanessa uttered.

They were at a stalemate. They retreated to their opposite corners to regroup. The automatic function on Alexis's voice recorder clicked off, rattling her, and causing her to knock her spoon to the floor. She immediately bent down to retrieve it. Both Willie and Vanessa jumped up as if to shield her from bumping her head yet again. They sat down gingerly when they were certain her head had cleared the edge.

"Look, I'm not trying to be difficult. I just don't want the integrity of God's church to be discussed in the court of public opinion; that's all. You can understand that," Vanessa said.

"This case has been ruled an arson," Alexis said as if she were running out of steam. "The news magazine I am attempting to report for is investigative in nature, so I am trying to figure out the truth about this fire, as I am sure we all are. It's the first time that I am attempting to cover something like this."

Vanessa sat stunned.

"Wait, did you say arson? Willie asked.

"I did the initial report," Alexis droned on. "I kept good notes. Then my sources confirmed the arson, and I have scarcely a day to break the story. The eggs sort of fell in my basket, and I am attempting to make an omelet. I need you to help me make the omelet. Please."

"Arson?" Willie asked again with a faraway look in his eyes that told Vanessa he was off in his own thoughts. "Do you mean someone purposely burnt down the church?"

"Other reporters will run the footage of whatever is out there on this story. Both print and broadcast journalists will be calling with their own inquiries. Some with no journalistic ethics like you talked about before. Some will have no desire to tell the whole truth or paint the entire picture. I have a unique vehicle like the *Inside* 7 segment to do that. Either you tell your story upfront or defend yourself later. With me, you can affect the way you are represented in the press. Pastor Vanessa, if not me, then who? Who would you prefer Pastor Willie talk to?"

She was good, Vanessa thought. Willie returned from La La Land and back to the conversation with a heavy sigh. He leaned forward, elbows up on the table to use praying hands to shield his face, and then wipe it. Vanessa looked into his eyes and read his intense expression. She felt the signal. She had said her peace. As she began to clear the table she knew her compassionate husband would share his story and trust this young lady with what he held sacred—the truth.

Vanessa cleared the table of their dishes in two trips. She didn't butt in or comment. She was busy thinking that their PR person must have a friend still practicing law that they could put on retainer.

Chapter 4

The Preacher's New Robe

Abe looked at his reflection in his dresser mirror as he toyed with imaginary cufflinks. He hunched his shoulders to shift his imaginary suit jacket and delicately tapped the lapel right over his heart to emphasize the sincerity of the point he just finished reciting.

"That's why I'm asking you to plant a seed into this ministry so that uncommon favor will flourish in your life," said a voice that came from just over his shoulder.

"Plant a seed and uncommon favor will flourish in your life," he parroted.

Abe watched a veteran televangelist through the reflection in his mirror. The man, known as much for his fancy clothes as his fancy rhetoric, had abandoned the Bible and pulpit altogether. He unbuttoned his suit jacket to place one hand in his pants pocket and point with the other. "This is your now moment. Get ready, prosperity is on its way."

"I know it may not seem like it, but prosperity is on its way. This is your moment," Abe embellished.

Abe knew the man had concluded his sermon and that the remaining ten minutes of the program would be used to solicit seed offerings and gifts into the televangelist's ministry. This wasn't worth the tape to record it, he thought. He was not going to pull out a sixty-minute sermon from this broadcast.

"Give Him His due, give Him your best. Give the Lord the first fruits of your increase. If the truth be told, you should be giving to the Lord even before you give to your landlord," the country preacher continued.

Oh that's good, Abe thought as he sat down on the corner of his bed to scribble the quote verbatim into his tablet.

Abe alternated between two remotes to halt the VHS tape and set the television back for regular viewing. His entertainment center was packed tight with audio and video tapes, DVD's, and several decades' worth of electronic equipment. He still put to good use his top loading Beta-Max machine, transistor and CB radios. A twelve-inch screen set inside a 62-inch floor model TV panel served as a coffee table of sorts piled with books. His home was his museum. These were his relics, and he was both curator and guest.

Despite the new sign out in front of his building that claimed luxury condo and studio rentals available, Abe lived in an efficiency. His was a spacious corner unit. He was awakened every morning by a crew of workers erecting dry wall partitions in other units to bring truth to their advertising. To Abe, they were all still efficiencies made suitable for the new chic and trendy district residents.

Abe stumbled upon this space in the now diverse neighborhood when he went back to school after leaving the ministry the first time. At the time he didn't believe his calling had been a mistake, but falling in bed with a married woman from his Sunday School class had. After being dismissed from his ministerial duties at Philippians Baptist Church for his impropriety, he took a two year sabbatical from the Lord and the Lord's work and became a student of life. At forty-five, he found himself taking as many non-credit courses as he could stand, trying to pick up a new cause. During the day he shelled out cash for desperation at one of the original pawn shops his parents owned and he operated, which became the source of his junk collection.

So when his Uncle Charley called him with the proposition to lead a small congregation that had recently been abandoned by their former pastor, he heard choruses of, 'you can do it.' It gave him a reason to come out of hiding. He wanted to be restored. He just didn't know how. He took over the pastorate of the Harvest Baptist Church for three months. There he had a transient congregation that was often off to the next religious experience before he got to know their names and/ or their needs. Every Sunday there were more new faces and less of the familiar. Faces oddly like the patrons he serviced at Capitol Town Pawn; grim, shamefaced, and conflicted. Ones he could tell had traded all that was precious for life's addictions. They showed up at Harvest on Sunday mornings pleading for their souls back. Try as he might, he wasn't helping them. He couldn't.

Abe was having a hard time hearing God's voice. He felt sure that it was because he had forsaken God, so now God was forsaking him. The spring that once flowed with God's anointing had dried up and no longer flourished in his life. So he trusted his Uncle Charley, a man that he had always viewed as a servant of God, to be his guiding light back to the fold. And he obliged Mother Shempy who didn't want to have to take the city bus to find another church outside her community, and Greg Johnson, the chief musician, who depended on what they paid him to play the rusty organ as a supplement to his income. They sang in his chorus even when the, 'you can do it,' sounded more like, 'you have nothing better to do.' Abe wanted to keep the lifeline going for these people. He wanted the consigners that visited Harvest from week to week to get back a portion, if not all of what they had lost in the world. He wanted nothing more than to be an honor guard for the Lord, but he felt more like a ringleader in the biggest charade imaginable.

Attendance that had been steadily declining had reached an all time low by Easter Sunday morning, a day when sinners of every variety usually came out of the woodwork looking for redemption. The church catching fire on the holiest of all holy days was all the sign he needed. The gig was up. He was both thankful and relieved.

Then he got two phone calls this week. One was from his uncle telling him that the daycare owner across the street from the church was willing to open her doors to his members to hold service in the interim. The other call came from a reporter that wanted to chronicle the resurrection of the Harvest Baptist Church from the ashes.

I could be that televangelist with the flashy suit, Abe thought, *or better yet, I could wear my new robe.* He stared at the garment hanging in a clear plastic bag just outside the closet door. It was another community donation from the local drycleaner. The friendly Asian man had seen the broadcast about the church fire and was looking to clear inventory that hadn't been picked up, while being charitable in the process.

Abe peeled back the covering and tried on the garment for the first time. It was like nothing he had ever seen before with its flowing ivory satin fabric, and a staunch gold collar with a deep crimson cross in the center of the front and back panel. He was a man of average height, but the robe was obviously made for someone much taller. Abe had to shrug his shoulders to shift the extra material to the back, which created a train behind him as he walked. It was ridiculous in its grandeur.

Once again, Abe heard the chorus. He toyed with the idea that his return to ministry after his fall would be televised. Maybe Marion Butler, the woman with whom he had the

adulterous affair, would be watching. He often thought of her
and how he was minutes away from proposing to the already
married woman when God pulled back the covers on her plot
to get back at her husband. He could still hear her insincere
apology and remember how he lived in fear of her husband
ever finding him with his own revenge in mind. He still questioned whether the sweet words and warm caresses were all
an act. Through the pain and regret he wondered did she still
think about him.

I'll show her, he thought. In this robe he would make his
comeback. But first he had to have a sermon. He dropped to
his knees after replacing the robe on its hanger and opened
his bedside Bible. He felt a nudging as he flipped through the
book of Isaiah and allowed the book to open to chapter fifty-
five. It was a familiar passage of scripture. It declared that, *'His
thoughts are not our thoughts, neither are His ways like our ways.'* It
also demanded that we seek the Lord while He may be found.
But where, God?

Tears began to escape his eyes seemingly without cause. He
knew he should meditate, but he had no time to tarry with
this passage—no time to study. He had less than twelve hours
before show time. Holding on to those words and trying to
build upon them was like trying to build a sandcastle with dry
sand. Abe knew the people in his church wanted to be impact-
ed emotionally, not taught. They wanted to sing their song,
tell their life's story through testimonials, and have the pastor
give them a catalyst for a good cry come sermon time. He
didn't have it to give. So he had come to rely on the words of
others to give him something he could relay to God's people.

His entire collection of audio and VHS tapes, CD's, and
DVDs were of God's Word through different messengers,
most of which he had used before. He scanned his row of
tapes and stopped at a cassette of a message by Pastor Willie

Green when he was asked to preach for the pastor's anniversary at Abe's home church.

He fired up the Sanyo stereo system complete with a turntable and cassette deck that was on the shelf under his television. He took the tape from the case and pressed play. A selection from the choir prompted him to fast forward. He stopped in time to hear Willie take his sermon topic, 'Seasons Change.'

"Some of you may or may not agree with me, but the seasons you find yourself in, in this lifetime, and how you fair during that particular season is based on the voice you decide to listen to and trust. Amen. The Bible says His sheep will know His voice."

Abe didn't notice the tape had stopped. He was trying to grapple with his memory to figure out from what book, chapter, and verse that quote came. He felt his heart accelerate the way it did back when God's Word would strike a chord. He remembered being at that service when this tape was recorded and marveling at how Willie Green served up God's Word with no additives and no fillers. He didn't use fancy words or catch phrases, just the meat of God's Word. Everyone left full. That was the kind of preacher Abe had vowed to be. But he had gone Hollywood for so long, going under the surgeon's knife in an attempt to transplant everyone else's anointing. He didn't know if he could turn back.

He approached the tape deck with disbelief when he realized it had stopped playing. He was hungry for more of what Pastor Green had to say, as if he, himself was on the verge of a breakthrough. He pressed several buttons to get the tiny wheels inside the player from spinning in vain and to eject the tape altogether. A violent whack on the side of the machine released an explosion of thin cassette film exposed from its casing that he pulled until he felt it catch on a tiny spool inside. He let the mangled tape dangle and cursed his luck.

He couldn't go on like this. Abe felt sure that he would stand in front of that congregation and those cameras tomorrow and everyone would know he was a fraud. He stared at the ceiling, suspended in time between his past and his future. With his eyes set upon heaven, he waited temporarily on his help. He shook his head helplessly, then wildly, defiantly. He knew he needed to make a decision, to move from that spot. He searched within this time, for anything at this point. The words of Shakespeare, Socrates, or Confucius would be better than nothing . *If a tree falls in the middle of the forest . . .* He almost laughed . Then he thought about it. *And there is no one there to hear it.* How would anyone know?

Abe turned his attention back to the television and surfed the channels with his remote, hoping that his all-access channels would help him locate the Lord. He landed on the string of channels that broadcast mega-ministries twenty-four hours a day. He took down notes, cut and paste sermon points, and modeled timing and execution. All the while he was hoping that once again, no one would know his shame. Later, as he practiced in the mirror with his robe, he imagined that he wasn't any different from the pastors and bishops who he had borrowed from.

Sunday morning, Abe had to strip down to his undershirt and slacks under his robe. The unseasonably warm weather did not prevent The Kid Street Daycare from running their heat. The camera crew was in place after a short pre-service interview. The tiny playroom appeared to be filled to capacity with the rented adult-sized chairs. The members of his background chorus were poised with their praise. The key member, his Uncle Charley, was able to get the word out to the old and some of the new members. The presence of the news crew could have possibly brought out the rest.

Abe was pitch perfect as he delivered the amalgamation of

adages and anecdotes he'd put together. He squelched the notion to deviate from his outline and impart what was on his heart once he felt the rhythm of his words. He reminded himself he was being taped and that the best television was scripted.

Abe shook hands and graciously thanked the reporter who said she would be in touch. His back was a pool of sweat and his robe was the perfect sponge. How long did he have to stay and greet the crowd? He felt himself judging the sincerity of everyone's commendation. He felt dizzy, but he held his mask in place.

A trustee approached with a sealed envelope addressed to him that was placed inside the offering basket. Abe broke the seal on the envelope as Mother Shempy and her teenaged granddaughter approached.

"Pastor Townsend," Mother Shempy said, "I'm so, so glad that y'all decided to go on with service despite the circumstances. I started to get worried. Lord knows what I would have done if I had to try and find another church."

"See, the Lord worked it out for ya." Abe leaned in for a church hug, which was contact with the arms and the chest, but none of the rest of the body.

"He sure did. You've met my granddaughter, Melanie, haven't you, Pastor?"

"I believe I have, Mother Shempy," Abe said, taking the young girl's hand and pumping it twice in a handshake before releasing it. "How are you, Melanie? Did you enjoy the service?"

Melanie shrugged her shoulders then added, "Nana's got District cable, and all she watches is the church channel. You better not change her channel before the *Bishop Robbie Robinson Show* goes off, although most of the time she is already asleep. I love to watch their choir. Bishop Robinson preached on almost the same thing that you did today, Pastor Townsend. Isn't that funny?"

Abe would have been embarrassed. He might have even fainted dead away if he weren't looking at the note just passed to him.

Pastor Townsend,

Great sermon. Seasons indeed change. What you need is a publicist to help polish your image and navigate you through your next phase of ministry, which promises to be fruitful if you plan for the Harvest. I'll be in touch.

A friend.

"It's funny how that happens, right, Pastor Abe?" the girl persisted.

"No. Actually, sweetie, it happens quite often. It's what you call confirmation," Abe said as he searched the sparse crowd for the source of his anonymous offer.

Chapter 5

A Tale of Two Pastors

Alexis rushed from the county Board of Education build-ing where she was covering a special school board hearing to get into the production van with Danny Mitchell, her cam-era man. Having a special report on the *Inside 7* segment to air in less than fifteen minutes didn't mean her job stopped. That was the hectic life of an assignment reporter. She had barely taped her wrap up on the Harvest story before she had to get set up in Upper Marlboro for the beginning of the school board session. She had cut the squares, laying the voice tracks for the promos, shooting the lead-in live with the anchor in the studio, and pre-taped the interviews, but left it in the hands of Martie and the crew to do the patchwork. She couldn't wait to see how it turned out.

They sat in rush hour traffic, but as far as she was con-cerned she had the best seat in the house. One of the moni-tors in the back of the van hooked up to roof-top satellites used to send live feed directly to the studio was also a televi-sion monitor. She didn't care about the five-minute footage of her with school board members; she'd watch that later on. Right now, the World Report was on mute. As the program rolled into its last station break, they aired her promo piece. She scrambled to find the right knob to turn up the volume.

"I'm Alexis Montgomery. Join me with Lizzy London on

the *Inside* 7 segment as we take a closer look into the myste-
rious Easter Church Inferno and the ongoing investigations
through the eyes of its two very different religious leaders in
a segment I call, *A Tale of Two Pastors*. That's the *Inside* 7 segment, tonight at 7:30."

Alexis was mesmerized by the title frame, THE EASTER
CHURCH INFERNO, etched out in computer simulated flames.
She could envision subsequent reports baring that same
brand. She remembered the thrill of sitting under the hot
lights coated with the heavy cake make-up for the cameras,
knowing that just the right angle would bring every pore on
her face into focus for all of D.C., Maryland, and Northern
Virginia to see. The make-up was so much different from the
mineral blush and tinted lip gloss she applied herself while
on assignment. Her hair was always a hit-or-miss and at the
mercy of the environment. When it was hot and humid, her
hair was usually a hot mess if it weren't freshly done. If it were
cold and rainy, and she was on assignment outside, she had
several hats to match her outerwear because her wind-blown
look could sometimes go awry. She could definitely get use to
the beauty treatment of an anchor.

Catcalls from the guys in the van congratulating her on
her upcoming investigative debut brought her back to focus.
She pulled out her cell phone to call her grandfather who
she had not seen since leaving Kannapolis a little less than a
year ago. Updates by phone were all they shared. He would
tell her he's praying for her and remind her that the world is
a wilderness without Jesus. To him she was on this quest to a
dangerous and unknown destination if it didn't soon lead to
a good church home and a husband to cover her. She wanted
to tell him about her story and convince him how good and
honorable it was to be committed to finding out the truth.
As the phone rang she realized it was Wednesday, the day her

grandfather practically encamped in church all day and night. She figured she could at least leave a message.

Just then one of the guys called out, "Who woulda thunk Milky Montgomery would be sitting across from Lizzy London?"

She extinguished the call before leaving a message. The nickname bringing to mind the disappointment she had brought upon her grandfather. One segment wouldn't change that fact.

"Call me Alexis, or don't refer to me at all," she shouted. *Morons.*

They hemmed and hawed and peeled off insincere apologies that Alexis tried her best to ignore. She felt her excitement returning as the theme for the *Inside 7* segment played, and the host, Lizzy London, provided an overview of the content and context of the night's show for the viewing audience. Then she introduced the special reporters. The format usually split the thirty minute show between two stories, the weightier of the two usually going first. The producers preferred to end with a warm and fuzzy story.

They did not know what to make of her story that was not quite a high-crime piece and not quite a human interest piece either, but certainly both. Alexis's story was allotted fifteen minutes, one station break, which was practically the whole show. She heard Lizzy whisper into the microphone during countdown that she hoped the interns had scanned the mail in the mailbag because if Alexis's piece turned out to be fluff, they'd have to cut off the second half and use the viewers' response as filler. Alexis didn't know whether to take the fact that she had the bulk of the show as the sacrifice of a slow news week or a bout of the station's confidence in the credence of the story. She chose to believe the latter. Forget Lizzy London.

"But first, a church and pillar of the community burns to the ground on Easter Sunday marking the end of one man's tenure as pastor and the beginning of another. Coincidental or circumstantial? For this we go to Alexis Montgomery."

Lizzy was known for stealing a reporter's thunder in her improvised introduction, especially if it were breaking news. She did it just to mess with the newbies who were slaves to the teleprompter. Alexis remembered sitting right off her shoulder scrambling to alter the words on the script so that her lead-in didn't sound like an extension of Lizzy's intro. It was like playing a game of Taboo as she tried not to repeat the same words while sounding poised and provocative at the same time. She watched herself blunder, but felt she recovered well on camera.

"A church ablaze on Easter Sunday could be viewed by many as a sign. A deliberate sign says fire officials. Fire crews were sent to a building that has been a part of the Capitol Heights community for fifty years, a church that just recently underwent a very drastic and dramatic leadership change. Who set the Harvest Baptist Church on fire? Investigators have ruled this case arson. Could the tension that was brewing on the inside just months before ignite someone, who once was or still is a part of this congregation, to commit such a crime? I start my investigation with the two men who knew and loved the church more than anybody—the current and former pastor of that church—as we take an in-depth look into *A Tale of Two Pastors*."

Alexis sighed a breath of relief as the story cut away from her live-in-studio to pre-recorded footage of Pastor Abe Townsend conducting service. He was preaching a message of prosperity to congregants forced to form tight rows between cots in a daycare classroom across the street from the old Harvest edifice. The scene shifted, and Alexis and Abe were out front walking along the gate of the badly damaged church building to set the scene for their interview.

The guys in the van with her had lost interest and began a noisy debate of their own. As the van inched along a congested 295, Alexis had to strain to hear the program.

"It's Sunday, and you are about to preach a message, no doubt filled with inspiration and hope. Is there hope for the Harvest Baptist Church family in the wake of this tragedy?" Alexis led him to their first stopping point marked beforehand so that the microphone buoyed above them could pick up their voices as opposed to using the handheld.

"Oh, I believe so, Alexis," Abe said, accompanied by nervous laughter. "Hope is the basis of our faith."

"Take me back, if you will, to Easter Sunday service. Was there anything unusual about that day?"

"Nothing whatsoever," Abe was quick to say. His eyes pleaded to know where her line of questioning was going. "Besides the fact that one of our trusty deacons was late with the keys and we got a late start, everything else was routine."

Late? Weren't fire crews on the scene by two o'clock? Alexis wondered while she watched. Why didn't she pick up on that earlier and ask him more about the time frame? *What Black Baptist church started late and got out early on Easter Sunday?*

"You came by your pastorate by unusual means. Your predecessor decided to move on to another church. A decision met with great opposition. The church was literally torn apart with some deciding to stay and some deciding to go with him. What made you step in under those circumstances?"

Abe was a bobble head doll constantly nodding to her inquiries. "God does His greatest work through our adversity," he said.

"Was there adversity even after you took over as pastor?" Alexis fired off.

"Let me put it to you this way, we had to reorganize and rebuild. We added some new members to the fold. Those members that I acquired kept the Harvest legacy intact. They loved their church tremendously and wanted to continue the work this church was known for in this community. Although, it appears now that we must begin again." Abe glanced over his shoulder at the charred church building for emphasis.

"Some would say that to petition a pastor to prevent a move, as some of your members have done, is extreme. Could there be anyone in that central group that could want to see the church destroyed?"

"I am not a judge or jury. That's not my job. It just seems unlikely and counterproductive to fight to stay at this household of faith, and then turn around and burn it down," Abe countered without hesitation.

He knew all the right words to say, Alexis remembered thinking. She was familiar with pastors who used the ideals of God's Word as a cover so they didn't have to relate to what was going on. Her grandfather was the prime example. She was raised to believe that God's Word was a shield and buckler, but every now and again she needed him to remove the cover and let her see the cracks and dents in his armor.

"There are some critics in this community that have complained that the church has not been the same warm and inviting place as it once was," Alexis said mainly to rattle Abe, who seemed to be answering on autopilot. "What do you say to those people, who used to rely on the food pantry and other resources from this church? They refer to you as just a placeholder as if someone else behind the scenes is actually running this church."

Pursed lips, and then a ponderous look skyward broke up the monotony of the Q &A. From the light reflected off Abe's hazel eyes, Alexis thought she could see a tear, for once showing a real humanity.

"People on the outside are always going to talk. I may not lead the church like it has been run in the past," Abe said, reaching out for the gate for support. "They've got to understand I am just a man. With the training I received, I do the best I can until I get my power and direction from God. I expect Him to cast new vision for this church. Hearsay is not going to squelch what we are trying to do for God."

"So you will rebuild?" Alexis asked.

"Yes, we will."

"In this area?"

"I don't see why not. This area has nurtured us in our time of need."

"Even before this fire, the church was facing financial difficulty. Tell me about that."

"Well, times are hard for everyone. The church is no exception. Some people shut down when times are hard, shy away from the church. We are a small church that has to rely solely on the regular giving of its members and donations, of course. We were prayerful, because between repairs that didn't get done after Tropical Storm Roberto flew in here late fall and the general upkeep, we had to cut back. Cut backs on weekday services to conserve energy, cut backs on printed programs and many, many of our services for the homeless in this community, just to name a few."

"So the church has had a recent claim through their insurance policy?" Alexis asked pointedly.

A blank expression and more mindless head-nodding told Alexis that Abe was lost.

"The other . . . um, my predecessor initiated that claim. Why the work wasn't completed, I couldn't tell you."

"Has your staff contacted your insurance agent, and are they prepared to pay out the half a million dollars you will need to rebuild your church?"

"That is the hope," Abe whispered.

"Insurance figures and scams are the major motive in an arson case. Who could stand to benefit from the policy taken out on this church?"

"The kingdom, Ms. Montgomery," Abe replied forcefully. "The insurance money, like all our offerings, will be used for the up building of His kingdom and the furtherance of the gospel. We just want to hold church and praise God."

There was a lot more she had wanted to ask him, but she remembered feeling like she would only be spinning wheels. She had done her job. She was like a prosecutor trying to show just cause, or at least plant enough curiosity in the story that the station would want to do a follow-up.

The producers decided to fade into another clip from Abe's sermon at that point.

"Get ready for spring. Plant your seeds now. Promotion is on the way." A cloaked Abe shouted from the pulpit as the program headed to station break.

Alexis temporarily lost possession of the television monitor as the guys voted to turn the station to one that might be reporting on the traffic nightmare they had found themselves in. Rather than play a game of keep away with them, she appealed to them to use the radio. She was anxious to see Pastor Willie Green's side of the interview. Without footage of him in his element, she had a fear that her piece would appear very one-sided.

When she regained control of the monitor, the second half of her piece was already in progress.

"I caught up with Pastor Willie Green who is the co-pastor here with his wife at what would seem like the reincarnation of his former church aptly renamed Pleasant Harvest Baptist Church. They are preparing to celebrate their 50th church anniversary this year with the theme—'Back to Basics, Back to Jesus.'"

Alexis was already unsatisfied and blaming Pastor Vanessa for not letting her get sermon sound-bites. They shot his interview in his office and the outdated wood paneling looked atrocious on camera.

"You have been gone from Harvest Baptist Church for four months now," Alexis started.

"That's right, since the first of January," Willie said.

"And you get the anonymous call that the church that you used to lead is on fire. Not even the current pastor got that courtesy. What do you make of that?"

"Sincerely, I don't know. Everything from that point was like a blur. I couldn't believe this was happening. I didn't question it. I just reacted," Willie reflected.

"Who made the dag-on call!" she shouted to herself on the monitor. She couldn't believe she didn't follow-up with that question.

"Then you, and what seemed like your entire congregation, were the first on the scene."

"Yes. We had just finished up service. It was like rushing to the hospital when you find out that one of your members or loved ones has been in an accident. We were simply overjoyed that no one was hurt. Praising God for sparing lives," Willie added before Alexis could ask a question.

"When I interviewed you that day, arson had not been confirmed, but I asked you then was there anyone you suspected who could have started this fire." Alexis, who was sitting across from Willie at his desk, referred to her notes. "You said whether someone set it or it caught fire itself, God allowed it. You also said God would reveal the truth."

"Yes, and I still believe that. There is a scripture that says, whatsoever is done in the dark shall come to light." Willie's genuine smile turned somber. "It pains me to know that someone was hurting enough to set a match to God's house.

I mean, what are we doing if we are not healing the broken-hearted?"

"You had plans for the Harvest Baptist Church building that didn't include another congregation holding service there. Tell me about those plans."

"Good job, Milky, cut him to the quick," one of the technicians said. "I hate fake sincerity."

"So who do you think did it?" Danny asked her.

"Huh?" Alexis asked annoyed. *Couldn't they see she was trying to watch?*

"I got my money on that guy right there. Didn't the other guy say he got money from another claim and neglected to get the work done on the church?"a second technician chimed in.

"I asked him that very question if you all would shut your traps and listen."

"Yeah, this guy has got way more motive," Danny agreed.

Alexis felt the floor of the van shift. She could feel the slant as if she were in a magic house where the floors shift and the mirrors create the illusion that a person is sideways or upside down. It was her story. Did it really favor one over the other? She had never really suspected either one of them of wrongdoing. She figured the matchman was some leisure-suit wearing or hat-wearing member that no one suspected was harboring a grudge about being denied a solo or leadership position.

"How can you say that?" Alexis defended, hoping to silence further debate so she could finish watching her piece. "I barely had time in the segment to ask him a question. Now, shush."

Alexis focused her attention back on the screen.

"Before you left you had a group of members opposed to the vision and direction you had for the church. What was that rift all about, and what do you think it means to this case?" Alexis asked Willie as the program continued.

Willie sat back in his chair as if he expected this question was coming. "The *rift*, unfortunately, sprung from a misunderstanding. I take responsibility as the leader of that church for letting it carry out the way it did. I had to learn that the vision that God had for me wasn't the vision He had for everyone. It was as simple as that. Your congregation is like your family, you fuss and fight. I love the entire Harvest Baptist Church family. Ultimately, I hated to part from them."

"See what I'm saying. You don't apologize for nothing," the technician said.

"It wasn't exactly an apology," Alexis lied. She remembered thinking that it was odd to use the interview segment as his opportunity for what seemed like a public apology.

That was it. Her time was up. A split frame of Willie's headshot and a still frame of Abe from the Sunday service filled the screen as she concluded her segment. Ironically, they looked like two mug shots for a line-up.

The van suddenly swerved to the right as the slow and steady creep forward gave them access to their exit. Bill, the van driver, took the free flow of traffic as permission to test the speed limit. His work day was over fifty minutes ago.

Alexis was far from through, she thought as she righted herself and held on to the bolted metal editing desk as an anchor. Over the next few days she'd be checking the ratings and viewers' responses to add to her pitch to continue her story when she met with the *Inside 7* producers on Friday morning. She had to get in contact with the infamous deacon and those members who orchestrated the rift.

She couldn't help but wonder what Pastors Willie and Vanessa Green felt after viewing the program. Pastor Willie was her link to everybody involved in this story. From their talk, she could tell he really had a pulse for that community. She needed to peel back the layers of a case by possibly interviewing Pastor Willie again. But in her gut, she felt she had ruined her chances of him ever opening up to her again, especially if his wife had anything to say about it. When she should be reveling in the glow of her investigative debut, she couldn't help but figure that she had just lost her biggest lead in the Greens.

Chapter 6

Darkness Becomes Light

Abe had the most curious morning. Everywhere he went there was someone who recognized him from last night's airing of the *Inside 7* segment. He received plenty God bless you's on his stops along his route to work. A few wanted to know how they could help the church. Abe was at a loss as to what to tell them. Even at the pawn shop a woman who had been in several times with the same broach, silver pocket watch, and gold wedding rings in a Ziploc bag said she saw the broadcast. This time she accepted his offer of $75 for the entire lot stating, "I don't feel so guilty now. I never heard of a preacher working in a pawn shop, but I'm sure you're giving me the best deal you can offer."

After she left, Abe sat down at an old desk crammed behind the counter. He didn't feel like becoming engrossed in inventory and playing with the newly acquired gadgets. He silenced the transistor radio he had set to WAVA Christian talk station. He needed desperately to put together the pieces of his life or at least the last few weeks. He felt oddly like a burgeoning celebrity. He figured he needed to start acting the part. He had brought his Bible to study for future sermons during his shift. This was his time, his rebirth, he thought.

Thoughts about Alexis, the reporter who interviewed him, and the anonymous note came to mind. Abe had changed his mind about her. She had been so hard-hitting with her questioning that he felt he had been deceived. Was this a set up, asking him about the church debt and the insurance money so that he would look guilty? When he watched it a second time on videotape he saw that it wasn't just his inquisition, but she was equally persecuting Willie Green, if not more. She had to know the notoriety, and in his case, empathy the broadcast would bring him. She was a reporter. She was used to building up and tearing down images every day. *Prepare for the Harvest,* the note had said. Maybe she was the one willing to coach him behind the scenes.

He searched his PDA for the number she had given him. The number he had for her had a familiar cell phone exchange. He dialed her number, and she picked up on the third ring.

"Hello, Ms. Montgomery, this is Abe Townsend."

"Oh yes, Pastor Abe, how are you? I take it you caught yourself on television last night."

"I sure did," Abe said, rolling the jewelry pieces out on a cloth to clean and inspect while he talked.

"Did you happen to talk to Deacon Thompson for me? That's your uncle, right?" she questioned.

"Yes, Uncle Charley," Abe said. Squinting to see the inscription written inside the wedding ring he was shinning.

"I've been calling the number you gave me. A woman picked up once, but I think he's been avoiding me. He's not returning my call."

"I'll talk to him, today, as a matter of fact," Abe said.

"Good, tell him this doesn't have to be an on-air interview. I'm just compiling facts now."

"I was thinking that maybe we can meet?"

"You, me, and him?"

"No, just you and me," Abe stopped what he was doing.

Realizing how suggestive that may have sounded to her, he tried to clean it up. "No, I mean to discuss what I should do next. You know, like in the note."

"I'm," she hesitated. Then there was an awkward silence. "I 'm not exactly sure what note you are referring to. I usually don't have time to meet and debrief with everyone that I've interviewed. Even now I'm rushing out the door to my next story."

"So, will there be another story about the church?"

"Lord willing, but right now that remains to be determined. Look, I wish you all the best with your church and your ministry," Alexis concluded. "Oh, but do try to find out how soon you can file an insurance claim and start rebuilding your church since this is an arson case."

"Insurance, right. I'll be working on that today," Abe declared.

"I'd be interested to know how that goes. I'll get back in touch with you if I need something," Alexis said, bringing closure to their working relationship.

Abe relinquished the call with a puff of air. He picked up the wedding bands again to check the weight of gold. The woman's ring said ''til death do us part,' and the man's ring had the inscription; 'love covers a multitude of sins.' *What weird inscriptions for a set of wedding bands*, Abe thought. He checked to make sure they were a matching pair and figured this guy must have screwed up royally in their relationship and she was bound until death to deal with it.

He filed the rings away in the storeroom with the rest of the ware that was on a countdown until they became legal merchandise of Capitol Pawn and sold. He looked around at a few items he wanted to add to his museum after their statute of limitations ran out. He was stalling for time. *Insurance, right*, Abe thought. *Call Uncle Charley*. All of a sudden the storeroom was too small. He felt the walls closing in on him.

This had happened to him before when he contemplated returning to ministry the first time. He ended up hyperventilating on the tiled floor behind the display counter.

He escaped the back room and rammed into his desk in an effort to make the front entrance before he met the same fate as before. He was barely outside before he began sputtering like an engine in need of fuel. He sucked in the air as the seat of his grey trousers met the concrete outside.

Abe felt silly sitting there. *What was he doing?* He was a preacher working at a pawn shop. A pastor that felt he hadn't been rationed his measure of daily bread in years. *Where was his help?*

He flung his head back hard against the brick base of the shop. He focused his eyes on banner sized ad that made a claim to his patrons to cash tax refund checks up to $5,000 like the banks. With a hefty hidden fee, of course, not spelled out on the flier. It was a flashy promise of fast cash that offered a false sense of security, at least for a while.

Once again, Abe thought about the note, but also about the church that lay desolate and destroyed no more than twenty minutes from his place of business. He inherited the business like he inherited that church. He had to get in contact with the insurance agency. People expected him to make a claim.

"I think that is him, Delores. The pastor I was telling you about from that story." The woman waved her hand at him as if he should recognize her while her friend openly stared. "We'll be praying for you, Pastor."

"Thanks, darling, God bless," Abe said, jumping up and dusting off his rear end. "All right now, we all fall down, but we do get up."

Abe returned the affectionate wave before turning to go inside. He pulled down the banner, balled it up as best he could and tossed it into the trash can before going to the phone

again. He called his aunt and uncle to give them the heads up
that he would be coming over.

When he arrived at 912 Monroe Street, as usual, the door
was left open for him so he went right in. Abe hoped his Aunt
Elaine had left a plate for him as well. Neither of them was
in the well preserved front room where his Uncle Charley's
favorite chair and dinner tray were strategically placed to view
the television and bay window. His aunt and uncle reminded him of June and Ward Cleaver from the popular sitcom,
Leave it to Beaver. He remembered her serving his uncle meals
in his chair, which was in the direct path of the kitchen.

Maybe he didn't need a publicist, Abe thought. He needed
a wife.

Abe didn't bother to holler from this distance as he headed
up the hallway after peeking in the kitchen. Voices from the
back bedroom moved him in that direction. The door was
open. There he could see his aunt and uncle engaged in a
heated exchange.

"I asked her if I could help her since you were out and she
started asking me all sorts of questions," he heard his Aunt
Elaine say.

His Uncle Charley quickly closed the gap between them.
He grabbed his wife by the wrist and slung her around. They
moved from the sink in the adjoining bathroom to the doorway of the small walk in closet. "What did you tell her? I won't
have you defy me. I just as soon bury you if we can't stand
unified."

"What do you want me to do, Charley?" she asked.

"Think," he yelled. "Keep your mouth shut and help me
for once."

"I always want to help you." Her words strung along in a
heart piercing whine like a child in front of a parent anticipating her punishment.

What is she getting so upset for? Abe thought. *Why is either of them reacting this way?*

"Lord, Charles, what am I suppose to tell them if you won't talk to them. First it was the reporter lady, now it's an investigator."

With a firm grasp still on her wrist, Charley bent down and raised a shoe to her. She shielded her head with her free hand. She didn't make another appeal. She just wept openly and awaited his assault. Abe could not believe his eyes. He felt like a little boy whose innocence had been robbed by what he was viewing. The reality of what was happening left him temporarily paralyzed.

"You promised, not again," she whimpered.

Abe looked at the solid heel of his uncle's lace-up shoes aimed at the bull's eye of his aunt's head and found his voice. "Uncle Charley, no!"

Abe made eye contact with his uncle for a second before Charley turned his attention back on his wife. He looked at her wrist in his hand as if it were a foreign object.

"I don't want to talk to anyone," Charley said, giving his wife a final shove before pushing past both of them. His footsteps could be heard down the hallway and out the door.

Abe stood firmly in the doorway this time. He waited to hear if he would return before dealing with the aftermath. Instead, they heard the noisy engine of his uncle's car crank up and pull away.

"He said it would never happen again," she offered by way of an explanation. She backed farther in the closet as if she didn't want to see Abe's face as she talked. He allowed her that space. His *Leave it to Beaver* image was already shattered.

"When did all this come about?" Abe said, reminding her he was still there.

Just then he knew. This was not some one time occurrence

with his Uncle Charley and Aunt Elaine. This is what his mother and father whispered about at family reunions when they thought he wasn't listening. This was why Abe could never spend the night at their house. This was why their only son, Marshall, joined the Navy and stayed in Europe after his tour of duty there and never came home. Abe had no idea it was this bad.

He stepped forward and waited for her reply. She cowered in the corner. She stared curiously at something tucked back there and used the tail end of her skirt to pull it forth to make an unsteady stoop. Perched there she caught her breath and wiped her face.

"It's all right. It's just the stress that makes him act this way. I done right by your uncle, but something always comes along that makes it hard for him to return the favor. He had stopped for a time." He wondered if her soliloquy was for him or what she needed to tell herself. "I nursed him through a hernia, gout, and cataract surgery. Shoot, those were the good years. Then the unification put an end to my lucky streak. He's just been so angry."

He looked at her vacant eyes that were brought back to life by a wash of fresh tears. He didn't know whether he should hug her or kneel down and pray with her, so he did neither.

"He doesn't want to talk to anyone, so we won't," she said.

What he was witnessing was unmerited submission rather than support, Abe thought. "How can I help you, Aunt Elaine? He can't keep. . . Lord have mercy, this can't continue." He kneeled in front of her.

"He's an old man. He doesn't have that much fight left in him."

"I know but—"

"Please, Abe," Her entire body trembled with each word. "Forgive us. You're a preacher; just pray. God will take care of the rest."

This time she stood and made her exit, leaving behind a discolored and slightly disfigured metal box that she had sat upon.

Chapter 7

Three White Lies and a Gag Order

At ten o'clock Friday morning, Alexis was given the green light for another *Inside 7* exposé in her series, the Easter Church Inferno. The viewers' response had been tremendous, and she left the conference room with the viewers' emails printed and piled in a folder. She was amazed at the sentiments and generosity expressed toward Pastor Abe Townsend. Apparently a churchless congregation plucked a few heartstrings. Even a few people mailed in a love offering, hoping the station would be able to deliver to a church that presently had no address.

She dipped inside a private editing room to process it all and to begin structuring her next story. She had not been in there more than twenty minutes before Martie Hamilton escorted an official looking gentleman into the room wearing a bomber jacket that bore the shield of the Maryland State Fire Marshal's office. He was introduced as Chief Herbert Rich, assigned to investigate the Harvest Baptist Church fire case.

Alexis didn't have a good feeling about this visit. No sooner had he gotten into the room before the production manager, Mark Shaw, was calling him back into the hallway, leaving Alexis alone with Martie. She could see Mark handing a bulging padded envelope to the man through the vinyl vertical blinds.

"What's the deal with this guy?" Alexis asked.

"He wants to see everything that you have done on the Harvest story," Martie said.

"He'll have to wait on part two," Alexis said cockily.

"He says he can get a subpoena, Alexis. Mark said for us to just give him whatever he asks for. He says he doesn't need the headache." He continued in hushed tones as if the man could hear through the cinderblock walls. "Mark is probably giving him a copy of your report from Easter to see if it will produce still markers of the scene and the crowd watching. He also wants the unedited version of your *Inside* 7 piece too, as well as your notes. I have a feeling he'll be here for a while, but first he wants to interview you."

"I'm not handing over my notes to this guy. I'm working on another—" Alexis said, ending her sentence abruptly when the investigator reentered the room.

He was a stocky, hard-nose looking man with an unrelenting unibrow that made her question her last statement. Martie took that as his cue to leave, signaling to Alexis with his eyes that she had been warned. Alexis extended her hand to the empty swivel chair across the room for him to sit.

"Alexis Montgomery, I'm Chief Herbert Rich. I've seen your report. You're direct and to the point. I like that. You should work for us," he said. His brow relaxed into a sagging clothes line, which softened his face a bit.

"Thank you, but I think I'll pass. My job is stressful enough. What can I do for you?" Alexis crossed her legs at the knee to provide a perch for her arms to rest.

"I just have a few questions for you. I know you're busy." He took out a small memo pad, flipped over a few pages, and then placed it on his lap as if he might have to reference it later. "Since you were one of the first ones on the scene, I need for you to paint a picture for me of what was going on before you went on air."

"I just remember it being very chaotic. People were every-where."

"I talked to Danny, your cameraman, before he had to run out. I tell you, real caveman there. He talked a bit about stag-ing the story. I take it you were prohibited from getting too close, but I couldn't understand much else this guy was trying to say. I don't think those guys take their eyes away from the eyepiece enough to really see. He's like, 'talk to pretty reporter lady, she knows the details,'" Chief Rich said, amusing him-self at Danny's expense. He pointed to the editing monitor before saying, "So, pretty reporter lady, you know how to fire up one of these puppies so you can walk me through this footage?"

Alexis knew Danny all too well, and knew he would never refer to her like that. This was a man that thought compli-ments were the currency to buy her favor, she surmised. He pulled his chair up close to hers at the monitor. She got up and called out into the hallway under the premise of getting a technician to press play, pause, and rewind footage at the discretion of the Chief because she didn't know how to do so, but really, she didn't want to be alone with him. He went from being menacing to creepy to her in another way.

The tape started at a distance as Danny tried to set up a clear shot of the damage. He had at least ten minutes of foot-age of them setting up markers. Alexis pointed at the monitor once she sat down again to illustrate how everyone sort of converged on the scene at the same time. It was deafening because the church members broke out into a jubilant praise. Luckily, the mobile van was able to get a space at the corner as the group led by Pastor Willie Green began pulling up in their individual cars right at the curb past the police tape and walking over. The guys in blue hadn't taped the entire perim-eter and were manually pushing the crowd farther back for everyone's safety because the building was still smoldering.

She noticed the chief making notes and couldn't help making an inquiry of her own. "You found something?"

"Just noting what the fire looked like in its final stages. The blaze is sending out its last will and testament, but the smoke color and positioning lines up with the physical evidence we've collected there."

The chief fired off more questions as they watched. Alexis found it difficult to be on the other end of the question mark and hoped that the phone would ring or Martie would come and rescue her with another story scene to rush to. Chief Rich wanted her to ID as many people as she could in the crowd and rationalize why they interviewed who they did that day as opposed to others. More often than not, she simply did not know the answer, and there was no way she knew all the people standing around. Thank God he didn't want to view the *Inside* 7 piece too, she thought. He did ask where she planned to go next with the series.

Alexis played her hand close. She didn't know how much he had been told already. He could have talked to her producers sometime before or after the production meeting just like he caught Danny, the cameraman, before a run. She thought about her Harvest file in her bag that contained shorthand notes from her conversation with Willie Green and Abe Townsend. There were also leads from her initial report to follow up on in her spiral notebook.

The technician ejected the tape and turned off the monitor after satisfying the chief's curiosity. Alexis nodded her appreciation before she left.

"There is more to this story," Alexis said, "and I plan to tell it."

"You bet your pretty little head there is, and I guess it is both our jobs to uncover it. Hopefully we can work together. In fact, it will be my pleasure," he said, running his hand through his beard as he inched the wheels on his chair a little closer. "Here's the deal. I am going to need your notes."

"Notes?"

"Yeah, I have transcripts from the show, but I need your handwritten notes on each story unless you used a voice recorder, then I need that also. It will be returned when the case is solved."

"What am I suppose to do without my notes until then?"

"That's the thing," Chief Rich said. He stood as if preparing to bring this interview to a close. "The pastors are hot, which means they are live witnesses of the bureau, which means they are off limits."

Alexis laughed at the absurdity and looked at him closely to see if he made that last comment in jest.

"I have a job to do, Chief. Taking my notes and my witnesses is not allowing me to do my job. There is such a thing as The First Amendment," Alexis said, thinking back to her undergraduate days. Cops weren't the only ones that could lean on their shield; journalists had their support as well. She was not going to allow herself to be intimidated.

"Look," he started.

She was waiting for 'toots' or 'dollface' to follow. She raised her hand to silence him. There would be no more attempts at flattery. She got it. He had come to silence any further reports. "The Federal Shield law protects anyone who helps disseminate news to the public. It says that you have to do more than claim a subpoena before I should feel compelled to give you anything."

"I have been a fire marshal almost as long as you've been born. I get arsonists off the street so people like you don't wake up like a human torch, or at the very least, keep your personal effects at home and your degree-laden walls of your offices from being an open barbeque pit. If you think I'd let anything come between me and that responsibility, you've got another thing coming." He was not shouting. His mob boss swagger was helping him prove his point. "Everyone cooperates with Herbert Rich. So yes, I know about your law, just like I know the law that protects the medical community from breach of confidentiality and letting us look at their oh-so private medical records. Let me tell you that doesn't stop me from dragging one of those non-complying doctors through court for infringement either."

You can't bully me, which was exactly what he was doing. She couldn't believe this was happening. What would this mean for her story? She was given the go-ahead just a few hours ago. She had to keep the momentum going on her story.

"The way I see it, the law says I need probable cause that your sworn testimony and documents are necessary for the completion of my case. Sounds subjective to me. There are so many ways around it. I am telling you if you try me and sneeze in the direction of the church and its members while I'm conducting my investigation, you will catch some kind of charge. Now, tell me, darling, do you have time to go through the legal system?"

"But, but . . ." That left her sputtering.

"Now, where are the notes, and I'll be on my way."

Alexis pushed over the voice recorder already on the desktop that she prepared to review for brainstorming. She walked over to her satchel like a kid asked to show a parent a bad report card. It wouldn't do any good to protest. Martie had already shared the station's position. She was on her own. When she looked inside the bag, she almost smiled remembering her initial notes tucked inside her spiral notebook. She handed him the folder.

"Is this it?"

"Yes, Captain. That's it."

***

At one o'clock, Abe was playing solitaire on a late model computer when two people entered the pawn shop. One was a possible consigner and the other was a burly investigator from the Fire Marshal's office. Chief Rich wasted no time getting down to business after scanning the display cases, waiting for Abe to finish with his customer.

"I think this is so cool, really, a man of Christ like yourself who has time to provide a decent service for the commoners in these tough economic times." Chief Rich nodded his approval.

"Yeah, it's sort of a family business," Abe said.

"You don't say," Chief Rich said, staring at a pair of binoculars through the glass. "You got much family running the church with you too?"

Abe bit his lip. "No."

"I hope you don't mind me asking a few questions. I'm sort of on a tight schedule." He didn't wait for a response. "Who opens the church on Sundays?"

Abe hesitated, not because he wasn't used to investigators, like reporters, coming out of left field by now. He couldn't think of his Uncle Charley without thinking about what he had witnessed earlier in the week. "That would be Deacon Charley Thompson." He couldn't bring himself to call him uncle.

"Give me a timeframe of a typical Sunday schedule from the time you get to church in the mornings until you lock up."

"Since we've stopped sunrise service, which was really at seven A.M., we are usually in by 9:30 preparing for eleven o'clock service. Service usually runs a little over an hour and a half and we lock up after that and go home."

"What was unusual about Easter Sunday?"

"Nothing, other than arriving before Deacon Thompson, and since I don't have any keys, I waited."

Abe was taken back to that day. He remembered waiting on the front step of the church like a kid locked out of his own house. He thought about walking away for good at that moment. He remembered he kept timing himself by thinking, *If Uncle Charley is not there within the next five minutes.* His plan was to get back in his car and go hide out at the pawn shop until the day was over, no explanation or anything. That's when members of the congregation started showing up one by one. They all had the same question, and Abe anticipated that the chief had the same inquiry.

"How does a pastor not have his own key?"

"I do, but I usually don't need them, so on this particular Sunday I left mine at home."

He did not. There was something sad about admitting that he wasn't given any keys. He was sure the fact of whether or not his Uncle Charley cut him a key or not didn't affect the case either way, but he felt bad about lying. He didn't know who he was becoming, or maybe he'd never really had to face who he really was.

Abe wondered how long this interview was going to last. He watched the chief's massive hands flip the pages of his notebook, and then tap out a rhythm on the glass display case. The rhythm was methodical. Abe was sure his thinking was equally so.

"Can I trust you with some information? We think the back of the church is where the fire originated." He stared at Abe. Waited for that tidbit to sink in. "Anyone can see that the back is where the most damage is. There was only a thin drywall division between the back offices and the sanctuary. Very incendiary."

Abe felt more comfortable now that some of the details

were finally being leaked. He said, "I think there was only an office and a utility closet back there."

"Were there any inoperative alarm systems or sprinklers?" Chief Rich asked.

"Not to my knowledge."

"What were the conditions of the doors and windows back there?" Abe shrugged, prompting the captain to simplify his question from fill-in-the-blanks to yes-or-no. "Were the windows and doors broken?"

"No," Abe conceded.

"How often do you use the back?"

"I don't, really," Abe replied.

"You don't use your own office," he said as more of a statement than a question. He did some writing.

"The previous pastor used that office in the back."

"You're kidding me, right? He isn't enshrined back there is he? It's just an office, geez. What, this guy, uh," Chief Rich paused while he looked for the name, "Willie Green, is he your bitter enemy or what?"

"No, not at all, he's my predecessor. I like to think of him as a mentor."

"'Cept you never told him, right? I have a feeling this wasn't a pass the torch kind of deal. In fact, you probably don't even know the guy. Whose idea was it for you to take over for him?"

"I know of him. There are many pastors I haven't had the pleasure of meeting, but I have . . . uh, studied their ministry," Abe replied, ignoring the chief's question.

Abe wondered why they were standing as the chief tapped out another rhythm. Abe was beginning to see a pattern. Each time he referenced his pad he aimed from a different direction. He wondered if he could stand much more. He thought about Pastor Green and the poise of many other pastors he had studied. He remembered to stay in character.

"It's been more than a week and you haven't called in an insurance company claim," Chief Rich said as if he were thinking aloud. "Strange."

"Come again?"

"I said that's strange, Reverend. People typically call the insurance company immediately. An interview with the claims agent is usually the first stop on the road to recovery." Chief Rich said, "It's almost as if you don't want to rebuild. I guess that saves me a trip to the agency. Oh wait, no, I still have to talk to the agent who wrote the policy. Who's the policy with anyway?"

Abe faltered with a response. He had looked briefly at the contents of the metal box that he had taken from his Uncle Charley's house. Sure enough, his aunt had unknowingly handed him what he had come to the house for to begin with. The name of the insurer would not come to mind. He was too busy still trying to figure out how his aunt and uncle had possession of something that obviously should have been left for the fire officials to find.

"Just as I suspected," Chief Rich proclaimed. "Do you like your job, Reverend?"

Abe was unsure as to what job he was referring to, but he knew enough to nod in the affirmative.

"I love my job, but sometimes it's agonizing when these arsonists are on the loose. I lost quite a few friends when I was a firefighter in New York-219 engine in Brooklyn. Was there for eleven years. So many friends went down or were injured that I had to relocate to clear my head. I decided to be a fire marshal down here. I lived in hell. The fires in my own personal hell seem to burn so bright it outshined a heaven. Call me cynical, but I'm not certain if heaven exists."

Abe kept quiet, figuring the captain needed to vent. He could only imagine his loss. There were many days that he felt he was in hell himself, or worse, in purgatory.

"Insert sermon here," Chief Rich said, pointing both fingers back at himself. "Wow, not too many pastors could resist that lead in. Don't quit your day job, and please don't volunteer for any suicide prevention hotlines."

Now, he's was patronizing him, Abe thought. If that was a test, he had just failed like he did at saving his aunt from his uncle. He was still haunted by the need to do something more. He felt as if he, himself, should be arrested. He wondered if anything he had said today or failed to say labeled him as a real suspect in the chief's mind. He knew he would definitely feel the heat if the captain ever found out he neglected to tell him about the metal locked box. He just didn't know what to do.

As if reading his mind the Captain asked, "Do you know where any of the church papers are?"

"Yes," Abe was proud to say, "at home."

"I need a copy of the insurance packet. I'll come by tomorrow to pick it up." He took one last look at his notepad, and tapped out a ditty. "I better get the key as well for physical evidence.

Abe stared blankly as if to say, you caught me.

"Let me guess, Deacon Thompson has it?" He shook his head. "Don't worry, I'll get it. You, on the other hand, are not to talk to anyone about the details pertaining to this case—no reporters of any kind, got me? Oh, and by the way, don't take any unexpected trips."

At eleven o'clock, Saturday morning, Willie interrupted his study time to entertain questions from a Maryland State Fire Marshal. The chief looked as if he had been up all night and his earthy smell made Willie believe he had just left the fire scene. Willie introduced the chief to Vanessa, but got the impression he only wanted to speak to him. They settled downstairs in their home office. After a brief discussion with the two of them the chief sent Vanessa upstairs to write down members in the enlarged photos of the fire scene on Easter Sunday, while requesting a fresh brewed batch of coffee. Willie hoped that if and when she returned with the chief's cup, that it didn't accidently end up in his lap.

"We haven't quite figured out who discovered the fire and thought that you could help us out," Chief Rich said, looking uncomfortable on such a low couch. His girth hung over the edge as if at any minute he would fall off the end. Finally, he sat catty-corner against the arm of the couch and continued, "Who alerted you of the fire?"

Willie threw his head back in thought.

"A man or a woman?" the captain asked, prompting him.

"A man, no wait, a woman," Willie said. "I believe a man asked to speak to me, and then he passed it off to a woman. It was definitely a couple."

"Did you recognize the voices?"

Willie shook his head as he thought. He was more interested in what was said than who was saying it at the time. He knew almost two weeks later that he couldn't remember.

"I have to do many interviews, Reverend; everyone seen in that photograph is a potential witness. That is a lot of digging in rubble, and in this case, digging in church records, like the church telephone records."

"Telephone records? Wait a minute; are you serious?" Willie asked. He suddenly felt as if his rights were being violated.

"A call was made to your church. I am telling you as a courtesy, but it is already a done deal. A subpoena will handle all of that." Chief Rich shifted in his seat. "Do you get regular calls from members here?"

"No," escaped his lips immediately. It was more accurate

to say that he received a lot less calls from members now that he and Vanessa had a talk with their congregation. They also instituted a ministry tree to divert some of their calls to other ministry leaders in the church. Willie watched him scribble something in his notepad. This time Willie shifted. He played it off as if he were using the back rest of the leather couch to scratch his back.

"Let's talk now about the insurance. I just got the policy from your successor, Abe Townsend, this morning, so I haven't had much time to look at it thoroughly. But are you aware your name is still on many of the church documents including this policy?"

"I knew, but then again, I forgot." Willie said, shaking his head out of dumb luck, rather than contradiction. "I mean, I was advised to get that resolved when we went for arbitration, but I am afraid it never happened."

"Yeah, because my next question was going to be how the church handles a separation of this kind? Because you didn't just walk away from this deal alone. Then you and your wife had a merger of sorts. I've never heard of anything like it. Were you advised to get an addendum to your pre-nup just in case this church doesn't work out for you either?"

Willie didn't dignify that with an answer. He gave him that man-to-man eye contact that let him know he had gone too far and stepped into his dangerous territory.

"I'm saying, Reverend, the first split apparently wasn't smooth if you had to have arbitration. Tell me about it," Chief Rich said while writing.

"It basically was to settle whether or not I was going to surrender the keys and account balances over to the ones who wished to remain there."

"Obviously, you did."

"Yes," Willie said.

"Why were you holding on to it if it was your intention to go to another church?"

"I figured I knew that community best. I had dreams of having a full service pantry and community center as an extension of the ministry I share with my wife."

"You wanted to have your cake and eat it too."

"This was not going to be the selfish venture you are making it out to be."

"Okay, but you were skeptical that those that remained under the leadership of their new pastor could make the same impact."

"Not if they were putting up a front and playing church," Willie said, once again shaking his head. "Forgive me, I don't want to be judgmental. I can't speak on their motives."

Something in the captain's expression showed he understood. "Is it fair to say your perceptions could have caused this little oversight in the policy?"

"I've just been busy. Busy, doing the Lord's work down the road," Willie answered.

"And the Lord's work stopped you from making sure the work was completed on the previous claim. I don't know if you were aware, but it was apparent to us that the church was outdated and in disrepair. It took us longer than usual to discern whether it was an accident caused by a faulty electrical system or arson. Except for key evidence, this could have been ruled either way."

Willie couldn't say a thing. He felt as if he were getting a lecture from a parent about keeping his room cleaned. He was a preacher, not a repairman. Willie thought about the circumstances the chief presented, and it didn't look favorable on his part.

"Wait, am I a suspect?" Willie said, thinking about Vanessa's recent pursuit of legal representation.

Chief Rich placed a fist on the ground to launch himself off the couch. Willie stood as well. "On that note, let me know if anyone in your congregation, especially those street soldiers that marched up to the old church with you, gets the urge to shed some light on this case in the confession booth."

Willie was anxious for him to go. He didn't feel the need to tell him they weren't Catholic. His mind was in a swarm. He led Chief Rich up the stairs into an empty kitchen. He collected his photos with a sheet of notebook paper where Vanessa had written each person's name that she knew.

There was no coffee brewing. Chief explained the sensitivity of the investigation and warned Willie against talking to the press.

At the door Willie tried again. "Am I a suspect?"

"Everyone is either a suspect, co-conspirator, or witness. Have a good day, Reverend," Chief Rich said before leaving.

Chapter 8

A Consuming Fire

Vanessa was on fire. For her and Willie's return to the pulpit after their vacation, she evoked the Holy Spirit and preached everyone happy as if to say, "Whose house?" She led the appreciative crowd in giving God a standing ovation and doled out her famous scriptural prescriptions as souvenirs of the day.

She took a short break in her chair behind the preacher's desk before rising again with Willie to conclude the service with pastoral observations and blessings. She felt strange. Her face began to flush again with a tremendous heat that engulfed her. This time it didn't stem from the euphoria that filled her soul as she preached as if she'd be called up to meet the Master at any minute. The heat didn't emanate from a well of emotions she pulled from when she made a point in the pulpit or shared a timely testimony about her life and struggles. She was sick.

Willie was talking about the upcoming church anniversary and she wanted to add that their focus should be aligned with the theme, *Back to Basics, Back to Jesus*. She couldn't share that there should be more prayer and praise instead of gossip and concern over the recent media coverage and investigation of the Harvest Baptist Church fire. Vanessa felt it was important for them to reassure their congregation that the

Lord was in control of that situation, but Vanessa couldn't speak. Her gears were thrust in reverse, and she could feel the bile rising in her throat. She used her sermon outline that was still on the podium to fan herself and forced a smile to cover the turmoil within. She prayed that the Lord would be merciful and not let her taint her robe, her husband, or the sacred desk with the remnants of her breakfast. She silently heaved and prayed. When Willie yielded the microphone for her to speak, she shook her head as if she had nothing to say.

When church was dismissed, she immediately retreated to her office bathroom. Still in her robe, she turned on the sink and the exhaust fan and assumed the position above the bowl. The anticipation was worse than the waves of nausea itself. When she sacrificed all she had to give to the bowl below her, she didn't immediately feel better like in the past. She felt drained. She splashed her face with water and waited until the color had returned to her face.

A knock on the door startled her.

"There you are," Willie said. "I thought you had left me to go help your sister prepare. We had an invite out from the Wheelers, but I guess we've got to go to this dinner at your sisters, huh? I wonder if she will mind me inviting Wayman Brown over since he's new to this area. Hurry up out of there."

"You don't have to wait on me," Vanessa replied. *Just go.* "We drove separate cars, remember?"

She could feel him hesitate. "I see that chili from last night has come back to haunt you. I told you it wasn't any good. Use the deodorizer. Don't blow it up too bad. I pray that He who has begun a good work in you shall perform it before dinner." He could barely get out the entire statement before erupting in laughter.

His biblical humor was incorrigible, she thought. When

he left she came out of the bathroom. She thanked God that
Sunday dinner wasn't at their house this time as she hung up
her robe and slipped on her suit jacket. Before her sister became engaged, and even before unification, the three of them
would just crash after church and dine on what she called,
"congregation carry-out." It was her big idea to have a more
formal sit-down dinner with family and close friends after
church at least twice a month. Their family was expanding to
include Paul and his mother, Thelma Grant, long time members of the old Harvest Baptist Church. Willie took it also as
an opportunity to invite members of the congregation he was
still getting to know. The last Sunday dinner that was at their
home was on Easter, and it was half ruined because the newly
engaged Paul and Keisha decided to go out to celebrate while
the rest of Vanessa's guests were with them at the site of the
Harvest Baptist Church fire until well after seven P.M.

Vanessa arrived at her sister's apartment anticipating a
good meal she hoped she'd be able to enjoy. The aromas that
greeted her at the doorway told her she wouldn't be disap-
pointed. Her appetite had returned with a vengeance. As long
as they weren't eating chili, she was more than prepared to
chow down. She figured she should offer her assistance with
the final preparations and service of the meal, but with both
Keisha and Ms. Thelma onsite, Vanessa's help was not needed. Paul would never have to worry about going hungry with
those two around. Besides, she had just preached for an hour
and a half, so she deserved a break. She claimed a seat on the
couch.

Vanessa always felt Keisha inherited the best gifts from
their family. While Vanessa was playing pastor growing up,
and eventually promoted to pastor of the church, Keisha was
learning to sustain and preserve the home. She could see her
grandmother and her mother in her baby sister.

All the guests were called around the oval shaped oak table that had been in their family since both of them were small. The table could be expanded by pulling on opposite ends and inserting the inlet. Vanessa felt a tinge of jealousy that she, being the oldest, did not acquire the dining room set from her mother, but knew it was better served there with her sister. Thick sliced meatloaf was layered in a serving dish with gravy, and bowls of vegetable medley and Keisha's famous lumpy mashed potatoes, were set in the middle of the table.

"Everything is lovely, Keisha, really lovely," Willie complimented.

"Thanks, bro, "Keisha said, assisting with the service of the gravy drenched meatloaf. Everyone passed their plates in assembly line fashion in that direction after getting their share of side dishes.

Vanessa was leery of the meatloaf once her plate was passed back to her. The aroma assaulted her nostrils and her mouth began to water in an unsavory way. She had thoughts of her own chili that she insisted upon finishing the night before and could taste the remnants of it on her palate. Instantly, she had lost her appetite. She excused herself to the bathroom.

There, she stared at herself really long and hard in the mirror. *What was coming over her?* She splashed her face for the second time that day and searched Keisha's cabinet for mouthwash. She found a travel size bottle and used half of it to give her mouth a fresh perspective.

All she wanted to do was go home and crawl into her bed, alone. She couldn't think of a way to excuse herself without offending her sister and alerting everyone else's concern. She hoped and prayed she could make it through the evening without another episode.

Vanessa returned to her seat next to Willie, which was on the opposite side of the table from Paul and her sister. Ms.

Thelma had the place of honor at the head of the table across from Willie's guest, Mr. Brown. Everyone was so quiet from eating that they weren't suspicious of her absence. She decided to take it easy, only taking miniscule bites of her meatloaf.

"So, I know the question that is on everyone's mind—when is the big day? I admit, I had a major meltdown earlier this week. Thank you to everyone who talked me off the ledge. I think we are going with the fall," Keisha announced.

"That still doesn't tell us a month or a day," Ms. Thelma commented."We've got to give the folks down south some notice. Your soon-to-be-cousin, Ollie, and I were hoping you all would just do it this August at the Grant family reunion."

Keisha's eyes bulged out of her head as if a surge of lightning went through her body. Vanessa noticed Paul reach over and grab her sister's hand as if to temper her. Vanessa jumped in to voice what she knew her sister was thinking, "Oh no, Ms. Grant, baby sis has waited too long to share her day with any other occasion."

"Exactly," Keisha managed to say after taking a swig of her sweetened tea. "Plus, Mama Tee, I want to send out our engagement announcements with our picture on it, so if you don't mind, please don't tell everyone about it."

"Save your money on those fancy announcements. Since I left Carolina, Cousin Ollie has taken over my job as Mouth of the South. The whole family knows the two of you are engaged by now."

This time Keisha let out a heavy sigh of disappointment. Once again, Vanessa noticed Paul's massive hand pat her sister's hand gently to the tune of, calm down, dear, before cupping it entirely. They held on that way, both using their free hand to feed themselves. That simple gesture was so endearing to Vanessa, as she remembered a time not too long ago when subtle displays of affection in her own relationship were often better than compliments and gifts.

"Now, it makes perfect sense to dust down the Arbor in back of Great-Granddaddy's church where we have the prayer breakfast and get you hitched on the last day of the reunion. I mean the entire family will already be together. Brother and Sister Pastor can just drive down along with any other little friends you want to invite." Ms. Thelma's head swiveled toward her son, "Right, Paul?"

The spotlight was turned on Paul as all eyes rested on him, those most pointedly coming from his mother and fiancée. He cleared his throat first. "Hey, I'll let you ladies figure it out. Just give me the time and place and I'll show up."

"Smart man," Mr. Brown hailed, and Willie agreed.

They both waved off the men as hopeless. Vanessa felt they created an interesting dynamic, her sister, fiancé, and future mother-in-law. She wondered if Ms. Thelma's apparent possession over her only son and Keisha's possession over this wedding would ever click.

Vanessa forgot she was supposed to be eating lightly and had almost completed her entire chunk of meatloaf. She pondered if her stomach could handle seconds, but decided against it.

"I thought the hot topic of today was going to be my Channel 7 interview. It seemed to be at church today. Your pastor makes the news and no one here has anything to say," Willie said, changing the subject.

"I'm glad," Vanessa said. "I started to address it from the pulpit so that rumors about the fire don't start to fly like they did during unification."

"Why didn't you?" he asked.

Vanessa cleared her throat. She didn't want to get into the real reason. "It was your interview. I figured you were trying to play it low key."

"I admit, we were talking about it at church," Thelma Grant

added, using a yeast roll to soak up the leftover gravy on her plate. "We wanted to know why that Reverend Townsend got more time than you."

"Some people forgot to remind me to watch, so I missed it," Keisha said. "I was busy setting up our wedding profile on the Internet so I can talk to other brides-to-be."

Vanessa ignored her sister's comment. As far as she was concerned, now that her sister had a fiancé, she was no longer responsible for reminding her of things.

"Well, I felt the reporter grilled him enough even in the short amount of time," Vanessa said. She and Willie had this conversation the night it aired. Willie didn't see the interview as a scathing accusation like she did. To her, Alexis was eager to assign guilt.

"She had to ask those questions though, Sister Pastor. If you think about it, she has to ask the questions her viewers are thinking," Paul said.

"Or, she was swaying what viewers were thinking by asking pointed questions," Vanessa was quick to respond.

"Who wants dessert?" Keisha asked, standing. She counted hands as if taking a tally of orders for the ice cream truck. Most of them saw the lemon meringue pie on display in the kitchen when they came in and couldn't wait for the opportunity to sample it. Keisha left the room to begin cutting slices.

"Well, we know you didn't set that fire, Brother Pastor. Shoot, you were in the pulpit. You've got an entire congregation to vouch for that." Thelma Grant stacked the dishes around her in an attempt to clear the way for dessert.

"Well, the fire detective they sent yesterday is not so sure. He was the one that grilled me. Let me just warn you, it's a matter of time before he gets to all of you. He had me afraid I was going to jail. He asked me to stay in town and not plan any long out-of-state trips just in case they had any further questions to ask me."

"Arson is serious," Wayman Brown spoke up. "I used to work for the local volunteer department in Southeast when I retired from the Corps and moved to this area."

"Wow, really?" Paul perked up. Everyone looked at Mr. Brown with amazement as if he had just transformed into an action figure.

"I can't wrap my mind around the malicious intent of an arsonist. I wanted to believe it was an accident done by a passerby. But to have fire investigators interrogate me as if they suspect me is unreal," Willie said.

"They either suspect you or someone around you," Mr. Brown added. The comment hung out there like a sheet on a mild day. Everyone was stilted as if they wanted to, but didn't dare look at their neighbors around the table. "Those investigators have very little to go on sometimes. Fire often times destroys its own evidence and we, as firefighters, destroy the rest. They will question everyone. The guys at the firehouse would immediately know which fires were ruled arson when the detectives would come to the firehouse to question us."

"Why?" Thelma asked what was on everyone's mind.

"We knew they were trying to find out who was standing around the scene when we got there. Arsonists love to hang around a scene and see their own work. They probably figured the fire is either a revenge fire or a profit-oriented fire. One time, this young kid I worked alongside in the fire station got charged with arson. I was blown away. Come to find out it's not uncommon for guys like us on the volunteer unit to set fires too. I guess to try to stir up some action in between calls. When someone is trying to be too helpful or trying to play hero-now that's a vanity fire."

Vanessa felt a chill race up her spine as Brother Brown was talking. This time she wasn't infirmed. It was what he had said. It was scary to think that the person responsible for the fire could have been standing in the midst of all the people that came over with her and Willie from church, or could have been one of them. So that was why she was stuck playing the identity game with a bunch of photos.

"Well I'm glad we weren't there," Keisha said, returning with as many pie slices as she could balance on a tray. "We don't have time to be questioned, and we certainly don't have time for some investigator to tell us when we can and cannot travel. I have a honeymoon to go on."

"Oh no, Ms. Keisha, it's not going to take them that long. Fire is hot, but an arson case runs cold quickly," Brother Brown said. "They'll have this thing figured out soon or not at all."

"I'm following the story because I'd sure like to know who did it. I drive by there every day to see if something has changed," Paul said. "First it looked like they were trying to pull out all that they could salvage. Then it looked as if investigators were trying to recreate the sanctuary. I talked to Brother Jacques at the store on the corner. Now, he's got some theories," Paul said. "Keisha and I drove past there on the way here. It's still roped off, but from an angle you can see clear inside to the back rooms where your office used to be, Pastor."

"Well, the first person they need to question is that ole' Charley Thompson," Thelma charged. As sure as I'm born he had something to do with it. "

"People are innocent until proven guilty, Ms. Thelma," Willie reminded, dabbing the corner of his mouth where the whipped topping had landed.

"Deacon Thompson was dead set against leaving that church, Ma," Paul said. "He's probably half-crazy himself over his precious church burning down."

"He's not that tore up 'cause he was on the same television

show as Pastor this week, standing by the door like he was an usher or some type of guard while his nephew was preaching," Thelma said, using her fork as a pointer after pulling creamy layers of pie off of it with her mouth.

This was what Willie was looking for and what Vanessa was trying to prevent. This was a chance to ignite another huge conversation about Charley Thompson and the Harvest Baptist Church. She knew talking about it was good for Willie who was only trying to make heads or tails about the situation. Vanessa was concerned, though, with the speculations of a former firefighter and her future brother-in-law playing junior detective. She was also concerned with Keisha sharing updates with future brides on the Internet and the former Mouth of the South talking about it in church and reporting to family members down south. This story had the potential to consume them all like the fire did the church.

She looked at her husband to see if he could be thinking the same thing. She saw a mixture of fascination and devastation on his face. She inched her hand over and gently let it rest on top of his, letting him know he had a hand to hold through it all.

Chapter 9

A Game of Cat and Mouse

There was nothing like the solitude of the pawn shop to Abe. He did his best thinking there and was often caught singing, dancing, or talking to himself when the door chimes announced the arrival of a customer. Even then he could decide to what extent he wanted to interact with the customers. Sometimes he would empathize with those forced to make a desperate decision in order to get some cash. He would minister to those who were really wrestling in the spirit and would tell them that their situation was only temporary. For a few people, he even talked them out of selling their possessions outright. For those people he had a special shelf in the storeroom of items he would never sell. He'd pray for the owners to return and reclaim their property, and many of them did.

Recently, he felt his old life slipping away. Somehow he didn't feel authentic outside of those walls as if it weren't safe to be himself anywhere else but there. It had been almost a week since the *Inside 7* broadcast and close to three weeks since the actual fire, and he didn't feel any closer to the truth, any closer to God.

He looked around the empty pawn shop and wondered if it were a sign. *No customers on a Monday was rare.* The recklessness of the weekend and the cruel prospect of another week usually made Mondays his busiest day. It was also rare for his Uncle Charley to miss church. Abe called after church, and then again this morning with no answer either time. He wondered if his uncle was as remorseful and ashamed of his abusive behavior as Abe was for witnessing it and not doing anything about it. His aunt was adamant that she was okay. He found himself wondering what would Willie Green do, but he knew. As his pastor, he was supposed to pray for his uncle to help and bring him to deliverance. He had more praying to do himself, because at that moment, he wasn't sure he was willing to forgive his uncle yet, even if his auntie had. Abe wanted to see what his uncle had to say for himself.

The doorbell chimed. A postman distracted with headphones tossed a package on his counter and left without so much as a hello. The padded envelope was addressed from Alexis Montgomery from the TV station. The note inside explained that the contents of the envelope came as a result of their *Inside 7* report. Immediately, he noticed that the bold and deliberate strokes of her handwriting did not match up to the fanciful characters in the anonymous note he received in the offering basket. He carried that note around in his wallet as if it were an important clue to a hidden treasure.

He sat on his favorite stool behind the counter, opened the package, and immersed himself in the many cards and notes with a few checks for generous donations thrown in between.

"Important package?" a woman asked.

Abe wondered how she got in without him hearing the bell. He took a good look at her. She was functionally attractive, and well put together like his old oak table. Her medium length hair was curled all over. She wore a form fitted suit to display her curves with a peak-a-boo camisole to showcase her cleavage.

She cleared her throat, bringing Abe's attention back to why she was there. He stood.

"I was preoccupied, I'm sorry. Is there something I can help you with?" Abe asked, figuring from her appearance that she must be in the wrong place.

"How long do you intend to stay open?" the woman asked.

"We are open until five P.M."

"I had a hard time finding you." The timbre of her voice sent a shiver down Abe's spine. He had to tell himself she didn't mean that literally. She sashayed down the length of the front display case, looking down occasionally before returning to her spot directly in front of him. "You're that preacher, right?"

Abe's heart began to accelerate. "Yes, yes, I am."

"You plan on rebuilding that church of yours?" the woman asked.

He hesitated. "Uh, yeah." *Maybe she is another reporter,* he thought. He figured if she were a reporter on local network television he would have noticed. He didn't know what it was, but she definitely had appeal.

"How can you rebuild your church if you're stuck in here all day?" She stretched her arms out on both sides of her, using the top of the glass display case as a prop to gently lean forward, giving him another eyeful. "How long do you plan on staying here, doing this?"

The bell chimed before he could answer. A man stood in the door frame, pulling a kid's wagon with two enormous speakers in it. He struggled with keeping the cumbersome pair from toppling over while pulling the wagon at the same time. Abe knew he should help, but he was a deer caught in headlights with this woman. She looked over her shoulder at the customer and back at Abe before taking her goods off display. Abe put his index finger up to indicate that he would only be a minute with this customer.

He had to get a grip, Abe told himself as he willed himself

not to look her way. He remembered the last time a good looking woman flirted with him and the chain of events it set off. He never wanted to be that vulnerable again. He came from around the counter to assist the man the last steps of the way. Every time he looked up, he met her gaze. Abe inspected the speakers and offered the man his bottom line on the storage fee for them. The man promised to come back for them in two weeks. He didn't have time to haggle with this man who obviously thought he would get more. Abe could tell he was thinking about all the trouble of getting the speakers there in the first place before walking out in outrage. Once the man resigned, Abe went back to his post to complete the transaction. Again, he put his finger up, promising to get back to her just as soon as the agreements were printed and signed.

Abe escorted the man to the door, not because he was generally that courteous, but rather to inspect the woman's goods. He immediately noticed her toned legs and feet topped with steel grey stilettos. He backtracked to the second finger of her left hand. No band was present. He discreetly adjusted his belt and waistband before approaching her, in case she was doing an inspection of her own.

"How old are you?" She greeted him for a second time with a question.

"Forty-eight," Abe replied. He felt like he was being fitted for something. He halfway expected her to take out her tape measure to assess his inseam.

"You don't look a day over forty-five," she said, doing a commercial for her perfect porcelain veneer smile.

"You don't say." Abe felt sixteen. He had all his own teeth that were not badly stained or damaged and not even a notion of grey hair, so he accepted the compliment.

"What's your passion, pawn shop-preacher? Is this it?" she asked, looking around.

Abe, who earlier thought he couldn't stand the outside world invading the sanctity of his shop with questions and inquiries, suddenly didn't mind. "What is yours? You seem to know a lot about me, but I don't know anything about you."

"Oh, I dibble and dabble in a lot of things." She turned away from him, once again pretending to be interested in looking at something in the display case. She knew his eyes would trail her. She was like a Broadway actress making full use of her stage. She stopped when she was framed just right. This time she leaned back on the showcase as if she were about to kick up her heels in a chorus line. "But my main passion is helping people succeed. That's why I sent you the note."

It took a minute to process what she had said. He didn't know what to say. So this was the woman he'd been waiting to get in contact with. He was sleepwalking toward her and stopped when they were face to face.

"You?" Abe fumbled to get his wallet from his back pocket and produce the perfectly folded message, "wrote this?"

"I should have known someone from the Thompson clan would come to prominence," she said. "How is your Uncle Charley?"

"Honestly, I haven't seen or talked to him in a couple of days. He wasn't at church yesterday. I'm a little worried."

"Well, when you do, you must tell him I said hi," the woman said with a wink.

They were silent. Abe could tell she was waiting on him to say something. Her eyes seemed to bat in concert with the ticking of the clock. His heartbeat joined in. Everything adjusted to this woman's rhythm.

"So, what makes you want to help me?" Abe asked.

"You have potential." She was no longer leaning. In one fluid motion she had stepped toward him and was concentrating on his shirt that he had not ironed before putting on. She ran her hand down the button line of his shirt as if to smooth it, stopping at his navel. "There is nothing more alluring to me than a man with potential. I saw you on television. You have a genuine quality that people can trust. No one would ever believe you burned the church down."

"Because I didn't," Abe proclaimed.

The woman laughed. "I believe you. That was test number one. Your body tensed, your voice strained, but your face masked your discomfort. It's like a good make-up foundation that can protect your skin from the harsh environment, yet it can hold an array of shades. The beauty is that you have an innocence etched in your features."

She didn't believe in personal space, Abe thought, as she patted his cheek. He fought the urge to ease his hand on hers, holding it there. When she removed her palm, he immediately missed the warmth.

"People will trust you with their souls, and that's what you want. I think you did amazingly well the other night. How has the feedback been?" she asked.

"As a matter of fact, that was what the package was all about." He left her to retrieve the padded envelope delivered earlier from the other side of the counter. He dumped the notes from all the well wishers out on the counter for her to view.

"Hopefully, this is only the beginning." She inspected each check that was clipped together with a squint of her eye. "When is your next appearance?"

"On television? There aren't any other interviews scheduled that I know of. That particular reporter said that was it. They are only interested in finding the arsonist in this case. Plus, the principal investigator on this case told me to refrain from interviews."

"Oh no, you've got to stay in the limelight, Abe." She

shooed that notion away with a wave of her hand. "Your help comes in the light. You need the exposure to help you reach the next level."

"But how?"

"The reporter tried to paint you as a minister not interested in helping the community. You need to fix that, pass out turkeys on the street, hold a benefit at the daycare, do something that will get yourself noticed for giving back. I'll think of something." Her eyes lifted in her head as if she were already scheming.

"Giving back is expensive," Abe said.

"You do have some discretionary funds, don't you?" Her eyes wandered around the ceiling of the pawn shop as if she expected money to fall from the air. "Think of it as an investment."

"Then what?" As crazy as all of that sounded to him, he wanted to do anything this woman wanted him to do.

"We'll let the insurance policy build your church building and the media build your church membership. The bigger the church membership at the time you're ready to break ground, the bigger the church needs to be. Everyone loves an 'up from ruins' story and donations will continue to pour in. Trust me." She now had a hold of his arm across the counter while painting a picture with her right hand. Abe followed her vision in the sky as if she were a skywriter. "Don't worry, I'll be there guiding the way, holding your hand. I guess I will be renewing my membership at Harvest Baptist Church. For the record, I like my seat padded and my sermons short and to the point."

There was a silence, not at all awkward in anticipation, but rather complete in quiet contemplation. Abe was on another mission. The choruses of 'you can do it' that started out as chants at the beginning of the conversation had become full cheers. He looked at this woman who had become the answer to his prayers and thanked God she was devoted to helping him.

"Can I take you to lunch?" Abe asked.

"I thought you'd never ask." She grabbed her clutch, turned to the door and extended her arm for him to grab.

Abe rushed to the register to grab some discretionary cash for the best lunch a day's tally could buy. He didn't want to keep her waiting. "By the way, I didn't get your name," he said.

"It's Blanche, Blanche Seward," she said.

Chapter 10

Hope Not Dope

Curiosity got the best of Willie Green as he found himself steering his car right past the turn to Pleasant Harvest and into the neighborhood of his former church. He had gone to a D.C. hospital to pray with a member that was having an early morning procedure and couldn't resist seeing again the ruin that was the Harvest Baptist Church. The last time he was there fire and rescue crews were on the scene, and he felt like a loved one standing helplessly by as emergency workers attempted to revive a family member. He was there when they turned off the hoses declaring they had done all they could do. By that time they had taped off the perimeter, but like now, he wanted to cross those borders, touch and examine the place to see if it were really gone.

Willie didn't want to continue to gawk from out front, so he went across the street to get a cup of coffee from the convenience store. He expected to see Chief Rich probing around and figured he'd hang out while he drank his coffee to see if there was any activity. He greeted one of the two Haitian brothers who owned the place and prepared his coffee.

"You see what has become of your house of worship," the man said, following Willie to the end of the counter where the coffee condiments were.

"*Vous ont été maudits,*" came the native tongue of the eldest brother, apparently taking refuge in a low seat behind the counter.

"Brother said the place was cursed," the youngest translated.

"Tell Brother, I haven't been away that long. He knows I don't believe his voodoo myths." Willie remembered getting along with all the residents and proprietors of the neighborhood while he was pastor. He and the Brothers Jacques often talked about ways to improve security on Lincoln Avenue, but often had to part ways when they spoke of their superstitious beliefs.

"*N'en faire qu'à sa tête,*" The eldest brother used French derivative to communicate with his sibling, but more so to have a private conversation without offending his customers rather than out of a lack of English proficiency.

The brothers shared a laughed. "The priestess had her way and left everyone with this great mystery. Brother knew she was mixing up trouble, but he didn't want to anger her," the youngest said in all sincerity.

Willie slowly drifted away from the conversation thinking that the notion of a voodoo priestess casting a spell on the church was pretty farfetched even for them. *But, who could the church have angered,* Willie thought, still feeling very much a part of the Harvest family. He found a spot near the window. A woman with long hair rounded the corner to enter the store. He almost didn't recognize her in casual attire with her hair pulled back into a ponytail, but it was Alexis. He moved in the space between a sparse collection of magazines and the ATM machine in the corner to accomplish the difficult task of spying on the very person he was ducking.

He watched her go back and forth between the aisle and the counter, seemingly loading up on a variety of boxed food and snack items as if she were in a grocery store. She held onto an energy drink while the owner bagged up the other items. For a second their eyes met, but surprisingly they both looked away at the same time. They had spotted each other. There was no need to continue the charade that he was browsing the magazines.

"Don't tell my wife. I'm over here snooping at my old church," Willie admitted as she approached.

"I won't as long as you don't tell Chief Rich from the state fire department that I am here talking to you. I have enough to worry about," Alexis said.

"Oh, Chief Rich," said one of the Jacques brothers who apparently held the belief that every conversation held within the store was communal. "Please tell him we need our tape back. We told him we have one camera, one, that faces the opposite street. Still, he took our surveillance tape. The camera doesn't work without tape."

"We get another tape," the voice of the eldest coming in stronger now as he stood and looked around.

"But that was a perfectly good tape."

Willie and Alexis looked at one another and thought it best to continue their conversation outdoors. He took her bag from her as she struggled with the door that favored swinging inward rather than outward.

"So I guess they are still working on the case," Willie predicted once outside.

"It takes a lot to tear down the lies of church folk," Alexis murmured.

He looked at her, sure a comment thrown like that would come with some sort of explanation. "So I take it you have your own theory about who did it?"

"No offense, Pastor Willie," Alexis said, releasing a breath of pure frustration. "Aww, this case is driving me crazy!" She shook the can of her energy drink so much Willie thought she might crush it in her bare hands.

"Calm down, I have full confidence that Chief Rich and his boys will find the arsonist."

"I want to find them, him, or her," Alexis whined, "on primetime television."

"I thought I saw a promo for the second story in your series. I can't imagine how you've managed it."

"I'm not supposed to be talking to you," Alexis reminded.

"And I'm not supposed to be talking to you either. So as long as we are not talking about doing another interview, you can tell me. What are you working on besides lunch and dinner too?" Willie said, raising the bag of food he helped carry for her.

"I'm looking for the street preacher, Roy Jones," she huffed, taking the bag from Willie. "I thought he could use these."

"Roy Jones?" Willie questioned. He started to ask did she have an appointment to meet with him this morning, but knew that would be silly. The last he had heard, Roy was still homeless and preaching from storefronts. For the past three to five years before Willie left Harvest, it was the church that helped feed Roy, and Willie's personal desire to find him permanent shelter.

"Do you know him, or where he could be?" Alexis panted like a puppy waiting at the foot of his master for the possibility of a treat.

"I know him well, but you do know he's homeless, right? During the course of the day, he could be anywhere. Hopefully, he's going to one of the shelters I hooked him up with at night. That might be your best bet."

"I'm going to find him if it takes all day. I took the whole day off for this because if this doesn't work, I forfeit my series and I am back on the beat tomorrow." She was crestfallen at the thought.

"Well, I pray everything works out for you," Willie said,

preparing to excuse himself and go back to church. He wondered if faith or desperation was fueling her quest. "What
happened to not doing anymore stories on the church fire?"

"He said stay away from any church *members*. Technically,
Roy never went to Harvest Baptist Church, right?"

Willie could tell she was determined and had thought
things through. Like a parent, he worried about the unseen
dangers. Roy was flighty and unpredictable. Even in his re-
formed days he seemed to attract unsavory characters. Willie
remembered rescuing him from a dealer that was beating on
Roy as if he owed him money or at least his devoted patron-
age.

"I really don't think you should go down there by yourself,"
Willie said as if she were about to rappel off a cliff into a
mountainous ravine.

"I'm grabbing at straws here, so unless you're offering to be
an escort, I've got to, Pastor Willie."

Willie looked at his watch, up to the sky, and back at her.
He sighed. Then he used his hand to gesture for her to lead
the way. She tossed the energy drink in the bag and swung it
merrily beside her as if his accompaniment was all the pep
she needed.

They noticed two tables placed out in front of the church
as they started out down Lincoln toward the D.C. line, but
didn't tarry. It felt weird walking down the street as if it were
absolutely normal for the two of them to be searching for a
half-witted homeless man. Willie felt as if he should be trail-
ing a few steps behind her. They didn't want to be caught
together by Chief Rich or one of his associates who may view
this escapade as interfering with their case. Willie thought,
worse than that, he didn't want to be seen by anyone that
knew his wife and felt obligated to report back their version
of what was going on either.

He owed Vanessa the courtesy of a phone call. He indicated to Alexis to wait, then he walked off to the side to dial the church's number from his cell phone. Luella connected him to Vanessa's office. Vanessa was not too happy to find that he had scheduled the morning away from church. He'd forgotten this was their week of consecration before next week's 50th anniversary of the church. She had been preparing an emotional tribute for her father, and demanded he be present to start going over the logistics of the celebration when he returned.

When she asked what he would be doing, he warned, "You don't want to know." Surprisingly, she left it alone. She knew he was either being a Good Samaritan by helping someone, or involving himself further in the investigations of the Harvest Baptist Church fire. In this case, he was doing both.

Willie was anxious to survey the block and satisfy both their curiosity so he could get on his way. He linked back up with Alexis.

"Roy can be . . . different, eccentric. The last I saw him he was talking about preaching the gospel."

"Okay, but you sound skeptical." Alexis pulled out her voice recorder.

"He's been through a lot, drug addiction, homelessness. Time on the streets can take away a man's sensibilities," Willie offered, as he urged her to conceal the recorder from view.

The landscape of faces changed as they moved farther away from the church and closer to the D.C. line. Willie waved to a few that remembered him as pastor of the church up the street. He asked a few about Roy that confirmed he was a permanent fixture on these streets. More and more they saw faces of people not interested in social interaction as they walked by with hurried gaits, bags, belongings clutched tight, and downward gazes.

They came to the intersection at Division Avenue where all eyes were on them. Apparently this was a block where the attendance was taken and tourists weren't welcome. Willie wondered should they go any farther. Red brick apartment houses separated by narrow alleys dominated the next block. Willie checked his watch, which read five minutes past eleven A.M. and decided to conquer another block before giving up. They were almost run over by a rugged young man over dressed in layers and his scrawny sidekick crossing the street in haste. The pair seemed to converge with another non-descript man in front of the same building.

Willie and Alexis both did a double take when they spotted a man in a black knit cap resembling a young Marvin Gaye. He came from the alley beside the building to join the group as if he were the leader of a secret club convening on the corner. Alexis reached for her notepad inside her purse and flipped a few pages as if she had a strong desire to sketch the scene. Willie urged her to keep walking although they both couldn't help but take continued glances at the gathering.

Knit cap tilted his chin in their direction as if to ask who they were. They were in a brief eyeball stand-off with his crew as both sides made sure that the other didn't pose any immediate threat. Willie sighed with relief as the man with the knit cap smirked and waved them off as an unconcern as others gathered. Knit cap did an extended handshake with each of the men and just like that their meeting was over.

"That was—" Alexis said, consulting her notepad.

"Illegal drug distribution," Willie added, "from the neighborhood dealer-man." This was the man he kept from beating down Roy. This was also the man he had to continually ask to take his business somewhere other than the footpath beside his church. Why was he still on the street?

"Louis Crenshaw, I interviewed him the day of the fire."

Alexis said, staring at her pad as if it were playing the reel of her memory. "He spoke about a man admonishing people about hell from the church steps. I asked him about it afterward and he gladly gave up Roy's name. I wonder if Chief Rich has gotten to him."

"Well, it wouldn't be a good idea—" Willie realized he was speaking to Alexis's shadow as she stepped off the curb and proceeded to cross the street. He thanked God, Louis and crew dispersed. Willie could see his knit cap bobbing from side to side with his carefree gait and a few more loaded handshakes as he headed in the direction they had just came from.

Willie chased after Alexis's vigorous pace. He didn't want to call her name and make a scene. He had to jog and finally grabbed her arm as she dead-ended in a mob of people. Willie felt like an out of shape parent trying to keep up with his rebellious teenager.

"Where do you think you are going?" Willie fought to catch his breath. "There are things street thugs like him don't take too kindly to when conducting their business; police, police informants, and I'm pretty sure the third is nosy reporters."

This time Willie was asking himself what he was doing here. He took a timeout on the bench under the empty bus alcove and Alexis followed suit.

She sat down hard. "I figured if he were bold enough to deal drugs on the street, he might be willing to talk to me again."

"And say what?" When she didn't answer, Willie replied, "Let's just walk to the end of the block to see if Roy is hanging out up there. Then if you are hell bent to chase down Mr. Crenshaw, you're on your own."

There was a long moment of inactivity as both contemplated what this next hill meant. He looked left. It was an uphill climb. On one hand he could take this five minute walk up the hill. On the other hand, he had a fifteen minute drive to the dutiful sanctity of his church office. *Why do I feel compelled to be here*, he thought.

"Do you think Roy could have done it?" Alexis asked.

"Done what?"

"Burned the church. Even you questioned his sensibilities."

"No, not the way he took shelter there." Willie shook his head. "Even when the doors of the church weren't open, he took shelter there. When he wasn't *in* the shelter he was outside the church. He wouldn't come in. He wouldn't come home with me. He was outside the church with all his bags, his cart and his cardboard mat. Typical, no stereotypical, homeless sensibilities. Gosh, I regret leaving him to these streets."

"You think Crenshaw and his gang could have done it then? Maybe it was a turf issue, and the church was blocking his business." Alexis didn't rest.

"Maybe it was a curse like Jacque and his brother down at the corner store seem to think. I don't know, Alexis. I don't want to believe any of it is true, because in my mind that means the gates of hell prevailed against the foundation of the church. And I can't see how that can happen."

"Typical," Alexis finally sat back.

"What?"

Alexis couldn't hide her annoyance. "What's with you church people with your unyielding ideals that you flaunt as faith?"

"Excuse me?" Willie questioned. Who did this young woman think she was talking to? Willie was beginning to think it was time for them to part ways.

"I'm sorry, Pastor Willie, if I offended you, and I'm not talking about you, per se." She blew out a puff of air.

"So you separate yourself from us, church people. What happened to your granddaddy, Bishop Montgomery, and the small home church that you just love?" Willie gibed.

"I consider myself a Christian. That's right, I am a daughter of the kingdom and I know the kingdom of God is too big to be held indoors."

"That's just the excuse a wayward Christian gives for not affiliating with a church."

"I make no excuse, Pastor Willie. I say all that to prove that I know that the building is just a representation of the foundation of Christ you carry inside. Buildings burn, grow too small, or fall down to disrepair, but your spirit should thrive with Christ," Alexis said. "The question is, do these people who took over that church after you left have the spirit to come back so that the enemy does not prevail?"

They both seemed to exhale at the same time as they pondered the answer to that essential question. He could see the turmoil on her face. "Amen to that, Ms. Montgomery, but somewhere down the line you've been hurt, maybe even in church, which has left you with some unresolved issues," Willie said.

"We've all got them," Alexis stood and stomped her foot as if it had fallen asleep, "but this is not my exposé. Let's find the man of the hour."

"Certainly," Willie resigned. "I need to take my tail on, so I won't have any unresolved issues in my marriage."

They began a deliberate pace up the hill, looking periodically over their shoulders for the neighborhood boys working the block. Past an abandoned building that appeared to be burned out, Willie thought he spotted a familiar silhouette. He was standing with a haggard looking woman who gave him a hug in exchange for something in his hand.

Willie stopped in his tracks. It took a minute before Alexis, who was trotting beside him, realized he wasn't moving. Willie thumbed in the direction he was looking. Fear, humiliation, and anger took over him. Here he had been defending

Roy to her, just to find him dealing the same drugs that destroyed his life.

Willie screamed his name across the divide. The fear that showed on Roy's face after the sudden commotion turned swiftly to delight. Roy bid farewell to his customer and moved toward them. Willie had begun a visual inspection to assess Roy's well being. His usual fetidness was downgraded to a mild rankness without the reeking of liquor.

"I'm so glad to see you, Reverend," Roy greeted, squeezing tighter, causing his windbreaker to squish between them.

"I'm glad to see you also." Willie peeled away, remembering what he saw. "What are you doing out here, Roy? I saw you hand that woman something. I know you're not out here dealing."

"Dealing hope, not dope," he said with a sincere smile that never left his face, despite Willie's accusation. Roy turned toward Alexis. "Certainly, not dope."

"This is Alexis Montgomery. She's a reporter," Willie said.

"Nice to meet you," she said a little too loudly.

Alexis offered him the bag of food she had bought earlier for him as if she were a deaf mute and suddenly couldn't talk. Roy pulled out a snickers bar and a can of soup. A puzzled expression registered on his face.

"We'd like to talk to you. I, especially, would like to find out what you have been up to. Maybe we can take you to lunch at one of the fast food places and talk there." Alexis said.

To Willie's surprise, Roy expressed his preference of dining at the corner hotdog stand. He would have imagined a man whose next meal wasn't a certainty would pick something heartier like a loaded submarine and soup from the Sandwich Shoppe. Willie and Alexis watched as he piled relish and onions on two polish sausages already lined with catsup and mustard. Willie couldn't resist making himself a hotdog, chalking up the idea that he'd make it to church to share lunch with his wife. Alexis cracked open her energy drink. There were not many places to sit, so they found an empty bench facing the most pathetic looking park in the quad where they found Roy earlier. There was only space for the two of them on the bench where the wood planks of the seat were dismantled leaving the space equivalent to a loveseat. Willie stood.

Alexis explained the events of the past couple of weeks as it related to her ongoing investigation of the church fire on the *Inside 7* program. She didn't wait for Roy to finish his lunch before telling him, "I want to discuss the possibility of doing a story on you and your relationship to the church . . . and uh, Pastor Willie here; okay?"

Roy was nodding his head before she could get it out, and continued to nod as if he had been waiting for someone to document his life. Willie wondered if he understood what he was agreeing to. He wanted to clarify that Roy would ultimately be on television and possibly be seen by the friends and family he hadn't seen or talked to because of his addictions.

"Pastor Willie has told me you had to overcome so much in your life. Can you tell me about some of your struggles and how it has led you to where you are now?" Alexis said with all the patience of a pediatrician coaxing a child to describe where their ailment hurts. She was armed with a pad ready to record his every word.

"I was a certified junkie. I wanted the drugs more than air. Have you ever run out of air? It's a terrible thing. You get lightheaded. I've been choked right out here on the terrace by a junkie. One of my best friends and I were supposed to share some blow, and I took too much."

Every time Willie listened to one of Roy's stories, he found them heart wrenching, and the pauses in between torturous.

"When you're being choked you have to make a decision. Are you going to conserve energy or are you going to fight? Nine times out of ten you're going to fight. Fight for that last breath, and the next one, and the next one. Or you scramble to choke what's choking the life out you. That's where I am now."

"And where is that, Roy?" Willie knelt in front of him and patted his hand for support. "I thought you were turning your life around. I thought you were done with that life. I saw you stand right here and give that woman something."

Roy went into a knapsack, which was the sum total of his personal effects. Willie could see a dog-eared Bible he had given Roy some time back to read in the shelter at night. He produced two sealed top liquid containers similar to the mini servings of creamer Willie used in his coffee.

"What is that?" Alexis asked, taking one from him to examine.

"My daily dose of medicine given to me at the clinic to step down off the *horse*," Roy said.

"Heroin," Willie explained, knowing Roy's history with his drug of choice.

"Except, it was God that helped me get down. Some people take up to two years to recover. They make you take your dose at the clinic starting out, like a parent watching you eat your vegetables. After awhile, though, if you have consistently worked the program, and especially if you have a job, they hand you these to-go cups. I asked God one day, Reverend, to give me the strength to withstand my urges because there is someone like Mildred, the woman you saw me with, that needs this more than me. I've been storing them up. Then I just talk to people, describing that big monkey they are carrying around on their back, but can't see. I let them see mine, you know—testify. I keep them away from the dope man by offering them my dose."

What else could be in those cups, but another form of heroine—a less potent kind? Willie wondered if it were a drug at all. Maybe a placebo, Willie thought

"I can imagine it doesn't make you very popular with the dope man," Alexis said.

"Reverend, now you know, I've had my run-ins with him. I try to stay out of his direct line of fire." Roy, seeing the look of horror on their faces explained, "He's not going to keep me away from my mission."

"These people out here only need to know they can go a day without being on that stuff, just a day. One day where they don't have to hustle up the money for their next fix. They need just one day where they don't have to sneak into the hood for the blow before going into work — just one day. The day they taste true freedom they are not only ready to choke the monkey they've been carrying, but body slam the darn thing too. They feel so free. If they want more, I offer them Jesus and an escort to the clinic to sign up for the treatment program. So no, Pastor Green, I haven't left these streets. My ministry is five blocks between the alley down there and the clinic on A Street."

"How long have you been out of recovery? I don't understand. Don't you ever feel like you need your dosage?" Alexis asked.

"I'm not choking yet. I guess I can hold my breath longer without panicking." His grin was a testament.

"His foundation of faith is strong," Willie said, swelling with pride. *Stronger than he wanted to believe it could be.* He thought Roy had to be cleaned up, off the streets, and formally trained to minister. Like Alexis pinpointed earlier, he was starting to see the error of trying to cram the arch of God's influence inside a church house.

"It was this man," Roy said, pointing at Willie. "He never

looked down on me, never gave up on me. He gave me the Word, almost six months ago to the day."

Willie just shook his head dismissing the notion. Roy has grown spiritually in ways he couldn't have imagined were possible in such a short time. He thought how brave Roy was to remain in the trenches after his own deliverance. He wished he could see Roy in action, and wondered how Alexis planned to cover his amazing story.

Willie noticed that they had been talking rather than eating. He was sure his hotdog was getting cold. "Go ahead, Roy, eat."

Roy wolfed down the first sausage in two gulps and licked the condiments from his fingers. It shamed Willie to see a man so hungry. He took several bites of the second one before Alexis inquired about what he had seen or heard on the street about the case.

"The block is hot, but not from any fire. If anything, that part of Lincoln Avenue has become a dead cell to the dealers now with new cops and fire officials piddling around, but not for long." Roy patted his chest hard with the flat of his hand as if his last bite went down too fast. He succumbed to a coughing spell that seemed saturated with the city's pollution.

"Are you okay?" Willie asked.

Roy flailed his right hand about, as if to signal something. "Do you think I can get something to drink?"

"Sure," Both Willie and Alexis answered simultaneously.

"I can run back to the corner and get you a soda. Which kind do you want?" Alexis put down her pad and grabbed her change purse.

"I'd like to have one of those if you don't mind," Roy said in a raspy voice, pointing to Alexis's energy drink she had sat down between them.

"Here, take a sip of my water, and we'll all walk back down

to Jacques's to get you as many energizer drinks as you want," Willie suggested, cracking the seal on his bottled water. He handed Roy the bottle to take a swig in exchange for his bag. Willie led the way to the sidewalk.

"You should get a commendation from the city for single-handedly taking on the dealers on this block," Alexis declared, giving Roy a pat on the back. "I was so discouraged coming up here wondering why our tax payer dollars pay police salaries so men can deal drugs blatantly in broad daylight."

"You'd think they'd set up some type of sting operation to catch some of these guys in the act," Willie said.

Roy chugged half a bottle to finally make his coughing subside. The next time he spoke his voice was surprisingly clear. "It's a sting, all right. Quarterly they take the hoods off the street. Some of the runners even go to jail. They all come back though, thinking nothing can hold them, but in actuality behind closed doors the DA and police chief have a deal. The everyday junkie, or someone like me, is expendable, but the dealer has value to them. They want to find out who's supplying them. It's like chemical waste. They will allow the dealers to dump toxins into our waters to choke out the big fish."

Their pace was relaxed, and they walked three astride. Willie had walked this street many times, but knew he'd never view it quite the same. When they spotted the neighborhood dealer man making his way back up the block with his boys on the opposite side, they didn't duck and hide.

"Like clockwork, he and his boys are usually down by the church catching people off the subway who leave work early to get their fix before going home," Roy explained, discretely pointing at the man in the knit cap. "Something must be going on down here."

Alexis shook her head in shame. "If I could get permission, I'd blow the lid off of this whole operation."

"Woe, one story at a time," Willie said, stopping. "Is this an exposé on Roy or an exposé about the drug-infested neighborhood? Because the pretense you talked to us about was a story about Roy, the man."

"It's both. Am I just supposed to ignore what I've seen?" Alexis asked incredulously. Her gestures were inhibited by the pen, pad, and drink she carried in her hands.

"It's the backdrop, not the focus." Willie turned to face her. "Look, I know I can't tell you how to do your job. All I know is that Roy is out here alone. I've tried, but he is not leaving these streets. I don't want him to suffer repercussions on these streets for the story we put together."

"I'll keep that in mind. I work by a code of ethics that does say minimize harm," she pondered. "I certainly don't want anything to happen while he's out here alone either."

"I'm not alone, Reverend." Roy's giddy smile returned.

"I know, Roy, I see the Holy Spirit all up, down, and around you. He's protected you for this long. We've got to find out from Ms. Montgomery here how you can get prepared for your close up."

Willie knew how it felt to be a babe in ministry. New found faith, some would call wide-eyed optimism, often left people blinded to the tactics of the adversary. Roy was a definite target of the enemy. Willie made a mental note to pray his covering this week of consecration.

They resumed walking. Alexis began filling him in on the details of taping her show. Willie jumped in with his own suggestions for story angles and possible staging. Roy agreed to meet Alexis and her camera crew at noon the next day for taping. As they approached the intersection across from the church and Jacques's convenience store, they couldn't believe their eyes.

"Hallelujah," Roy said, reading the sign in front of the

church that read, "FEED THE STREETS," and written underneath a span of days they were giving out their rations. The table was manned by Pastor Abe Townsend. Willie craned his neck to survey the volunteers, which he couldn't identify from this distance. Roy quickly crossed the street with a wave of his hand.

"I guess we won't have to worry about him eating this week," Alexis said, holding up her peace offering of edibles that Roy ran off without.

"Obedience is better than sacrifice," Willie uttered to himself.

"Uh, uh,uh, Pastor Willie, you are just judgmental today," Alexis said in a patronizing tone. "Maybe Pastor Abe got the memo that God's busting down the doors of ministry."

"Somehow, I never had to advertise my missionary efforts though."

"It's a new day." Alexis smirked. "I know why I'm cynical, but I don't get you, Pastor Willie."

He blew a puff of air, feeling obligated to explain. "When me and Pastor Townsend, there, met, we were in an arbitration room; might as well say a courtroom. Let me just say, his uncle and my former deacon might as well have had him sitting in his lap with his hand in his back, because Charley was definitely doing the talking for the both of them."

"All that was missing was the stage, huh?"

Willie nodded his head once to let her know she had gotten the pun.

"So I guess you are not going over there with your fellow church folk," Alexis said.

Willie checked his watch that read a quarter after two. Four hours had passed. "No, thank you. I got my own church to tend to."

Just then, a mobile news van from another station pulled

alongside the curb. Willie looked at Alexis and couldn't resist pointing. "Here comes the puppet stage now. Look, Alexis, breaking news, you'd better go represent your station."

"It's my day off, remember?"

He laughed at her. "Tomorrow?"

"Twelve noon," Alexis confirmed.

As the traffic light changed, they crossed the street and walked off to their respective cars without another word. Their chance meeting adjourned.

Chapter 11
A Battery of Tests

Vanessa's best friend, First Lady Pat Rawls, gave Vanessa a litmus test some time ago to evaluate whether or not her relationship with her husband was in trouble. It wasn't scripture or verse from the Bible, nor was it deep and philosophical like the theories in any of the counseling books Pat had kept from her college days. It was more of a basic rhyme of a rap song that Vanessa had been replaying in Pat's Southern Belle drawl since yesterday. *Money in the bank, gas in the tank, and never hesitate to tell each other what you think.*

Her red flag was hoisted to half-staff. Willie's unexpected morning romp to God knows where confirmed it. Vanessa was gone to a Trinity Conference planning meeting at a neighboring church after debating the entire morning about a proper tribute for her father at the church's upcoming 50th anniversary. She wasn't sure if Willie even made it in to church at all. They hadn't connected all day.

That's when the ditty started in her head. *Money in the bank.* Vanessa didn't have to worry about that. They were both on salary at Pleasant Harvest, and their modest lifestyle afforded them a few luxuries every now and again. Money had never been the source of their issues. They passed that test.

Vanessa was beginning to feel like it was all in her head until later when they did a tango. Neither of them went into any great detail about their day, preferring to dance around any accusation or insinuation that would disrupt their peaceful mood. After dinner, she left Willie unwinding from the day, on the couch mindlessly watching television.

She purposely left her hair loose after brushing it and put on her beige and peach silk camisole with lounging pants after dusting with perfumed powder. True to form, and even though she could tell he was tired and only working on a half a tank of gas, Willie tried to reeve his engine under the sheets. As if he could stay out all morning, with no explanation, and expect to get some at night. Besides, she was exhausted. After she gave him the snub, he rolled over without much fuss, and like a lumberjack cutting logs with a hacksaw, he snored.

Theirs was a communication problem. It always had been. It was made painfully apparent during the unification of their churches, a time when they failed to bring their ministry fiascos to the table. Willie found out about a time when the church finances were brought into question under her leadership by an auditing team, and she discovered that there was an all out revolt happening at his church because they were combining.

Vanessa would like to think those days of keeping secrets and not addressing issues were in the past. She had participated in this cycle of aloofness for too long. She had concerns she had not voiced to Willie. She was tired all the time and irritable. She thought of the other day when she had gotten sick in the pulpit. She plugged all these symptoms into WEB MD and self-diagnosed herself as pre-menopausal. If this was pre-menopause, she wanted no part of the real thing. Vanessa could not think of the last time she had been to the doctor, but knew she could not prolong a visit much longer.

Thoughts of bringing all of that to the forefront with Willie made for a fitful night's sleep. She rose in the morning before

Willie and sat up in the bed, praying and meditating. As if he could sense she was awake and waiting for him, he awakened shortly after.

"What's up, baby?" Still groggy, he propped his head on his arm.

She turned her entire body toward him. "I need help." Vanessa had not rehearsed what she was going to say, so the conversation drifted like tumbleweed from her preaching schedule and her sister's wedding to the upcoming church anniversary and Trinity conference. She finally ended by saying, "It's a bit much."

"It is too much," Willie agreed. "Tell me again why we are pushing Mt. Pleasant to be a part of this new conference thing? When we first met I thought you were anti-affiliation, especially with those ole' boys' club pastor's leagues where they sit around and compare whose is bigger; 'I've got more members. Oh yeah, well, my sanctuary seats more people.' Then the one who wins gets crowned Bishop at the end. Now you-slash-we have been paying start-up dues for the past three years, and you are like one of the charter members of one of those very same clubs."

Vanessa couldn't believe Willie was being so snide. He of all people should know how she struggled as a woman pastor to be accepted and respected by her peers. She was one of just three women pastors in this entire conference. It was important to her that at least one of the females take on the leadership role and affect some of the guiding policies so that the conference didn't end up like the glorified popularity contest that Willie proclaimed. Couldn't he see she needed this?

"Churches in covenant with one another is a powerful thing. This conference follows a different model than many conferences out there. Besides the fact that this is a unique conference to the DC, Maryland, and Northern Virginia area.

We plan to train leaders, provide grants for ministry projects, and be agents of change in our communities. We don't plan to elect a bishop in the first year, but rather take nominations for the following year review. Everything works on a three-year cycle for the Holy Trinity. And before you say anything, as far as the election process goes, we use the biblical premise that a bishop is a pastor to pastors that have a ministry model to be studied. He's not a mascot, and not necessarily the conference leader either."

"Well, that's on you," Willie said with a yawn.

"Willie? C'mon, where is the support?" Vanessa threw her hands up on either side of her in questioning gesture before letting them drop hard on the mattress.

"You know I'll sit up beside you like a good husband with a T-shirt that says *I'm with her*," he said. "For real, I get it, and I understand that you will be preoccupied for a while."

"Me, preoccupied, what about you? I'm doing all of this and still holding it down at Pleasant Harvest. You didn't even show up for work yesterday," she blurted out.

He exhaled loudly and sat up, and she shifted back in the bed to make space for his secrets and her insinuations. "Yesterday, I went with Alexis Montgomery, the reporter, to see Roy Jones, the homeless guy that I used to help at Harvest. She's doing a story on him this week."

Vanessa digested his explanation, swallowing back her own murky feelings. "I'd be suspicious of you and her if I didn't know that *you know*, that I would break you down so fast and send your fifty-five year-old, mid-life crisis-having behind crying home to your momma."

"You know I love it when you talk tough." Willie winked at her seductively.

"Don't make me smack you," she replied. Nothing in her stance suggested she wouldn't.

Willie reached for her hand that she allowed to lay limply in his. His smile was broad, handsome, and infuriating to her all at the same time. "Baby, she didn't know where to find him, or what state of mind she'd find him in. She was prepared to walk all the way from Harvest to the DC line. She needed my help."

Vanessa just laughed to prevent herself from cursing. *Negro, did you not just hear me say I need help also?* "When did Alexis become our, I mean your, adopted daughter? 'Cause she's young, younger than me." Vanessa reminded him of their more than ten year age difference. "Are you praying, Willie, or just reacting? I sure hope you weren't being called into distraction, because you've sacrificed ministry time with people you were called to lead to be on the street with Alexis and Roy."

Vanessa half listened to him ramble on about his escapades of the previous day and ministry according to Roy Jones. Willie looked at the bedside clock, which prompted her to do the same.

"I'm going back out with them today when they shoot the segment. I can't wait for you to see the piece." He made haste to the bathroom.

"What about the anniversary?" she said, going from sitting Indian style to a kneeling position like a lover not ready to leave the bed, beckoning her partner to stay awhile longer. "It's the Sunday after next, you know. We haven't designated anyone for the order of service, nor have we tossed around any sermon ideas. Pat and Ben will be here on next Friday, and we haven't made hotel reservations for them and their people. We've got a lot to prepare. This is a hallmark year. The celebration should reflect that."

"You can just fill me in on the preparations," he said from inside the bathroom. "You don't need me for the planning of the service. I haven't been at Mt. Pleasant a year. You've been there for forty-three. Heck, Keisha should play a part; she's been there thirty-four, thirty-five, or however old she is. I'll just wear my T-shirt over my robe. You know the same one I'm wearing to the Trinity Conference that says *I'm with the beautiful one that is running things.*"

The sudden movement and overall audacity of her husband made her insides quake. She rushed to the bathroom that Willie was occupying as he was coming out and simply hollered, "Move."

"Don't be like that, Vanessa. I was going back in there," she could hear him say beyond the running faucet and closed door used to hide her eventual eradication. "Can I at least get my toothbrush?"

Vanessa used all her strength to grab his toothbrush, face cloth and any other toiletry of his within her reach before thrusting it through the small crack she made in the door. She fought the warmed-over wave of nausea forcing her to bow down to the toilet bowl idol. She prayed for forgiveness and mercy from her God.

"I'm going to church now so I can get a few hours in before meeting Alexis and Roy at twelve. This shouldn't take all day. Okay? After today, I promise, you've got my undivided attention," Willie said, as a final peace offering.

She didn't answer. She wanted to call out to him, to tell him that she needed him right now, but an invisible hoodlum had her hovering over the bowl threatening to dunk her head in if she didn't pay her debts. She panted and prayed. When she heard Willie's footfall go in the other direction, she wept openly.

After the nauseating feeling subsided, Vanessa entered her room and sat down nearby at her vanity. She didn't want to look at herself. She took deep breaths hoping to slow her breathing, but it didn't help. She felt panicky and near hysterics. She wasn't quite sure if it were from her insecurities in her relationship with Willie or the uncertainty of her recent ailments. She needed an opinion, and since she wasn't anywhere near her purse to find her doctor's number, she decided to dish it all to her girlfriend, Pat.

She climbed in her bed as if she were going back to sleep, grabbed her bedside receiver, and dialed the familiar number. Pat answered the phone on the third ring with an enthusiastic sister-girl greeting that made Vanessa feel better immediately.

"Girl, less than ten days, I can't wait. I know it's the church's 50th anniversary, but I declare, gold is not my color. I'm thinking about sportin' purple. That's a divinely regal color, right? The hat, hear me when I tell you now, the hat, shoot, the whole darn ensemble is Pat Rawls fierce." Pat snapped out the last few syllables.

"Do you, diva," Vanessa said, "I wouldn't expect any less."

"So what's up, sweetie? What's blessed, and what's messed?" Pat sang.

"Trying to figure Mr. Green out, that's all. We just had a spat, and now he's gone to church. I probably won't see him until later this evening."

Vanessa could hear Pat kicking her husband out of the room so he would not be privy to the conversation. "You never quite figure them out, honey. You just learn how to co-exist. Are you going to be all right?"

That was the million dollar question. "I guess. It's been hit or miss recently. Now that the anniversary is upon us, I think we need to be on one accord. Willie, on the other hand, has other priorities," Vanessa said.

"Have you all, you know . . . taken a spin lately?"

"Vroom vroom," Vanessa said, satisfying her friend's thirst for details. She thought about it, outside of last night's miss, their sex life was pretty consistent, but far from full throttle because she was always so tired. They'd been stuck in first and second gear for awhile now. Joy rides in the middle of the day were out of the question.

"Oh well, you all don't have a problem then."

"It's probably me. I'm so moody most of the time. Lord have mercy, I am a moody minister," Vanessa reflected as she sank down in her sheets to a reclined position. "There is no need to rent a helium machine next weekend. Give me a bunch of balloons, 'cause I am blowing everything out of proportion these days."

"Must be your time of the month," Pat offered.

"That's just it, it's not. I don't think." Vanessa draped her left arm over her head while keeping the phone firmly in place with her right. She struggled to think about when was the last time she had a regular cycle. Her stomach dropped a notch. "What does menopause feel like?"

"How should I know, honey? I'm just two years older than you. I can tell you it is serious business. We have a whole ministry slash support group at our church devoted to talking about hot flashes and hormone replacement. You know, I'm nosy and will drop into any meeting at Dominion just to say hey, but I stay clear of those meetings, girl."

"I just assumed you were pre-menopausal when you told me that Aunt Flo didn't visit you anymore . . ."

"Hysterectomy," Pat said, cutting her off. "I had cysts and fibroids popping up all the time, having their own party in there."

"So they took it out completely?" Vanessa asked.

"Might as well; I was done having kids after Ridell. After all the ups and downs that boy put me through from the terrible twos up until his teenage years, I prayed to God to close down the shop. Girl, that boy guaranteed he wasn't having a sister or brother," Pat said, laughing at the memories now that had her calling for intercessory prayer in the past. "Seriously, my doctor made the recommendation to take out my uterus before the growths began mutating, and then I'd have another thing on my hands. But that's me, what's all this talk about? You can't possibly think you are going through the change."

"I don't know, girl. I've been feeling crazy lately."

"Are you experiencing your own personal summer?" Pat asked.

"Only when I'm nauseated," Vanessa said.

"Nauseated?" Pat asked with great concern in her voice.

Vanessa began filling her in on the waves of nausea that swooped down on her in the pulpit and this morning. She told her how she took to carrying crackers in her purse because the salt seemed to calm her stomach. She also shared her plans to investigate these symptoms with her doctor as early as that morning if she could get a last minute appointment.

"Nausea, mood swings, and exhaustion," Pat confirmed the list of ailments.

Vanessa felt her stomach drop with each item on the list like she was on a ride at an amusement park experiencing each small drop before the big fall. She hadn't mentioned the bloating.

"Well, I'd say you could spend your time, money and energy going to your doctor and running a battery of tests, or you could go to the corner drug store and pick up your own pregnancy test. If it ain't pregnancy, I don't know what it is."

Although Vanessa sat straight up in the bed, she felt as if she were free falling.

Chapter 12

The Rightful Renegade

Willie set up a private viewing party for him and Vanessa to watch the *Inside 7* segment. She had been rather indifferent toward him since his return from Lincoln and Division Avenue where he watched Alexis and her crew tape the footage that would be part of the program. Willie was thankful that she was no longer angry enough to throw tantrums and barricade herself behind bathroom doors. Surely, her attitude would come around after she watched Roy's amazing story, Willie thought. He felt like they were on a date as he tossed around their giant decorative pillows and other throw pillows to create a cozy effect. He was hopeful that this quality time could revive their scheduled date night idea that they both had been too busy to initiate and follow through on. He picked up Chinese food that they could eat in containers on the floor in front of the television.

After insisting they leave work early, Willie put on an old polo and jeans. Vanessa also changed to a soft yellow scoop neck tee and gray nylon sweatpants with yellow stripes up the side that made her look quite youthful and beautiful. They couldn't resist the aroma of their carry-out and began eating before the program began. Vanessa asked for one of his fried chicken wings and then shortly after reached for another.

"No." Willie moved his cartoon out of her reach.

"C'mon, honey, love is about sharing," Vanessa reminded him.

"Love is understanding that tonight your husband is hungry and wants all of his food. I got you combination rice because that's what you always get. You've told me many times in the past that Lucky Starr and other such carry-outs should leave fried chicken to church ladies and KFC."

"Humph," Vanessa resigned.

The credits were rolling for *The World Report*. Willie, watching Vanessa struggle to stand from her position atop a jumbo pillow, reached out to assist her before she and the combination rice toppled over.

"I can get up," was her curt response.

"Where are you going, the program is about to come on?" Willie could not believe his wife was being this petty. "Here, you spoiled brat, you can have another wing," Willie compromised.

"I'm not worried about your chicken wing. I'm calling Keisha to remind her to watch the program. Besides, I got a Jamaican beef patty in the freezer with my name on it," Vanessa said, traipsing off to the kitchen.

Willie certainly wasn't going to miss a minute of this report. He hadn't had time to think since yesterday's taping, let alone tell people to watch. Willie thought about Charley and wondered if the *Inside 7* segment was in his evening line-up of television programs. Now that was someone he wanted to call. Charley never understood why Willie wasted time on what he considered a homeless bum who didn't want anything better for himself. Willie knew this program was set to change many people's perception of homeless men and women.

"In our continuing story of the Easter Church Inferno at the Harvest Baptist Church, we discovered a man that used to take refuge on the streets just outside the church; a man that is now conquering these very streets in his own unique way. Roy Jones, former telephone technician and drug addict, knows Lincoln Avenue and this corridor of the city very well. It was the same street that fed his addiction to heroin and the same street he has lived on since his addictions stripped away his old life. What I found when I talked to Roy Jones was not a man guilt-ridden and tormented by his past, but rather a man very focused and determined to make a difference in the lives of people who are just like him," came Alexis's voice.

Willie was enthralled by the introduction that must have been taped some time after they gathered live footage. Alexis was in a swivel chair opposite the show's host with a huge framed shot of Roy simulated on the green screen behind them. Vanessa returned with a beef patty inside the lid of her combination rice. Without looking up, Willie extended his hand to help her back to the floor beside him. She ignored his hand, and he ignored her inquiries of what she had missed.

Willie smiled broadly and he sat up a little straighter as the scene changed to the taped interview he had experienced firsthand. Roy told a tale of inconsistencies that made him lose his job and the damage his addiction inflicted on his family, leaving him with nothing to salvage there either. His only resort at the time was the streets. His only resort had now become his life's calling.

"We went with Roy to a courtyard between a lot of dilapidated and abandoned apartment buildings. This was a place known as the terrace, code word for a place where he would score illegal drugs. Even after his own spiritual awakening, it has become a routine of his to return here daily to see who he can influence to trade off their drug of choice for a sermon and a substitute. He's a threat to the dealers, and some who realize that shy away from him. Still, there are others who gather and wait on his message of inspiration."

The same happened when Alexis and her crew set up the scene in the midst of a gathering either waiting on him or waiting on a fix. The thought of being on camera was either frightening or fascinating. Willie explained to Vanessa that the sparse crowd of no more than ten dwindled down to three. They were told their faces would be bubbled out, but if they chose to talk in the footage, Alexis would need a release form. Willie and the crew, not essential for the shot, stepped back about ten feet, leaving only Alexis and Danny, the cameraman to simulate a more authentic experience.

"Hey, Roy, are you preaching today to get your own TV show?" someone taunted from outside the frame.

"I'm just an ex-junkie talking real talk. You better come over and get you some," Roy called out, positioning his bag on the ramshackle bench. He sat it down next to the same woman they saw Roy with the first day. She had brought a friend who appeared weak and jittery from his infirmities. Both Willie and Alexis didn't think it would be wise to show or offer one of his self-serving cups from the clinic on camera, but rather wait until they were off camera or onto the next scene outside the clinic. They prayed the man could make it that long.

Willie could envision where he was standing outside the periphery of the shoot and thought about those behind the scenes moments as he watched. He remembered praying as he did when he sat in the pulpit as other ministers approached the sacred desk. He prayed for the saving power of the message and messenger.

"I have something I always carry with me," Roy said, withdrawing an old photograph from his bag. Willie noticed that the picture of his children now had their faces hidden from view like the blurred faces and brand name logos of his congregants standing around him.

"These are my kids. I look at this picture every day." Roy measured his words. "If they were to see me, they would see a shadow though. I'm scary to my own kids because I wasn't there for over five years of their lives, and it haunts them. It haunts me."

Willie recalled Roy's wife telling him when she remarried that it was best to have her new husband raise the kids as his own, that she would leave it up to his son and daughter when they get older to decide if they want to make contact again. That was a dark period for Roy when Willie wouldn't see him for weeks on end. It was also the time his then alcoholism opened up the gateway to his drug addiction.

"You ever thought you were fooling someone; your family or your co-workers? Come to find out you had remnants of your hit on your upper lip? You all saw me. You know how out there I was—chalky white skin, smoky gray lips, big bug eyes," Roy said.

"And tube socks," came Roy's heckler who Willie noticed had crept closer but was still off camera. They all laughed. Little did they know he was preaching already, Willie thought.

"I was a ghost, for real. A ghost in high-waters and tube socks until I gave it up. I gave up the ghost. Now, that's a biblical term, y'all. I read the Bible in the shelters at night. It helped me in some really difficult times. 'Cause ghosts are cool only in movies. So like when they talk about giving up the ghost in the Bible, they mean dying. Even Jesus Himself said in John, 'It is finished,' before He died and gave up the ghost. In His case He fulfilled His purpose."

"None of us are meant to be a slave to this stuff that is killing our bodies and brain cells at the same time, or lose everything and be sketched out in a chalk outline on these streets when we die a violent death. Give up the ghost, for God's sake."

There was a lone 'Amen' shouted in the midst of silent head nods. A few more could be seen now when the focus of the camera's lens shifted from Roy to the back of the crowd. The man on the bench was rocking back and forth. Willie did not know if it were from withdrawal or something Roy said that had struck a nerve.

Roy knelt in front of the man. "Give up the ghost, man. Even if you say you don't believe in God, He believes in you, and you used to believe in yourself also. That habit of yours has got to die or you will. Talk to me after. For real, I can show you how I did it."

"When we return, we learn more about what Roy Jones calls his Tube-socks Theology, and why he thinks more drug treatment programs should take their services to the street. When the *Inside 7* segment continues," came the voice over.

Willie turned from the television to Vanessa. Her hand was over her mouth as if she were trying to capture her voice before it left her body. She appeared speechless. Willie nodded his head sideways toward the screen as if to say, what did you think?

"There is a voice crying out in the wilderness," Vanessa said.

"Indeed," Willie replied.

"Did he just take a text and topic?"

"Yeah, he executed a sermon and hit the main point in under," Willie consulted his watch, "ten minutes. He even got a convert. We had to take a fifty-minute break while he helped the man on the bench. He gave him one of his doses, and I drove them to the clinic instead of them walking. Roy convinced me to give him my spare Bible that was in the car. I think the man registered for the drug treatment program. And you thought I wanted to hang out with Alexis. I was in Roy's back pocket the whole time. I learned so much about true evangelism and meeting people where they are in these past two days."

"Our missionaries need to be watching this," Vanessa said. "My Lord, Jesus."

Willie watched his wife draw her knees into her body and keep them there with her hands clasped tightly around her legs. She dropped her head like a turtle reverting into his shell. The piece was certainly praiseworthy, but he had never expected her to be so moved.

"Are you all right?" he questioned.

She tried to wave off his worry with her hand. They hadn't noticed the program had come back on. Roy was being interviewed in front of the drug treatment clinic. He described how the program works and shared that even in his own recovery he has on occasion given up his dose to get someone to the place where they could register themselves for treatment. Willie remembered this next part, but assumed it would hit the cutting room floor..

"Here is my mentor right here." There was an awkward pause where the cameraman panned to find Willie in the crowd despite Alexis's frantic hand signals. "Willie Green was the Pastor of Harvest Baptist Church, right next to the alley where I used to sleep at night. He taught me that the true measure of God's love comes from how you treat bums like me — cast-offs or what the Bible calls, 'the least of these.'"

Roy came over and stood by Willie. The camera tightened in on that shoot, which was the last frame of the report. Alexis's voice track wrapped up this installment with something insightful. He was in shock.

Vanessa came out of her shell at the mention of his name. "I thought you were supposed to stay off the television."

The phone rang, and they both looked at it, and then at each other. Willie felt for sure it was Chief Rich calling him to come down to the station like in one of those 1950's cop shows. He stretched to the fullest extent of his reach without getting up and tipped the telephone base with his fingertips. It was enough to cause the cordless mouthpiece to fall. He caught it and depressed the talk button.

"Hello," he answered cautiously.

"Pastor Willie, I guess you saw yourself on TV," Alexis said. She was winded as if she had finished a jog before making this call. "The producers thought we should leave that part in. Although Roy's story was compelling on its own, they felt that it should have some sort of tie in to the other part of the series."

"I guess you all are not concerned about Chief Rich and his threats."

"I brought all of that to my executive producer's attention. You were on camera for only sixty seconds. Plus, he talked about court orders, but never produced anything. I guess we are just calling his bluff."

"I wonder if he'll go looking for Roy next."

"Or if he'll take you along with him as an escort into the underworld," Alexis emphasized like a movie trailer announcer.

Willie laughed and that's when he felt his wife's hot gaze boring a hole on his profile. "Forget Chief Rich. I am satisfied as long as I am no longer in the dog house with my wife."

"I do need to write you an excuse note for having you out and away from church business for two days. Let me talk to Pastor Vanessa," Alexis joked.

Although Alexis was patronizing him, he really needed that note. Lately, he didn't know why he was in the doghouse with Vanessa and what he should do to get out.

"Let me put her on speaker," Willie said before she could laugh it off or object. He searched the receiver for the speaker button and quickly pushed it.

"Uhm, I want to thank you guys, really. Pastor Willie, I

don't know what I would have done or how the piece would have turned out if I hadn't run into you on Monday. Thank you also, Pastor Vanessa. I know you were skeptical about journalists and wanted to kick me out of your house that day, but I think it was worth it."

Vanessa looked at Willie in confusion, but answered, "You should be proud of that segment. Roy's story needed to be told."

"Oh, and did I tell you guys that the station put Roy up in style in a suite at the Four Seasons Hotel for the rest of the week, 'cause I belly ached that Roy, who gives back so much to his community, may not even have a place to watch his own segment?"

"That's great," Willie and Vanessa said almost simultaneously.

"The combination of meeting Roy and you all have really renewed my faith, in a lot of things," Alexis said.

"Well, speaking on faith, since I have my husband back to focus on our church anniversary which is a week from Sunday, we expect to see you at Pleasant Harvest on our big day without the camera crew," Vanessa said. "I mean, you can bring the crew, but not the camera. Isn't that right, Pastor Willie? We got a special seat for her right up front."

"Amen," Willie was happy to join in.

"I can't hear you, Sister Montgomery," Vanessa said. "Can I get an amen?"

"You guys, I've got to ease back into this church thing," Alexis pleaded, not ready to make a commitment.

"Pastor Willie, did we or did we not help this girl take every egg thrown in her *Easter* basket and make not one, but two tasty omelets from them?"

The old sassy and perky Vanessa was back, and Willie was prepared to back her up. "Yes Lord."

"Okay, okay, I'm there, amen," Alexis appeased.

Chapter 13

Dinner with Bridezilla

There was no personal fellowship dinner planned for Willie and Vanessa the Sunday before the big church anniversary, but that didn't stop Keisha and Paul from planning to show up on Willie and Vanessa's doorstep. Willie and Vanessa were sprawled across the bed by four P.M. with their own section of the newspaper to read. After ten minutes, it was more like the paper was reading Vanessa as Willie noticed his wife doing a nose dive into the Metro section when he heard the doorbell ring.

Willie shook Vanessa awake before making his way down the stairs to greet their uninvited guests. Keisha bounded through the door as if she lived there, followed by Paul carrying what appeared to be a glass display case that he supported from the top and bottom. Willie wondered what show-and-tell item they were in for as he mounted the first two steps off the foyer to call to Vanessa to join them.

"What you got there?" Willie asked, rejoining them in the living room.

"Oh, you got it," Vanessa called out from her descent down the stairs as she spotted the case now resting on their wide coffee table. "I'm afraid that's not going to be big enough."

"You sure?" Keisha said, looking down on the case then back at her sister.

"Wait, let me get the dimensions. It's written in my folder."

Vanessa disappeared around the corner before Willie could ask, "Does anyone mind filling me in on the mystery case?"

"Sorry, Pastor." Paul stepped around his fiancée to move closer to him. "I'm just the delivery guy. I came over to Keisha's house and she said, 'Here, we've got to take this over to my sister's house.' So here we are. I take it that it has something to do with the anniversary presentation."

Vanessa walked in with a 3X5 clip-out from a magazine with a photo attached on top of her red to-do folder. She walked past Willie and Paul and showed Keisha the advertisement.

"See, it would work length-wise, maybe height, but the width is too narrow."

Willie was getting annoyed with their dilemma without even knowing what it was about. He felt Vanessa and Keisha were talking over them like he and Paul were invisible or there was no way they could help. "Let me see what you're looking at."

Vanessa showed him an advertisement for a memorial bust made from some sort of casting material and polished a pewter color. The $399 price tag before taxes and shipping fees was not lost on him. They had discussed renaming the fellowship hall at church in dedication to her father who had been pastor for thirty-nine of the church's fifty year history. Vanessa was big on the symbolism. It had been a hard sale just a few months back to get her to consider re-naming the church to show the merger of their two churches into one. She had surprised him just a couple of weeks ago on Easter by acquiescing and presenting the whole church with the new name, Pleasant Harvest, which she and a committee had come up with.

"It should be here no later than this coming Wednesday. All we need is two of those pedestal thingamabobs." Vanessa had her index finger up to her chin in a pondering gesture.

"You told me to find a case. Why do we need two?"Keisha asked.

"For Daddy's big house Bible. I figured I can part with it from my personal library if it will permanently be on display in his memory."

"Awwwwwww," Keisha sang in a way only a female can to show that the sentiment had touched her deeply.

"Wait; the best part is it will be set to his favorite scripture," Vanessa added.

"Romans eight," Keisha yelped. Her hands were raised and quaking on either side of her mouth as if she were about to holler from excitement or have an emotional breakdown. "That is going to be so nice, sis."

They were all still standing around. Willie decided to let them have their moment and took a seat. Paul followed suit. Somehow he didn't think it was a good idea to order a product sight unseen. Willie looked over the advertisement and headshot once more and prayed the real thing was as sturdy as the one in the advertisement and looked remotely like the picture of her father staring back at him.

"So that is why I need the display cases to be uniform and bigger all around," Vanessa added.

"What happened to the simple lettering outside of the hall that says 'JM Morton Hall'?" Willie asked.

"What happened to 'you and Keisha can make the plans?' The signboard people are coming tomorrow with the lettering. Besides, once you are in the hall, you still need a reminder that it is named after and dedicated to Daddy. Simple? C'mon now," Vanessa smirked.

"Well, who is going back to the store to exchange this case for the two enormous ones you want?" Keisha asked, her hands poised on her hips.

Vanessa didn't quivel. "You are. Next week is hectic enough for me, since my husband and I put off some essential planning for this week. I need the cases by Wednesday afternoon, Thursday at the latest."

"Paul," Keisha said.

"So what's for dinner?" Paul asked, hiding the fact that at the mere mention of his name and an exchange of looks, he had been designated the task.

"I have turkey wings warming in the oven and rice on the stovetop, but I'm not sure I have enough. I wasn't expecting company," Vanessa said.

"I know you are not even trying to be stingy with the food as many times as I have fed you when we were living together." Keisha headed for the kitchen, and they all just naturally gravitated in there also. "Not to mention those meals you took home to feed your husband, here."

"And I appreciate it, sis," Willie said, still holding on to the photo of his father-in-law.

"Uh-huh, look, she's got at least two packs in here. That's enough to feed a small team. What kind of portions are you all used to eating here?" Keisha asked, looking inside the oven where the turkey wings were covered in cream of mushroom soup and baking. "These are ready. Shall I serve?"

"Move, girl." Vanessa swatted at her sister. Willie knew she was particular about anyone disturbing her display of dishes in the cabinet. She had her plates and bowls equally stacked on either side of her honey oak peek-a-boo cabinetry. She pulled down a service for four. Keisha, being the consummate host, assisted Vanessa in pouring drinks and serving the guys before sitting down with them.

"Since you were trying to act stingy with the eats, you'll just have to listen to me rant about the wedding," Keisha said.

"Well, that was going to happen anyway," Paul said.

Keisha gave Paul a sharp looked that Willie noticed completely melted away from Paul's apologetic eyes and affectionate grin. She began a conversation with Vanessa about another glitch or snag in her plans.

"Do we know a date?" Willie asked Paul in their own sidebar conversation as they ate.

"Sometime in October," Paul replied.

"I believe you have got to get more specific than that if you want people to show up."

"I don't know what the big deal is, Pastor. We pulled out a calendar, right? She had me close my eyes and run my hand up and down along a vertical line of Saturdays and I landed on the sixth. She immediately moved my hand to the thirteenth. I was cool with the date being the thirteenth, either day was okay with me, but then she started getting indecisive. She said she'd have to see what date was open for this super high priced photographer she wants."

"So, you're basing your wedding date on a photographer?" Willie asked.

Paul scooped up as much of the rice and mushroom gravy as he could with his fork before saying, "Sounds silly, huh?"

"To me, yes, but what do you say?" *Do you even have a say in any of it?* Willie thought.

Paul shrugged his shoulders as he took in a mouthful of his dinner. Willie thought when the two of them got engaged that his mentee would put an end to his sister-in-law's self-seeking ways, but now he saw his thickset friend was squished in Keisha's back pocket. He saw himself in Paul, and wanted desperately for Paul to assert himself so that he started off the marriage the same way he wanted it to play out for the duration.

"Excuse me," Willie said, interrupting the ladies' private chat. "Paul tells me you are getting married in October. You

know we do six months of pre-marital counseling at Pleasant
Harvest to cut down on urgent shotgun weddings that have to
be performed before due dates or court dates. Being the first
Sunday in May, that gives you scarcely enough time to get on
Vanessa's calendar for your sessions."

"Or your calendar." Vanessa aimed the same glare at him
as her sister did to Paul earlier, except hers wasn't melting
away. "TRIN-I-TY conference, remember? Plus, they can't
handle my inquiries, nor can I handle hearing my own sister's
intimate details."

"There shouldn't be any intimate-intimate details yet," Willie interjected quickly, then he turned to Paul. "Are there any
intimate details?"

"No no no. NO intimate details here," Paul declared. "I've
been a perfect gentleman."

"Gosh, bro, I can't believe you just asked us that." Keisha
blushed.

"See, you are already embarrassed, and we haven't even gotten into past partners and relationships," Vanessa said, noticing Paul's eyes grow wide with surprise. "Oh yeah, we clean
out the closet."

"Call Luella tomorrow to set up your first appointment,"
Willie said.

"Remind me, okay, honey?" Keisha said to Paul, stripping
layers of turkey meat off the bone and cutting it into her rice
with her fork.

"He doesn't have to remind you because your fiancé here is
going to handle it," Willie added.

"Whatever, Caveman Willie. Getting back to the wedding
itself, I'm trying to figure out how you all can officiate the
wedding and be attendants at the same time. I still want Vanessa to be the matron of honor."

Vanessa laughed out loud while Willie shook his head.
Next thing she'll be asking him to walk her down the aisle

also, Willie thought.

"I guess you figure I should wear a bridesmaid dress under my robe too," Vanessa chided.

"As a matter of fact, I do. I actually saw a nice coral-colored dress in a magazine that would look gorgeous with your complexion, but you have to lay off the turkey wings and rice, chicken and waffles, or whatever else you've been eating, in order to get into a decent size by October."

Willie winced at that jab because he was not completely convinced that one of his wife's evil-eye looks could not kill somebody if aimed correctly. He heard the clang of her fork hit her plate and thought for a moment she had struck her sister. When he looked up, Vanessa was biting down on her lip with a trail of walrus-sized tears streaming. She departed the table quickly and retreated up the stairs, leaving the rest of them in stunned silence.

"Not cool, babe," Paul said. "I know she's your sister, but she's also our pastor. You hurt her feelings."

Willie stood, but Keisha stopped him. "I'll go talk to her. Lord knows I didn't mean anything by it, as much as we play around with one another. "

Willie put up a hand to tell her to save any further explanation for his wife. Vanessa was a lot of things, but overly sensitive was usually not one of them. He had noticed the extra pounds hugging her frame, but had thanked God then for the extra cushion and thanked God now that he never brought it to her attention if it would upset her like this.

Willie didn't sit until Keisha went the way of her older sister after taking one last bite from her plate. Then he plopped down with a perplexed huff.

"What just happened here?" Paul asked.

"Well, your future wife was being extremely rude and inconsiderate, and my wife overreacted. I guess?" Willie sighed at the futileness of trying to figure out women. "Let me tell you about Morton women."

"Please do," Paul said, turning his chair slightly toward Willie while continuing to eat.

"They are head strong and used to running things. Before you came along and started dating Keisha, even before the churches combined, both of them used to sit right here every Sunday and discuss everything from personal work to church business. It was as if I weren't even here. I'd try to help them with a dilemma, but couldn't get a word in edgewise. Then on the rare occasions that they listened to my opinion, they were awestruck like they never considered a man's viewpoint before."

"I know what you mean. Keisha has clearly got some very concrete ideas as it relates to the wedding and our lives together as a married couple. Then on the other hand, she can be real indecisive, especially when it comes to her current job and decisions about her calling and career. When I try to mull over the options with her or help in the planning of something, she shifts to something else. It's as if she wants to have things totally worked out before she discusses it with me, and that's not the way things work in a relationship. I tell you, it can be both fascinating and frustrating trying to reason with her sometimes."

"Sounds like a power struggle in the making," Willie said, wiping his hands through his mustache and goatee to capture any loose rice particles that could be nesting there. "We, as men, are supposed to lead them, our wives and families. When their parents died, the burden of responsibility fell on Vanessa and trickled down to Keisha. They had Daddy's church to run. Now that they have men in their lives, it is hard for them to hand over that authority. You have to set the tone in the relationship and let her know in no uncertain terms that there is no major decision made about the two of you that is not run past you first for your okay or veto."

"Yeah, okay," Paul said doubtful. "How's that working out for you and Sister Pastor?"

Willie chuckled at Paul's comeback and raised his glass of white cranberry juice as if to say, 'you got me.' "I have a Morton woman, and I can confirm that it is both fascinating and frustrating." They shared a good laugh.

"This week, Keisha called me again balling her eyes out. Her job is beyond stressful for her. She has to deal with a difficult boss because she feels at any minute her position can be outsourced from underneath her. You know how it is hearing your baby in misery. So I told her to quit. I'll take care of her."

"No," Willie said.

"I did," Paul confirmed.

"With no discussion?"

"She was in misery."

"And no wedding date on the books?"

"Trust. It's going to happen this October, Brother Pastor."

"Well, did she?"

"Did she what?"

"Quit," Willie said exasperated. "Did she quit when you told her she could?"

Paul looked uncertain. "I think she gave her two weeks notice."

"You think?" Willie questioned. "Well, I think you all needed to be in counseling like yesterday. The idle mind is a playhouse for the devil. What is she going to be doing while she's not working except planning this wedding? Oh God, it will be like attack of Bridezilla every time we see you guys."

"Look, Pastor, no disrespect, but what was I supposed to do? We're talking about the woman I love. Keisha is not the only one who has made concrete plans. I've been working stock piling my resources and positioning myself for job security. I am fully prepared to take care of her. Keisha is it for me, and I know for sure she is devoted to being my wife and the mother of my children. Together, *we plan* to make both of those a reality real soon. I made an executive decision. You can't fault me for wanting to protect or even rescue her from a bad situation, even if it seems a little premature before the actual wedding day."

"Awwww," Willie tried to mimic Keisha's sentiment from earlier. He began to clear the dishes away. He doubted Vanessa was coming back anytime soon, so he covered her plate with foil. "Seriously, that's very honorable. I feel like Daddy Morton now. I'm proud of you, and I'm sure he'd be proud that his baby girl found one of the good ones."

"Well, thank you. Plus, it will give her time for her studies. She's taking one of her first classes at the Washington Bible College — The Old Testament survey, I believe."

"Non-credit or degree seeking?" Willie asked.

"Here again was another case of something she couldn't decide. Her job was going to pay for some training, but she felt swayed in the direction of ministry. She took this and another class over a winter session this January and got an incomplete in the Survey class. So she's retaking it."

That stinker, Willie thought. He wondered why she hadn't told him about taking classes at one of his old Alma Maters. He knew the prerequisite curriculum well and would have surely tested her knowledge of the Old Testament and Pulpit Etiquette before she even got a chance to make demands on them about her wedding or trample over people's feelings.

They heard a heavy stomp come down the stairs that halted their conversation. Willie wondered if a truce had been made upstairs or were the two sides retiring now to their separate corners.

"Let's go, Paul. Grab the case," Keisha said as if she had

heard their conversation and now he was in trouble. "I don't know what is wrong with your wife, but I hope she gets over herself before the anniversary."

Willie hoped the same thing. Paul gulped the last of his juice at her request while she gathered her belongings. Willie leaned in to Paul before he got up. "I guess you all will be scheduling your counseling with me."

"Willie," Vanessa hollered in an urgent tone from upstairs.

"Be up in a minute," Willie replied.

He noticed Keisha roll her eyes. She led the way to the door and let herself out. Willie opened the screen for Paul and the glass case. He wished him God's speed with his Morton woman before closing the door and tending to his own.

Chapter 14

Blanche is Back

"This is not a game, Mr. Townsend," came a voice that made Abe realize he wasn't dreaming, but in fact had answered the phone.

Abe pulled his sheets into a ball under his chin with one hand as if to protect himself from the hostile voice that had awakened him on the other end of the phone. He looked at his clock again that read a quarter past six in the morning and wondered if Chief Rich was putting clues together like a puzzle at this hour, or was this part of his terrorist tactics to catch him off guard.

"I got a four-week-old case and two people of interest, who happen to be ministers, trying to get a guest spot on *Letterman* by making appearances in every daily paper and dish 'em show out there."

Abe swallowed hard at Chief Rich's reference to Harvest's recent 'Feed the Streets' campaign, which was highlighted in the Metro section of *The Washington Post*, and the Sunday local magazine, *Parade*. He knew he was pressing his luck when those articles subsequently translated into a remote interview on the 5:00 P.M. news. In print was one thing, but on-air was quite another. Blanche was right when she said publicity begets more publicity.

Blanche's strategy since offering to help him was to continue the legacy of giving back that the church was known for before he became pastor. The fact that the church was homeless made the story more compelling, made the sacrifice that much greater, and made the public more inclined to help in their efforts. Blanche had even contacted founders of a southern organization called the Sabbath of Support designed to organize churches to collect a special offering on a particular Sunday to help churches throughout South Carolina that, like Harvest, had been damaged by fire. They were going to replicate that effort with participating DC, metropolitan churches on the fifth Sunday of next month, classically known as Missionary Sunday. Most churches had a missionary outreach program; she just provided them with their next worthwhile cause.

"Hellooooooooooooooooo," Chief Rich said. "If I'm not mistaken, I asked you to stay out of the limelight."

"With all due respect, Chief, it is very early," Abe pleaded. "I can call you back later, and I'll be more than happy to answer any inquiry you may have."

"Oh, we are so far past pleasantries," he said, ignoring Abe's request. "I also recall asking you to get in touch with Charley Thompson. Funny, but nowhere in my notes from that visit do I recall you mentioning that he was your *Uncle*. Where is he?"

"I don't know." Abe was suddenly hot and stripping back covers. "He and his wife haven't been in church for the past two Sundays. Honestly, ask anyone."

"I've interviewed a whole lot of people. I don't need to ask anybody anything else because you are going to find him. Call all your other long lost relatives. Heck, call the entire family reunion committee, but find him," Chief Rich demanded.

"I'll try," Abe said, swallowing hard.

"You'll do more than try. I expect you in my office at twelve

noon. Don't make me come to you," the captain spewed.
"This moves you back to the top of my list. I didn't believe
before that you were capable of a Capitol crime. Now you
have to prove to me all over again that you're not concealing
something from me or in cahoots with your uncle. You can't
cash out your insurance claim and start work on your church
until I close my investigation. Let's see if that lights a fire under ya. Let me tell you, if it comes out that you are somehow
involved, then you won't have to worry about shopping for a
crucifix for the new church. Get me? Twelve noon, don't be
late." The chief extinguished the call before Abe could say
another word.

Abe was almost certain it was not proper protocol for a fire
chief to call and threaten him the way he had. Sure, Chief
Rich was the principal investigator on this case, but this was
ridiculous. He sat up in his bed with new indignation. He
had a mind to call his bluff, go into work and use the storage
room of the pawn shop as a sort of panic room to hide out
in. Would he actually come find him? Better yet, he got the
mind to march into the station at noon and file an official
complaint against the senior officer. But then reality hit him;
the chief *would* find him and he most definitely *would* comply.
Abe didn't have the heart not to. Abe never possessed that
kind of bravery. God always supplied him with the courage
he needed in the past, but now, he hid behind God's name.
He just wasn't certain that God would back him up this time.

Where was his Uncle Charley hiding? He rubbed his forehead with the palm of his hand in an attempt to activate his
brain to come up with a solution. He thought about what
the chief had said about him being in cahoots with his uncle
and wondered was that comment a slip of the tongue, letting
him know that they had found some incriminating evidence
that proved his uncle's guilt. He was a batterer. Although he

thought it unlikely, he couldn't assume arson was out of the realm of possibility for his uncle now.

Abe folded his arms across his body and rocked as if he were a child awakened by a nightmare. "Lord, have mercy." The burden of knowing what he knew about his uncle was almost unbearable. It occurred to him that if his uncle had run off somewhere that he had taken his personal punching bag. He couldn't help but be overwhelmed by the fact that he had put his aunt in more danger by keeping silent as she had wanted.

Abe remembered going past his uncle's house Sunday after church to find his aunt's car in the carport as usual and at least a week's worth of newspapers in various spots on the front lawn. They knocked and knocked, but no one answered. Blanche had gone with him, anxious to talk to with his Uncle Charley again.

Blanche, that's who he'd call. Abe figured if anyone would know what to do, it would be her. He looked at the clock. It was barely past seven o'clock in the morning, and he deemed it too early to call her. He didn't want to do anything to inconvenience this woman who had been so helpful to him in just a week's time. He had spent more days with her since meeting that day than he had working at the pawn shop. At least three days out of the work week he was with her, setting up the 'Feed the Streets' effort and other publicity, always treating her before or afterward to a lavish lunch or a five-course dinner. Mainly he was putting in so much time trying to find a reason not to fall for her.

Blanche was giving him something new that no one had given him before, companionship. It was more than just a physical attraction like he'd experienced with Marion Butler. He was interested in her viewpoint, amazed by her intellect, and amused by her wit. She seemed to feel the same about him. Although his very nerve endings were telling him to be leery, his heart was doing an override.

She had joined the church that was still holding service at the daycare across the street and had basically become the administrative assistant if not the CEO. She had told him to call if anything new came up, he rationalized, so he picked up the phone and dialed her number.

"Abe, what's on your mind?" Blanche asked, sounding surprisingly fresh and alert.

"Look, I'm sorry to call so early, but something has come up," Abe said.

"It's entirely all right. Who needs beauty sleep? What's going on?"

"Chief Rich, the primary investigator of the church fire, called again this morning." Abe relayed all that was said during his early morning call.

"Oh boy, Charley's in trouble." She yawned. "Did he do it?"

Abe, who had been in the midst of a yawn himself swallowed down the end of it to consider her question. "I don't believe he did."

"See, it's that hesitation that's going to kill us, Abe. We've got to be sure about our position. Why? Why do you believe your uncle did not do it?"

"Because he's in love with that church," Abe said without hesitation.

"He certainly is, and he went to great lengths to remain there. I was there the night the rift was wedged between the folks who wanted to leave with Willie Green and the ones, like your uncle, who wanted to remain at Harvest."

Abe had heard the talk about Blanche since her return to Harvest. Some who remembered her from before said she dated Pastor Willie Green, and then aided her uncle in setting him up. Abe chalked it up to church gossip and could only imagine what they said about him behind his back.

"It got ugly. But that's enough about that," Blanche said. In her silence, Abe swore he could hear the wheels in her brain turning. "See, that officer knows that anybody is capable of anything if circumstances and opportunity presents itself. Okay, so we have to paint your uncle as a Bible-toting saint with a fierce devotion to his church."

"Yeah, but—" Abe grew uncomfortable.

"No buts, Abe," Blanche demanded. "We've got to paint our own picture or that investigator will have us filling in the colors by number on his own sketch that he plans on showing a grand jury. We've established relationships this past week in the Christian community with people, churches and ministries willing to help us. We've got to protect our brand, which includes your Uncle Charley."

There was silence as Abe contemplated opening the family closet and letting the secrets fly out.

"What?" she questioned impatiently. "Look, Abe, I'm going to need complete disclosure and honesty if we are going to work together."

Abe told. He described the last time he saw his aunt and uncle at their home and how he stopped his uncle from assaulting his aunt with his shoe. He told her what his aunt had told him coupled with those recessed memories that would indicate that abuse was nothing new in that household. He explained how adamant his uncle had been about not talking to anyone about the fire. He stopped short of the metal lock box discolored from the extreme heat of fire still in his possession.

Blanche didn't react in shock like he expected. She sighed, "Oh well, crucify him then. I did like him, but I have no sympathy for an abuser. If the old monster can put his hands on a woman, then he can sit in jail. He's going down. He's got to take the rap for this."

"Even if he didn't burn the church?" Abe shifted.

"Regardless," Blanche said definitively. "I say put a nail in his coffin before you are banging from the inside of your own. I wish I could see your expression right now. Put that bewildered, yet handsome game face on, Abe. We'll have to meet up before noon, if only for a minute, so I can prepare you to do damage control with the chief and paint yourself as a brainwashed nephew who couldn't see past his uncle's deception, but you've got to find him. From the short time I've known your uncle, I know he's a man all about his routine. Think, Abe; where would he be right now? What would he routinely do before retiring and getting in the habit of hanging at church, watching game shows, and knocking his wife around?"

At that moment he knew Blanche was an angel from God. Just talking with her freed his thinking. He knew where his uncle had gone, over 14,000 miles away to Abe's grandparents' house and his Uncle Charley's childhood home in Lake Chamberlain, Louisiana.

"Blanche, I'll call you back. I think I might know where to find him." Abe was so excited he didn't wait for good-byes.

He called Momma first. She was his Uncle Charley's sister who had retired to nearby New Orleans. She said she hadn't been past the rickety house raised on stilts sitting just north of the Delta's flood pan with crawfish swimming underneath. The upkeep, taxes, and utilities on the place was a thorn in her side, but her siblings, who were just as stubborn as Charley, could not agree to sell the place. It served as a family refuge. Not too long ago his cousin had taken temporary shelter there until his wife could put down the butcher knife long enough to work out the terms of their separation. Abe took a chance and called the old number to no avail. The phone just rang. He would have to call back to make sure that number was still assigned to that house and nowhere else.

Abe prepared himself for the day ahead. He was careful with his clothes selection, not because he would be seeing the chief, but because he would be meeting up with Blanche. About a quarter to eleven, when he was on his way out the door to meet Blanche, he said a prayer and called again.

"Hello," a shallow voice came.

"Aunt Elaine!" Abe shouted.

"Wrong number," the voice persisted.

Abe knew that voice. He knew it was her, and there was no way he was letting her go again. It was time to recapture his bravery. "Listen to me. Say yes if Uncle Charley is there."

"Yes," she replied matter-of-factly.

"Okay, okay," Abe thought. "Pretend I'm one of those annoying calls from the parish trying to shut down Grandmommy's well in the back."

"Okay," his aunt said.

"Just say yes if you are living there. Have you packed your clothes and are planning to stay in Louisiana for awhile?"

"Yes."

Abe could hear his Uncle Charley say something to her in the background. The voice grew nearer as he continued.

"I'm sorry, we're not interested," she stammered.

"Wait, I'm sending someone for you," Abe said. *I'm going to save you.*

"Who is this?" his uncle demanded, apparently yanking the phone from his aunt.

"I'm from the EPA of Tangipahoa Parish. I was just telling your wife about the human health risk of using well water for any purpose," Abe said in his best Creole accent. "We offer a service to houses that still have functioning—"

"We're not interested," Charley said before hanging up.

Oh, but I know someone very interested in you, Uncle Charley.

After meeting Blanche at the corner, Abe arrived at the Maryland State Fire Marshal's office fifteen minutes late with a color palette and an easel ready to paint the chief a picture.

Chapter 15

Can you keep a secret?

Vanessa could see Pat's wide southern smile from behind the sun-activated tinted windows of the Rawl's Mercedes sedan. She almost wanted to cry because only the two of them knew the reason for her crescent moon grin. A secret in her womb that she knew was true since the best friends' last telephone conversation was confirmed by her doctor only yesterday. Willie was clueless. Four months of oblivion.

She met her guest on the landing just outside her house in an attempt to head off her inquiries, but Willie was on her heels. They passed hugs around. Like a slow motion reel, Vanessa saw Pat's hands extend toward her mid-section. She grabbed her hands and held them firmly between the two of them. Making eye contact, she shook her head ever so slightly.

"You didn't call me back last night," Pat said through her teeth. Her smile was still in place.

Vanessa hugged her again and whispered in her ear, "I had nothing to tell you that you didn't already know."

"Oh, darling," Pat sang.

Their embrace was prolonged. Vanessa could feel Willie and Ben's eyes on them. She dabbed her eyes and pulled away to engage the others before they became suspicious.

"I wondered why my wife insisted upon us staying in your guest room. Looks as if we've kept our women locked up.

We've got to stop being so selfish and get them together more often," Ben said, unlocking the trunk with his remote key chain.

"I think you're right, except it's Vanessa that has kept me locked up. If you know what I'm saying," Willie winked.

Vanessa swatted her husband out of embarrassment. While the men pulled the hanging bags off the top, Vanessa grabbed Pat's mid-sized Coach suitcase from the side of the trunk. Pat tried to snatch the bag from her and they played tug-of-war with the handle for a while.

"Ladies, there are enough bags to go around," Willie said incredulously.

"Yeah, Vanessa, why don't we let the guys get that," Pat said, plucking her knuckles until Vanessa let go of the luggage. "We've got some catching up to do."

They trotted around the now discarded suitcase arm in arm, climbed the stairs, entered the house, and climbed more stairs. They didn't stop until they were behind the door of the guest bedroom. Pat scanned the room with her eyes as if she had not previously seen the lilac and blue décor.

"I guess this will be the nursery, huh?" Pat said.

"Girl," Vanessa plopped on the edge of the bed, "I haven't even thought that far."

"You're going to be a mommy." Pat approached her again with her hand extended as if she were Buddha, and to rub her belly was good luck.

More like mommy dearest, Vanessa thought to the degree that there was no reason she needed to be a mother.

Pat sat beside her and rubbed away on her belly, although Vanessa felt it defeated the purpose since her belly wasn't really protruding, everything else was.

"I haven't told Willie yet, so I hope you haven't blabbed to Ben."

"I didn't want to say anything until you went to the doctor. I just figured he'd get a big surprise this weekend. But why on earth haven't you shared the good news with your husband?"

"'Cause I don't know how," Vanessa whispered. She didn't really know that it was good news. Her chest began to heave as she felt herself getting emotional yet again. Being pregnant explained a lot of things that were going on with her physically, but she wondered what she could do to cut off the waterworks.

"Oh, honey, you just tell him." Pat wiped Vanessa's tears away with her hands. "I don't have to tell you that you are blessed among women, and blessed is the fruit of your womb."

Vanessa rolled her eyes at the biblical cliché. "Next you'll be telling me you're pregnant also. Just know if this baby starts leaping and beating up on me from the inside, I'll be too through. So stop, hear?"

They both laughed. Vanessa could hear Willie and Ben on the ground level and knew it was a matter of time before they came upstairs after them. She got solemn again.

"Seriously, this whole thing hasn't even set in with me. I want to tell Willie, and the world, in my own time. It's got to be the right time," Vanessa said.

"Like this weekend?" Pat's eye's twinkled and Vanessa knew that meant she was excited.

Vanessa didn't answer, but rather raised her brows and tried to replicate that sparkle of excitement. This wasn't just her moment. This pregnancy was not just her pregnancy once her husband, her family, and their entire congregation knew about it.

"You know what this occasion calls for, right?" Pat sat up inspired. "Shopping!"

Saturday morning, Pat assisted Vanessa with breakfast. Vanessa was mindful of eating too much for fear of getting nauseous. They then headed to the church with their husbands to observe ministry meetings, but mainly to view the JM Morton Hall complete with new lettering, podium, and memorial bust encased in glass. They all prayed together; a prayer of consecration. As much as Vanessa wanted to pick Ben's brain about Trinity Conference business, at one P.M. they left the guys to talk ministry while they hit the mall.

Pat was not a fan of walking the mall or necessarily shopping for bargains. She had expensive taste and every store they wandered in, she managed to find and buy something. Vanessa felt like Pat's personal assistant, following her around, except Pat wouldn't let her carry a bag over two pounds. Pat wore a safari-green belted pantsuit with ease. Vanessa felt doughty in a denim wrap around skirt. She already took to wearing bigger shirts to hide her midsection and at least slim her hips and rear end. They crisscrossed the t-shaped mall, hitting each anchor department store before leaving to find a boutique recommended by a store clerk.

The place was called Eden's Closet, and it was designed for a diva like Pat. Although it was a small shop, it was organized to be shopper-friendly with accessories like purses and hats along the wall and a few racks devoted to everything from casual pantsuits to formal wear stocked in the middle.

"This place has less selection than I am sure you are used to back home," Vanessa said, scanning a price tag on a butter-yellow suit with cream saddle stitching around the lapel. She figured the limited inventory added to the exclusive price.

"That doesn't matter," Pat said, flipping through each suit in her size. "What matters is I am two hundred miles from any other woman in my congregation. So the chance she shows up one Sunday as my twin is lessened greatly."

Vanessa was going through the motions, but not really looking. She wasn't even sure what size she wore anymore, and knew for sure she was a different size up top than on the bottom. She had turned into a pear. "I saw that gorgeous new suit hanging over the door this morning. Now, I know when you bought that you didn't buy just one. So what occasion are you shopping for today?"

"For life," she replied.

"Don't you mean for sport," Vanessa corrected.

"You're right, I don't need anything." Pat reviewed the three suits she had over her arm. "I should be helping you. What have you added to your wardrobe lately?"

Vanessa had settled a long time ago that they had two very different views of wardrobing. She felt she didn't need anything as long as her bases were covered with the basics. She had no particular style although she leaned toward comfy casual these days. As far as new closet investments, she thought about the two jogging suits she bought when she noticed she was picking up weight. Her goal was to make Willie go with her on a nightly stroll after work.

"Pick something and come to the dressing room with me," Pat continued. "Better yet, let me find you something. They have all sorts of maternity places now. When I was pregnant I almost went into a depression over the horrible frocks that were labeled maternity. What about tomorrow?"

"I'm wearing my—" Vanessa started.

"I know, you are wearing your robe in the pulpit. Honestly, I think that is so played out. Do you see Joyce Meyer or Paula White in a robe? What happens at the banquet? I bet you didn't even think about that. Do you and Willie sit up in robes while you're eating? If I were you, I'd have my 50th anniversary ensemble and might do a quick costume change before the banquet too, okay. " Pat snapped her fingers. She stopped to size Vanessa up over the top of her tortoise shell glasses that were on the tip of her nose. "What size are you now?"

Vanessa shook her head. "That's just it, my hips have run for the border, and my butt is trying to catch up with them." She attempted to look at her tush from over her shoulder.

"You need something in a jersey material. It is so forgiving."

In a matter of minutes Pat had made a few selections for her and was leading the way to the dressing room as if she had been there before. Vanessa dutifully tried on each one although she had a strong desire to lie down on the bench inside the stall. The last one was a black and white sleeveless v-neck with a pale blue ribbon woven in at the waist to resemble a wide belt. Vanessa looked at herself from all angles.

"Don't be afraid of it. It's called your shape. I'll admit this dress reveals some things, but you are going to reveal some things tomorrow, right?" The gleam in her eye let Vanessa know she had growing momentum. "Oh my gosh, this will be so perfect. Everyone is going to be loving you in this dress, and so excited, and loving *on* you and the little one in your belly when they find out."

"Pat, I can't." Vanessa knew there was no way she would reveal her pregnancy to Willie tomorrow, let alone her congregation. Wouldn't he be mad to hear something like that in front of everyone? Then she thought about Willie's nature, and knew he would be delighted. He was famous for, 'my wife is going to kill me when I tell you this,' inserts into his own sermons. They lived a transparent life. They shared just about everything with their congregation, but it wasn't going to happen tomorrow, she thought.

"I know, I know, you're not used to going sleeveless. I have the answer. Voila." Vanessa barely looked at the white sateen bolero with ruffles up and down the edges before Pat had her spinning like a revolving door to get into it. "It's called a diva collar, diva."

Vanessa turned around and had to admit she loved the way she looked. Pat convinced her that her black sling backs with the peak-a-boo toe that she already owned would go perfectly with this outfit. The forecast called for rain, she thought, and there was nothing worse than cold feet.

The next day Vanessa was having cold feet about telling her husband and congregation her secret. Pat was so bubbly and excited, that Vanessa knew she had to consider telling everyone before her friend let the cat out the bag. The thought alone gave her a bout of nausea. She made it through the morning on orange juice, two Krispy Kreme doughnuts, and high praise for the Lord. She enjoyed not having to worry about the order of service in preparation of preaching the gospel. She got to chill out in her own pulpit since Ben was preaching, which was a treat, but each time she looked over at her husband or at specific faces in the congregation, she thought they deserved to know.

She hadn't wrapped her mind around what was going on inside of her body, what they had done, what had been created. During the closing prayer and benediction Vanessa zoned out. She got panicky thinking about being pregnant at 43, an age that seemed much older to her now in her present condition. She wasn't sure about anything anymore.

Between morning service and the dedication banquet, when Willie was allowing their guest minister to wind down in his office, and the congregants saved seats and greeted each other, Pat was performing a transformation on Vanessa. She felt like she was back stage at the Apollo. She stepped out of her robe and into her diva collar. Pat loosened her bun and fanned out her hair before applying a tinted gloss to her ample lips.

Vanessa excused herself for the third time to use the bathroom. She surprised herself when she looked in the mirror.

Her hair looked as if it had grown a full three inches. What was more surprising was that she didn't recognize herself. She knew then that if she went in there and admitted she was pregnant, she would no longer be the Vanessa Morton Green she had come to know.

When she came out of the bathroom she met Pat's approving smile with a grave admission. "Pat, I need you to support me in my decision to postpone this announcement."

"What? Why?" Pat said.

"I'm forty-three, I'm old, and I just don't know," Vanessa said."I thought that the possibility of motherhood was behind me — that I had successfully dodged that bullet. Now look at me, messing around with that Willie Green."

"Honey, you're just scared, but you are past your first trimester. God has smiled on you, and He will see you through this pregnancy." Pat held her hand. "I understand if you do not want to do this publically. Forget my little fantasy. You and Willie need to talk this over privately."

"I don't know if I will carry this baby." Vanessa turned away from her friend's gaze.

Pat grabbed Vanessa by the shoulder and turned her around so she could face her again. "Wait a minute, what do you mean?"

"I thought about it. I'm sick and throwing up all the time. This is past morning sickness. Something might be wrong, and I can't take that risk."

"Vanessa, you're just letting the devil make way with your senses," Pat said, grabbing her hands in hers.

"No, Pat," Vanessa snatched her hand away from her friend and shook her head to refute what Pat just said. "I can't be a mother."

"I'm going to get Willie now," Pat announced, heading for the door of the study. "Forget the banquet, the two of you need to talk because you've gone crazy."

"Stay out of it, Pat," Vanessa shouted. She gathered herself and studied the door as if to sense if someone was on the other side. She checked her watch. "I'm going to check with my sister to see if we are ready to get started. Then we're going to go in, and I'm going to do nothing more than what I had planned in dedication to my father."

"You want me to stay out of it while you talk crazy about not carrying the gift God has placed inside you. What's your alternative Vanessa, abortion? You want me to stay out of it after we prayed in agreement to your consecration to God as leader of this house while you deceive your husband. How long are you going to hold the truth from him?"

Vanessa stood stoically. She didn't have an answer to any of her friend's questions.

"I can't do it. A true friend calls you out and tells you when you're wrong. Ben Rawls taught me to get it straight before you stand before God's people. I love you dearly, but I'm not taking part in this — not today, not any day. So we can say our goodbyes now," Pat said with her hands on her hips. "I'm going to get my husband, and we are going to go in there and do nothing more than say goodbye to your congregation, thank them for their hospitality, and tell them we've got to ease on down the road. I'll let you explain our departure to your husband later."

Vanessa watched her friend of twenty-five years turn on her three inch stiletto heels and leave.

Chapter 16

A Bump in the Road

Willie woke up thinking maybe he was the only mature one in his circle. The past few weeks seemed to be filled with petty squabbles and disagreements between he and his wife, between his wife and her sister, and now his wife and her best friend. He didn't find out about the latter until his guest minister left in the middle of their anniversary celebration. He was surprised that Ben fell prey to the nonsense and offered no other explanation than, "Normally, I wouldn't play like a celebrity that preaches one minute and is led out early by his entourage the next, but I've got to back my wife up. We love you guys. Just talk to Vanessa, man, and I'll call you next week."

Vanessa was the common denominator. To say that he was turned off by her current behavior was putting it mildly. He feared the twelve years that separated them was finally making a difference. When they first got together, his outlook on life met her intensity and fierce independence somewhere in the middle of that gap. Now he wasn't sure they were relating like they used to.

After spending the remainder of Sunday afternoon waiting for her to come to him with some sort of explanation, which did not happen, he planned to confront her. He wanted to know details about the weekend's ordeal this morning, but she popped up with some sort of mystery doctor's appointment. Willie went into church although the administrative offices were closed. He needed to prepare himself for the next day's non-negotiable joint board meeting that maintained the church's checks and balances system and integrity of operations. He left Vanessa an I-need-you message in an attempt to lure her to the office as well since she had the preliminary figures from the anniversary for the budget report.

She arrived at church after lunch and had a nerve to complain that Willie was in his office working instead of the main study connected to her office. Her dress was casual and her disposition was reticent. She stood in the doorway as if she didn't plan to stay long.

"You know you are not on the network server. Whatever you work on down here will have to be recreated by Luella in the morning in order for her to print copies for the board tomorrow. That doesn't make sense," she said.

"What doesn't make sense is why our best friends in ministry left the banquet like they were being run out of town," Willie replied.

"It was a disagreement that escalated between Pat and me, okay? I'll call her this week and straighten it out," Vanessa said dismissively. "That's not what we are here for right now. Unless you or I have a hard copy of the last agenda, then it's on Luella's computer. There was quite a bit of old business we didn't get a chance to discuss. We will never get anything accomplished if we keep tabling things to the next meeting."

"Just like these disagreements, these rifts you keep getting into with everyone around you including me. When do these things ever get discussed? I don't know what's going on with you lately, Vanessa. You're up, you're down, one minute you're reclusive, the next you're throwing tantrums. What's going on? Let's clear the air."

Willie watched her look down while brushing wisps of hair back toward her bun. He could tell she was thinking. Hopefully of a way to relay the truth, Willie thought.

"We can talk about this later, when we get home," she finally said.

"Let's talk about it now, Vanessa," Willie demanded. "'Cause it is slowly driving a wedge between us and the people around us. We are alone, in the House of God, with nothing but space and opportunity to straighten it all out. Heck, we've even got an altar."

He met her on the other side of the desk and sat with her in the chairs there. She brought her purse down in her lap and had a hard time positioning it so it wouldn't fall. She pulled out a yellow booklet with a woman's silhouette on the cover and handed it to him. The cover read, "Welcome to Motherhood, Your Pregnancy Guide," But it might as well have been written in hieroglyphics because he couldn't immediately interpret its meaning. Every female that he had been in contact with for the past two weeks flashed through his mind before he finally got it.

"Sweetheart, are you . . .?" He noticed her head nod before he could get it out. "Are we?"

Willie stood and resisted the urge to pull her to him in a crushing bear hug. He realized what everything had been about and vowed then to take care when handling her, when touching her, even when talking to her. Now he realized that while everyone was being impatient with her, including himself, she was crafting the blueprint God designed for both their lives.

"God be praised." He stood, giving God praise. His spirit got carried away, "Woo," he yelled out in disbelief at God's favor toward them.

Willie realized Vanessa was not standing, nor did he hear

her voice lifted up in praise. She was still sitting in the same position. A pained expression covered her face. He kneeled before her. "Is everything, okay? You went to the doctor this morning, right? I mean, could they tell if the baby is all right?"

Vanessa was back to nodding, chasing some of his dread away, but she was so overcome with emotion he couldn't read her.

"What is it, baby?"

"I can't do this," came a low hollow voice he did not recognize.

Willie pushed off of one knee to his chair. "You can't?" He wished she would just tell him what was wrong. What would prevent her from bearing their child?

"It's not so much that I can't do it, but rather I never thought I could. I'd see pregnant women or other women with their children and think I couldn't do the whole birthing and nurturing and mothering thing." Her eyes pleaded for him to hear her out — to understand. "I know it is a subtle difference that doesn't mean much to you, but I have to carry this baby at forty-three years of age. I have to breast feed or bottle feed the baby when I should be preaching. I've got to wipe the child's nose and tail when I should be leading this church, not to mention the Trinity Conference. You know how much that means to me."

"You're being silly," Willie reasoned.

"Oh yeah, Willie Green, you may have scored the goal, but I have to be the mother. And don't think I won't be judged as old as I am. I will be left cleaning up the stands and fields while you are treated like the MVP, receiving repeated pats on the back."

Willie was hurt, as if he had gone to hug her and got stabbed instead. "Is that really how you feel?"

"You wished this on me," Vanessa continued, ignoring

him. "I distinctly remember having a conversation not too long ago about your mother wanting me to produce a grandchild. Like she will be willing to babysit from a nursing home. I guess the prayers of the righteous do avail much, huh Willie? I told you then that I was not cut out for this."

Willie sat back as if to really look at her. Where was all this coming from? "Wow, you sure do know how to take all the beauty out of this situation." He got up and stepped back a few feet to see if he ever really knew who she was. "Now I see. This is why you've been moping around. How long have you known you were pregnant?"

"Dr. Sanchez confirmed it last Thursday. I went to a new doctor today who's both a gynecologist and obstetrician. I'm nearing twenty weeks," she sighed. "I guess subconsciously I've always known."

Give her the benefit of the doubt, let her rest, let her gather herself, Willie thought, but he wasn't listening to himself either. "And everyone else knew except me? Keisha? Pat? Ben?" Willie questioned, "everyone except the father."

"No," Vanessa was bound to the chair, and she craned her neck to follow Willie who was pacing now around the office. "Only Pat knew. That's why they left early, because she knew how I felt and thought I should tell you."

Willie stopped pacing and kept silent, remembering what he said earlier about treating Vanessa gingerly. She was visibly upset. He wondered how much of that stress was affecting the baby. He thought also how easily blessings can turn into curses and decided to change gears.

"Let's both just calm down. This is supposed to be a joyous time in our lives, and no devil in hell is going to take that away. I'm just sorry I've missed over half the pregnancy. I could have been there to hold your hand," Willie said, talking to the back of her head now.

"Yeah, well you were out on the street playing detective and reporter," she said.

Willie walked around the front of his desk so she could see his face. "C'mon, Vanessa, don't even blame this on the *Inside 7* reports. You were keeping secrets. You knew where I was."

"After the fact," Vanessa added.

The telephone rang up the hall, causing the light on his extension to blink. They both shifted to find their cell phones, realizing if it were an emergency with one of their members, that one of their personal phones would be going off next. They waited and regrouped.

His cell phone buzzed instead of rang because it was set on vibrate. He was tempted to ignore it, but knew few people had that number and it could be important. He flipped the phone over and recognized Alexis's number. They had just seen her in church the day before, and he wondered what she could be calling about now.

Willie answered the phone under the watchful eye of his wife and could not help but react to what Alexis was telling him. Roy had apparently been picked up by the police with a few others for drug possession, and the police were trying to tack on a distribution charge. She was waiting to see if they posted a bail for his release until his arraignment. Willie couldn't believe the timing and asked Alexis to call him back when she had more details.

He looked at his wife across the desk from him, which brought him back to reality.

"Another crisis," she declared as if she had been on the phone. "Go ahead, go."

After a few minutes of stalemate, Willie said, "Forget that for right now, forget the report. I think we should go into the sanctuary and pray."

"Don't you think that is counterproductive if we are praying for different things?" Vanessa's words sounded like pure venom to him.

Willie turned in his executive style chair and shut down his computer. He picked up his cell phone and shoved it hard into its belt holster. He walked around his desk and the set of chairs Vanessa sat in.

"I'm leaving before I say something guaranteed to upset you," he said once he reached the door.

"Yeah, right, and you want me to believe it has nothing to do with the phone call you just received."

Willie thought about what she just said. Sure, he was concerned about Roy, and would help to raise the money to pay his bail, but his family was more important right now. They both needed space and a clear perspective. He couldn't sit there and let her gut him out anymore with her words without a few of his own.

"You know what, Vanessa? This isn't about anyone else. It's about us. You are talking as if you don't want to bring our baby into the world, which right now sounds the same as you don't want to be married to me. You decide," Willie said, leaving her with her own puncture wound.

Chapter 17
The New It Girl

The death of an international superstar of stratospheric proportion preempted the regular broadcast of most televised programming, including the *Inside 7* segment, as never ending probes into his death, dizzying amount of tributes, and his footage played 24/7. As a young boy on the rise, this star came to Washington DC to attend a gala of the then president, Jimmy Carter. A perky Channel 7 special assignment reporter, Lizzy London, got to meet and interview him. The current production team of the *Inside 7* program elected to run the vintage footage in memorial.

To any other reporter that hiatus would mean death to a series of stories based on lesser known individuals. But to a rising reporter like Alexis Montgomery armed with conviction about an investigative probe of her own and breaking news on her Blackberry, there was no stopping her.

"Well, that's the kind of meeting I like, short and sweet," remarked Lizzy London, who in her seniority no longer felt it necessary to pitch ideas. Alexis wondered why she even bothered to show up. She usually upgraded a top story handed to her from the nightly news anchor desk and used that as the lead-in story for the *Inside 7* weekly broadcast.

The large conference room that was chilly when Alexis first entered with her Frappicino, and last minute research was

now warmed with the energy of the *Inside 7* production staff.
A large calendar with tentative show ideas was written in red
marker on a white board.

"Well, I have some ideas to kick around, so I will know in
what direction to move in for my series next week," Alexis
said. She figured since Mark Shaw, the Executive Producer,
and his assistant, Martie, looked comfortable in their chairs
with their share of sugar-rush snacks at their side, that she
should go for it. She held up her all-important Blackberry.
"My source at the department told me that they are in the
process of extraditing Charley Thompson, who is the deacon
at Harvest Baptist Church, from Louisiana. They are charging him with arson in the Harvest Baptist Church case. They
think they've got their man."

Alexis placed her Blackberry directly in front of her on the
table as was the custom of everyone else in attendance in respect to their unofficial keep-your-device-where-we-can see-it,
no texting during the meeting rule. She couldn't help but
smile at how she bought someone off in Chief Rich's office
after the captain himself called to ream her out about forcing
Willie Green in the frame of her last interview to spite him.
And Martie said her Starbucks gift cards wouldn't work as a
bribe. She was no longer afraid of his threats. They were hollow at best. He was just desperate to solve his case.

There was rambling around the table from some of the
other writers and production assistants. Alexis heard one say,
"I guess she's never going back to the beat."

"Great, so next week we'll be wrapping this horse and pony
show up," Lizzy said, spinning her finger around for emphasis.

Alexis's thoughts were swarming. "Not yet, I don't think we
should rush it. I hate those reports that show shots of a suspect
taken in the jail or taken to and from court before anything

is officially ruled. Then you have barely enough footage to be called a photo and barely enough accurate information to be called a caption. We might as well be print journalists for that kind of reporting. There is a process to formally charging someone and a window of time before that information becomes official. But in the meantime—"

"Basically, you are going to drag this out as far as possible, and we are supposed to reserve airtime for you," Lizzy said, cutting her off. She looked to Mark for back up as if Alexis had just made a ridiculous request.

"So do they think Abe Townsend is involved?" Martie Hamilton asked with a wink in Alexis's direction.

"Oh yeah, that's the lunched-out preacher, right?" someone else commented.

"The website got so many hits after that interview of people trying to access the back-story, and emails doubled trying to help the poor cat out," Martie continued.

"Pastor Abe, I'm sure, is making plans for a bigger church. His membership has increased, and they have already outgrown the daycare. They are holding service at Central High School auditorium now.

"You could do a follow-up on him or that other preacher that left the church, Green," commented Maisy Day, the technical assistant.

In Alexis's excitement, she shared that Pastor Willie and Pastor Vanessa were expecting. Willie had shared the information with her in confidence when she called back to tell him they had Roy's bail set at $5,000. He seemed consumed by the time he met her at the station. She felt guilty overshadowing his happiness with such bad news. Their concern was where Roy would go when they paid for his release. He couldn't stay with her, so she left that burden on Pastor Willie as they left Roy with the 'three hots and a cot' for the next night or two down at Central Booking.

"That stud. What is he like, fifty?" someone called out and roused scattered laughter.

"Wait a minute, guys, let's keep that under wraps. I shouldn't have shared his business," Alexis said, although she doubted any of the people she worked with hung in the same circle as Willie or Vanessa Green.

"Maybe Alexis should do a recap of the pastor's ending with a follow-up since the public was generally interested. Get their reactions on this new information about the deacon. Plant a flag on this exclusive information so the other stations will know we had it first. That would give enough time for charges to be filed against this Thompson fellow and a trial date to be set." Mark swiveled his chair toward Alexis. "Congratulations, Montgomery," Mark Shaw said to a modest round of applause from everyone except Lizzy.

"But sir, I have an even more pressing story. It's an investigative probe into the supposed Drug Taskforce and the subsequent sting operations between the DC mayor's office and surrounding Maryland counties," Alexis said, using finger quotation marks to highlight the hypocrisy.

A few aides had come in at the same time to whisper messages to their respective staffer who would have received the message if they were allowed to use their phones. She paused until Mark, who had an aide glued to his right side sifting through his Blackberry, signaled for her to continue. "Well, just like prohibition didn't decrease alcohol consumption, this task force has spent thousands of tax payers' dollars and has done little to clean up our streets. I dare say from my research that the police are perpetuating the problem with their unfair arrest history. They are ten times more likely to convict a person for possession than they are for distribution or higher drug crimes. Any Joe Friday can arrest an addict. Take that same corridor from Lincoln Avenue that snakes down to the district line for instance. It's a known fact that drug users walk into court and get time-served in a detention center or probation with a record and the dealers walk scot-free. They wrangle the users or runners together with trumped up charges to pad the files to justify the cost of the program."

"What?" Lizzy said as if Alexis was speaking a foreign language.

"I'm with Lizzy, way too much altitude, Montgomery" Mark said, then laughed, and when he laughed, his flunkies did also. "Bring it down to earth for us."

"Hear me out," Alexis said, rising from her seat. She could feel the blood coursing through her veins as she struggled to make it more palpable to the show's producer. "My piece would be a follow up on our last show because Roy Jones, the homeless preacher that I interviewed and the viewers loved, I might add, got caught up in a drug bust. They arrested him since our last show for drug possession, and I believe they are trying to tack on conspiracy charges too. He's got five co-defendants. He was swept up by these task force goons who know full well who the dealers are on this street, but won't touch them. He's getting arraigned next week. Roy told me about these quarterly sweeps and how the DA has got incentive to let some of the big fish go to continue dealing on our streets."

"A part two?" Martie assisted.

"Yes," Alexis said.

"Now she's Mother Theresa." Lizzy looked as if she was about ready to slap herself she was so outdone.

"She's done her homework. Now you all know how I like the whole jailhouse interview," Mark claimed.

"Well, he will be out on bail soon. Pastor Willie and I met with a bail bondsman, and Pastor Willie needed a day or two to petition the church for the money. The state is building a case against Roy, and he could be wrongly accused," Alexis said, holding her breath. "Any drug that he would have on him would be the sealed single-serving size issued to him at the rehab clinic I featured in my piece."

"I can see it. One week he's on the street preaching, the next he's taking us into the drug underworld," Martie explained.

Mark sat back and let his executive style chair drift in her direction. "You think you're ready for something like this, Montgomery?"

"I am. I played it too safe last time. I will present the court statistics and keep the interview strictly first person. It will be from his lips to the camera's lens."

"Extend an invitation for someone from the taskforce to respond. Don't let them off easy either. Drill them about the Jones case in particular. See what you uncover. Who knows, you might just get him off," Mark said.

That was her intention, Alexis thought, taking his comments as the go-ahead she needed. With that she sat down.

"It's the *Inside* 7 segment with Alexis and Lizzy," someone remarked.

Lizzy shot a threatening look around the table, stopping, of course, at Mark.

"She has redesigned the format since doing her series. Instead of the three seven-minute segments where we barely covered anything thoroughly, Alexis has covered a heck of a lot in ten to fifteen minutes," Mark boasted. "What you got for your lead-in, Lizzy?"

This caught her off guard, but she quickly recovered. "I think I should cover the extradition of the arsonist at the top of the show. It's only responsible journalism to keep the public updated on an on-going story."

It was Alexis's turn to pass out a threatening look. How dare Lizzy try to finish off a story that she had begun. Lizzy met her stare with a smug look of her own.

"All right then, keep me posted," Mark said, waving the Blackberry that was now in his hand as he adjourned the meeting.

A sense of dread came over Alexis as she gathered her things from the table. Forget Lizzy London and her insecurities. Let her have the Charley Thompson story if Alexis could pull off the story she just pitched and prove Roy innocent in the process. She had bigger fish to fry; if only she had the pan of hot grease.

Chapter 18

A New Attitude

The moon traded places with the sun as day gave way to night. It was so bright and so high in the sky, yet to Abe, it didn't seem unattainable. He was with Blanche. Being with her started his ascent toward the sky. Then she clasped her hand with his, and he was there. He didn't know what to make of this obvious step toward affection and decided to get comfortable in this new spot in the universe.

Blanche had arranged for him to get measured for a new robe earlier in the day at the insistence that his old one was hideous and unacceptable. She accompanied him to the uniform shop. There he received a call from his Aunt Elaine to say that his Uncle Charley had been turned over to state police and that she was home for good after being forced to Louisiana with his uncle. He was held on the grounds that the state had enough evidence to prosecute him for the arson of the Harvest Baptist Church fire. Blanche was gracious enough to go with him to pay his aunt a visit instead of dining out as they had planned.

Abe felt oddly like a man who was bringing his girlfriend to meet the family for the first time as he held her hand there on his aunt and uncle's front stoop. For a split second he questioned his decision to bring Blanche into his family's turmoil, especially not knowing what physical state they'd find his aunt in after being secluded with her batterer of a husband for two weeks. He was still squeamish at the vision of his Uncle Charley aiming the heel of his shoe toward his aunt's head. All fears were put to rest when they were met with a surprisingly fresh-faced and hospitable Elaine Thompson who acted as if she had been waiting on company all day.

No introductions were necessary as Abe soon realized that Blanche and his Aunt Elaine knew each other from the church before the rift and split. They exchanged words that could be considered pleasantries. His aunt immediately fixed them a plate of fresh pulled pork shoulder and coleslaw on a Kaiser roll and served it on two TV trays so they could join her in the living room.

"I was watching the news in here half way expecting to see your uncle's face and hear them talking about bringing us back from down South. I tell you them parish police swarmed on us like bees to a hive. Your uncle was driving and decided to take a light. Tell me why he did that? He didn't see that police car sitting in the cut to the right as we passed. I thought we had gotten away, but they must have run his tags, 'cause before you know it, he came after us. Then two other cars came. Seem like from every direction. When Charley finally stopped they told him to get out the car. They had a warrant out for his arrest back home here," Elaine Thompson said without prompting. She had her dinner napkin in hand pressed against her heart to still it. Her soft and airy voice was stretched to capacity trying to relay the emotions.

"We spent like six hours at the station down there. That was Thursday night. Then they loaded him up like lettuce on a produce truck and took him off in handcuffs."

Abe noticed her grab her wrist and begin rubbing it as she spoke. The terror of the situation was apparent in her eyes. He was unaccustomed to her being so chatty.

"They took me down to the station and asked me more questions than they did on the street there," she continued. "At first they were going to release me until I told them I didn't have no place to go without the key from your uncle; that Maryland was my home and not your grandmother's property. I wasn't up for no two-day drive. Come to find out Maryland State Police wanted possession of the car anyway. They helped me get my things and got me on a flight to Charleston, South Carolina. From there I got on another flight home. I just got in something after nine this morning."

"I'm glad you are all right," Abe said.

Everything from the beige floral print wallpaper to the threadbare carpet was the same. It was just strange to see his aunt sitting in his uncle's chair staring into the TV screen the way his Uncle Charley had every time he came to visit. Abe wanted to uproot her, but it was too late. That transplant should have taken place a long time ago. He wished she could know how guilt-ridden he was. "I'm sorry you had to go through all this, Aunt Elaine; really, I am."

"It must have been horribly frightening," Blanche threw in on piggy-back.

"Frightening is being in this house alone. I didn't expect that." She looked around at the walls. "Sure didn't expect to miss him."

"Well, he's still your husband no matter what has happened or will happen," Blanche tried to reassure her.

His aunt stared at Blanche and slowly nodded her head in agreement with that statement as if Blanche had read her mind. "They've got him now and his car too. Didn't even let me have that. Doggone it if they didn't know the moment I would arrive before I get a call from the station asking me to come in later on this morning for questioning. I could hardly sleep, and I declare I only ate one time between Louisiana and the time I got home. Twenty-three hours. I came in hungry as the dickens, and ate just about everything I could spot. I saw that shoulder I started two weeks ago." Elaine pointed toward their plates. "We left in such a hurry, you know, I had to shove it in the refrigerator. That shoulder has been sitting in vinegar relish all that time, so I know it's tender. I put it on as soon as I got in, turned the stove on low, went to sleep, got up and went back down to the station. Let it cook all day. I wish I could have brought some to Charley. See if he'd like that. Yes indeedy, see if he'd like that. "

"It's delicious." Blanche's eyes wandered as if she didn't know what else to say. They traded smiles like they had formed some kind of kinship.

"Aunt Elaine," Abe said, trying to focus her attention back on the case. He couldn't believe she even wanted to think about her husband let alone cook for him. He chalked it up to battered woman syndrome to continue to cherish a man that had hurt her.

Abe wasn't certain if his uncle had burned the church down and didn't want to carry his aunt back to painful memories of her abduction to find out what she knew. He needed to know that his uncle wouldn't be released to harm her again, that his punishment would be more then missing out on a pork shoulder dinner. "What are the police saying? What did Uncle Charley say?"

"Your Uncle Charley ain't saying anything. He said he didn't want to speak to anyone, so he's not, and they're not letting him go neither. Heard the officer say they was waiting on the chief to formally charge him with something, 'cause they couldn't chance letting him go."

"He's a flight risk," Blanche commented. "He's proven that, and that alone is enough to keep him."

That seemed to make his aunt breathe easier. "I answered

all the captain's questions, and I suspect I'll be answering some more questions before it is all said and done. They said they would be putting Charley in touch with a public defender. Hopefully by then Charley would stop being so stubborn and speak."

"If not, then I figure the facts will speak for themselves," Blanche interjected.

Abe wondered what the facts were. They had two separate cases here; abuse and arson. Even though one didn't necessarily have anything to do with the other, it spoke to his uncle's character. Abe figured if his aunt could hide the reality of her abuse from her family and friends at church, what was to prevent her from holding some vital piece of evidence to protect her husband?

"Did you tell them?" Abe said, being purposely vague.

"About the metal box?" she questioned.

"No, about you and Uncle Charley," Abe said, trying to spare her feelings in front of Blanche although he had already told her of his uncle's abuse toward his aunt.

"I think you should bring the metal box back here where you found it. I was wrong for letting you take it. They might search the house."

"Yes, ma'am," Abe said.

"What metal box?" Blanche demanded to know, her eyebrows forming sharp peeks with concern.

"Bring it tomorrow after church, you hear?" His aunt's eyebrows made their own peaks to show she wasn't playing.

"Yes, ma'am," Abe assured.

"What box?" Blanche persisted.

Abe's eyes pleaded with her to let it go until later. He knew she'd agree with his aunt not to be caught dead with such a critical piece of evidence. But since the police didn't have the box yet, Abe wanted to know what they did have that would hold his uncle in jail. "Aunt Elaine, did you tell them that Uncle Charley hits you?"

His aunt swallowed hard and hung her head in shame. "I wasn't going to. In fact, the parish police was relentless. They wanted to know why I would willingly leave my home if I didn't know my husband was a suspect. Made me feel like I was going to jail with Charley for a minute. All they knew is that they had a fugitive, and when I opened that car door, they thought they had two."

"At that point I could no longer be your uncle's protector. I just told them like this, I never liked Louisiana. See this scar, here? I got this in '83 when I told Charley I didn't feel like going with him to Louisiana to his family reunion." She brushed her hand across the inside of her forearm at a scar only she could remember and see before sweeping her hair behind her ear to reveal a fading blue-black mark between her cheek and eardrum. "But this one here I got the other day when I questioned when we would be returning home to Maryland."

Abe rushed to her side to comfort her. Although this bruise was more than likely from his uncle's fist, visions of the shoe heel once again came flashing back. He couldn't help weeping right along with his aunt. They took a moment to get themselves together. Blanche patted him on the back and lent her support as he sat on the couch next to her.

"The chief told me earlier today to say the word and he'd add assault charges on top of the abduction and everything else he got coming to him," she said and looked at Abe as if it were his decision to make.

"This latest development is sure to make it on the news soon. Tomorrow is Ministry of Support Sunday too," Blanche said as if the implications any story on the church would have on her pet project was clear to everyone.

"I'll see you all in church then. You know your uncle ain't even looked in the direction of a church while we were away. That is one of the things I missed the most about being away from home; that along with central air conditioning."

"Maybe she should think again about attending church," Blanche said, turning toward Abe. "I've sent out press releases to all the major papers."

"Why in the world would I stay away from church after what I've been through?" Elaine Thompson said, her right arm rising to her hip.

"You know church folk with their snide comments and gossiping. I'm trying to think about your feelings and privacy. It may be too much for you to deal with considering the circumstances. I strongly suggest you reconsider and let a little time pass before rejoining the congregation."

"Did I miss something?" his aunt said with a brassiness he didn't recognize. "Does Harvest Baptist have a new first lady I wasn't aware of? Although I know this one here has been vying for that position long before you came to be pastor."

"Blanche has been helping our church regain its integrity and image since the fire. She's responsible for the increase in membership and support to our congregation," Abe said in her defense.

"Uh-huh, well, I appreciate her concern, but tell her I just got out from under one thumb, I don't need the fingerprint of another one," his usually meek aunt said to him as if Blanche had all of a sudden disappeared. "I plan to make my own decisions, and I plan to go to my church. If anything, people should see me praising the Lord my God in spite of what is going on."

His aunt grabbed their plates and excused herself to the kitchen under the spotlight of Blanche's astonished stare. Like the picture on the wall above the television, something was slightly askew. Abe certainly understood where the burst of assertiveness in his aunt was coming from, but wondered why it never burst free before now.

"That woman is a loose cannon. Talk to her, Abe," Blanche said. "I'm serious. No one wants to support a church with a lot of chaos going on. The family scandal needs to stay under wraps as long as possible, or at least until after The Ministry of Support Sunday. We've worked too hard to have your aunt be the center of attention airing her dirty laundry at devotional."

Abe signaled to Blanche to calm down as he checked up on his aunt in the kitchen. He didn't know whether he agreed with Blanche or his aunt. Surely he could see both sides. He laid his hands on his aunt's shoulder. The rest of her arm was elbow deep in sudsy dish water.

"Y'all gone now?" was her way of asking were they leaving. Her voice saturated with her cares. He did want another glass of sweet iced tea, but kissed her on the cheek instead as a good-bye gesture and told her he would see her tomorrow.

Abe was thankful for the quiet drive back to his apartment, and even more thankful that Blanche had not questioned him about the metal box. He had a lot on his mind, including what he was going to do for sermon material the next day. This entire situation with his aunt's emancipation had him thinking about the Beatitudes. *A New Identity and a New Attitude*, he tried out as a sermon title. *Blessed are the poor in spirit, for theirs is the kingdom of heaven . . . Blessed are the meek, for they shall inherit the earth.* He immediately thought about his aunt. There were many highs and lows ahead of her, but God had her covered with the fruit of inheritance. But it was the next verse that kept playing in his mind. *Blessed are those that hunger and thirst after righteousness, for they will be filled.* The verse wasn't talking about the thirst satisfied with a refill of iced tea.

Thirsty? Came a voice he almost didn't recognize. It was the Spirit of the Lord.

"Abe," Blanche called out while pulling on his sleeve. He hadn't realized he was passing his building. "Are you all right?"

He had gone too far and had to circle back around. "Yeah . . . zoned out." He didn't tell her he was having a revelation. God was telling him his well had been dry for so long that he had forgotten how to thirst.

They found a space out in front of Abe's building and he prepared to walk Blanche down the street to her car where she had parked earlier, except they didn't move. She lingered.

"Thanks for coming with me this evening. I guess I better get upstairs and do what I do to prepare for service." Abe was anxious to hear what the Lord had to say and to be filled. "I sort of have a ritual."

"Can I watch?" Blanche asked. "I've seen every operation at Harvest. I might as well see how the magic happens. It's only nine thirty. Plus, I'm not ready to go home yet." She shrugged. "So be a gentleman and ask me up."

Abe was being pulled in two different directions. On one side the Lord was calling him into communion. The Holy Spirit was whispering to him in a love language and he had scriptures on the tip of his tongue to speak in return. Spending time with God would give him a fresh Word for his congregation. On the other side was this sultry siren who quite possibly wanted to take their close association into a true courtship. Spending time with her might prove that she actually felt the same way about him that he did about her. Maybe to another preacher this would be an uncontested fight, but it had been awhile since he had felt either of these sensations.

Abe stalled for time, fiddling with his keys until they eventually fell on the ground. He took that opportunity to look her up and down. She wore a blouse in the most divine shade of blue and high-waisted trousers that accentuated her small waist and caressed every curve thereafter. She coaxed the bundle out of his hand after he had picked up his keys. She stood upright and dangled the bunch in front of him by one solitary key. She held *the* key.

Abe didn't think about his apartment's appearance, the blown entryway light, the stacks and stacks of audio equipment, not to mention practically his entire wardrobe strewn across his bed. His only concern was the woman who trailed behind him down the hallway with his key. He allowed her to open the door to his apartment and had to lead her in the dark to the lounger in front of his bed and the lamp nearby.

"Wait, let me get this light," Abe announced.

When he reached up for the dangling cord, he was surprised to feel her hand there too, halting him. He felt the heat of her body next to his, and then her lips were on his. Finding her mark, she slowly, sensually, sucked the life out of him. He was reeling, and he stumbled backward toward the vent, taking down a pile of books he kept there. She was like a sexy vampire going for his neck as soon as he regained his balance.

He finally pulled the cord to see if she would recoil in the light, and noticed the top two buttons on her blouse were open. "Blanche, woo, what, what's going on?"

He could tell she was taken aback by the capacity of his apartment and sheer volume of his stuff. She recovered quick as she approached him. "I'm making myself available to you in every way imaginable."

"I see," Abe said while she nibbled on his neck again. "Lord God, I see, but–"

"I think you understand what that means," Blanche said, this time it was she that was leading him to the bedside lounger. "C'mon, we spend so much time together, and the church is growing because of our partnership. This was bound to happen, right?"

Abe's defenses were steadily weakening. He let his mind believe that this was a natural progression in their relationship. He introduced her to the non-cluttered side of his bed. This time he was the aggressor, covering her with his unbridled desire.

"Yeah, I like a man that calls the shots," Blanche panted. "We call the shots."

He thought his mind was playing tricks on him. The Spirit of the Lord was no longer speaking to him, and it wasn't Blanche's voice he was hearing either. This was an extreme case of déjà vu, because he was hearing Marion Butler. He rolled off of her, but she persisted to grab and pull at him, so he gave her a slight push. "No," he said.

His vulnerability scared and shamed him. "We can't possibly call the shots. Do you know how disastrous that would be if we did?"

He rose from the bed to get some distance. He tried to put things in reverse by zipping, fastening and re-adjusting his clothes.

"I guess you never heard of letting a girl down easy." She bent at the waist where she sat to find her shoes. He took a seat next to her on the edge of the bed, hoping to make contact with her downcast eyes.

"Many days when we were out together I'd wonder what you really thought of me. I'd like to think that I was really that witty when you'd laughed at my jokes, and I would love to believe I am really that irresistible that you actually wanted to spend all that time with me. This is who I really am." Abe pointed to the packed ledges and shelves around the room. "I'm lost in my own world most of the time. I hide behind stuff; I'm a fraud. I haven't written my own sermon in God knows when. Just when God was speaking to me again, tonight, of all nights, I end up here with you. I can't. I got to play by His rules."

Blanche hastily re-buttoned her blouse and rose to her feet. She smoothed her clothes and managed brief glances with him. "Well . . . umm, I'll be going then before you begin to think any lesser of me than you probably already do. It's just that . . . I thought, and well, this has been one big mistake. Thank God I didn't cause you to sin. You're a good man. I don't know what came over me."

He had already sinned. They both had crossed the line with their intentions. He was just thankful the Lord was merciful, because he felt doubly guilty for choosing her company over the Lord's this evening.

"I hope this little incident hasn't ruined our partnership or The Ministry of Support," she said, moving toward the door quickly. Abe marveled at the tempter's form. She could have bought him for five cents a year ago, but he knew he was worth more in God's eyes. She was worth more also. He suspected no one had ever told her as much. She was just as confused as he was, he thought.

Abe grabbed her arm, determined not to let her go. "You don't get off that easy. I get that your motivation is to take the church to new heights, and my natural man surely wants to get swept up and go with you, but you have to know who I am and I have to know who you really are. I still want to get to know you, Blanche. That is how we see if we mesh in the spirit. You have to tell me who you really are though."

She turned to face him, this time less ashamed, yet less assured. "I don't know." She looked to the ceiling to gain composure, and then at him. "I'm sorry, I can't do this." She bolted from the apartment before he could get himself together to chase after her.

Abe stayed there until her scent and touch were a distant memory. He didn't hear from her when she arrived home as was their custom. He didn't hear from the Lord anymore that night either.

Chapter 19

An Elevated View

Vanessa awoke temporarily unaware of what day it was. The light shone through the sheers that covered the blinds at her bedroom window, which meant it was well past seven A.M. She heard a doorbell ring and thought it was in her dream, but now the knocking was an unmistakable reality. It coincided with the throbbing in her head. Willie and their new house guest must have gone out, she thought. If he told her where he was off to this morning, for the life of her, she couldn't recall it now.

Her pregnancy had brought about selected amnesia. At church, both Vanessa and Willie forgot to mention to everyone around them in ministry that she, the co-pastor and esteemed first lady of the church, was with child. Surely they could use the prayers of the righteous, because they were struggling to come to terms with it. He was walking on egg shells and she on tissue paper not to divulge anything. Once inside their own home, they forgot how to love one another. Willie went out of his way to let her know how much he disapproved of everything from the general care she gave herself to her overall attitude. He resented the fact that she made him keep the pregnancy a secret. He didn't realize that the contempt he expressed wouldn't breed happiness. She couldn't muster up the energy to be anything but indifferent. They were becoming married strangers.

Vanessa carried her fuzzy robe with her down the stairs and covered herself before opening the door. She caught Alexis's backside heading for her car at the curb. She hesitated for a moment before calling out to her.

"I'm so sorry, Pastor Vanessa; I hope I didn't wake you. I guess Pastor Willie hasn't gotten back from taking Roy to get some clothes and a suit for his arraignment tomorrow," Alexis said, back-tracking.

I guess he checks in with someone, Vanessa thought. She crafted her tissue paper smile as she held the front door open for her. She chose the kitchen table to entertain her guest although she had no intention to cook for her.

"I was over at Starbucks, I should have called. I could have bought you something."

"I can't . . . I'm trying not to drink coffee," Vanessa said.

"Right," Alexis said, swallowing quick as if she felt guilty for sipping her coffee now.

That son-of-a-gun husband of mine told our secret, Vanessa thought. Vanessa tightened her robe around her. Both sets of eyes did a roaming view of the room in search of the next awkward topic. "Help yourself to that Danish over there. You're practically family." Vanessa tried to keep the sarcasm out of her voice. She would have gotten it for Alexis, but her bottom half had become an anchor that was not so easy to hoist these days.

Alexis took her suggestion. Vanessa had to ask for forgiveness for her disdain toward this ridiculously skinny sister. "Are you losing weight?"

"I'm not trying to, honestly. It's this job. I'm sure Pastor Willie has told you that Roy's public defender wasn't optimistic at all about isolating Roy's case from his co-defendants, which means they will be tried together, and Roy could do time for their crimes." Alexis returned to the table with a section of Danish on a paper towel.

Vanessa was clueless. She remembered nodding her head or mumbling something when Willie asked if Roy could stay with them, at least until a trial date was set. Every morning Willie and Roy left out together, leaving Vanessa to drive herself around during the day. Roy kept to the spare room off the basement when he wasn't sitting around talking with Willie. Vanessa made sure they were all fed at night. Roy was a welcome distraction.

Alexis fanned her eyes before rubbing them. "I'm sorry. It's just not looking too good. Then I am covering this for *Inside 7*, which might not have been such a good idea. My executive producer said he loved a jailhouse interview, and it looks as if he'll get his wish. I thought I had this in the bag."

Vanessa got up this time to get a tissue. Upon closer inspection of her countertop, she noticed the blood pressure cuff sitting beside her bottle of pre-natal vitamins and the travel case it came in. It was her husband's subtle reminder for her to check her numbers daily as the OB/GYN suggested the early part of this week when he insisted upon going with her to an appointment. The doctor was worried that she was having pregnancy induced hypertension. She tried to ignore her husband's constant worry and over protectiveness. Just like she pretended not to know that he palmed her belly at night.

Vanessa brought a box of tissues and the equipment sticking haphazardly out the top of its case back to the table. "You're going to need one of these if you don't stop. You are a journalist, Alexis, not a judge and jury. That is why we have a High Priest and Supreme Judge in heaven. You and my husband might have chosen to help Roy, but apparently you were divinely assigned this case, and it ain't over until God says it is, you hear?"

Alexis nodded, sniffling into her tissue. "I know; it's so easy to give up. I'm a good writer. I could fudge a report for next week's show, but I was supposed to do the definitive investigative work that would make the prosecutors release Roy and take a good look at the system as a whole. I'm supposed to prove that I am talented and deserve to be an anchor, not because I am pageant-queen privileged like all the men, and even that hater, Lizzy London, seem to think."

"I know what you are talking about. Preaching is still very much an ole boy's club as well. You feel as if you have to work twice as hard to prove yourself, to be accepted as a spiritual leader even in the body of Christ."

"It may seem men and women are equal in broadcasting, but the men give up very little control behind the scenes."

Vanessa nodded her understanding, resting her hand innocently on her belly. She noticed Alexis staring at her and immediately withdrew her hand. She sighed, "I guess Willie has told you."

"Yep," she replied sheepishly. "How many months are you now?"

"Almost five," Vanessa replied.

Alexis leaned over to get a rub. "You're going to pop like a top in a minute. You must be elated."

Vanessa's stomach growled, causing Alexis to remove her hand. "I'm a forty-three-year-old woman. Should I be elated?" She rose to find herself something to eat, because being pregnant took her from zero to famished in no time. She pulled a piece off the Danish loaf to nibble on before checking the refrigerator for something more substantial.

"That isn't so old. Wasn't Elisabeth from the Bible up in age when she—"

"Don't go there," Vanessa warned.

They both chuckled, but it got quiet quickly, causing Vanessa, who was cracking eggs for an omelet, to turn around. *I know this girl is not crying again,* Vanessa thought. "Lord, chile, you'd think you were the one pregnant the way your emotions are up and down."

This seemed to make Alexis cry more. Vanessa felt her headache returning. She cut the stove off, but brought the Danish with her to the table.

"What's going on?" Vanessa asked.

Alexis tried to pull herself together. She was at the end of her tissue. "I'm all right. If anything, you've given me hope that there is another chance for me to conceive. "

"Sure you'll get your chance," Vanessa stroked her back. "Wait . . . another?"

She nodded her head and sighed. "Four years ago I made the hard choice to get rid of my own baby."

"Adoption?" Vanessa asked.

Alexis just looked away. "I was new to the city. I didn't have a husband or any support. I thought I had no other choice."

"What about the father?" Vanessa said as if she could now offer her an alternative. "Or your grandfather and church family?"

Her laugh was loud, almost sinister. "The father was the son of the bishop's good friend who wrote me a Dear John letter before I could tell him. The good bishop, on the other hand, was the one who told me, 'Strait is the gate and narrow is the way. It doesn't widen for anyone, Alexis, especially one in your state. We have to be examples. We can't let our actions and our decisions prevent others from passing through.' That might be ambiguous to anyone else, but to a twenty-four-year-old admitting she had made a mistake and seeking forgiveness, it told me in no uncertain terms that he wanted me to get rid of it.

"So I took the first thing smoking to DC, determined to break into television broadcasting here like I had always planned to do, and raise my child." She sighed heavily. "But competition was stiff and my break didn't come immediately, neither did my forgiveness."

"Wait, let me stop you there." Vanessa leaned in. "God's forgiveness is immediate. Your problem was you were looking for forgiveness from the wrong person."

"To make a long story short, Pastor Vanessa, I terminated the pregnancy. Do you know I talk to my grandfather almost every week and he has never asked me about the baby and I have never told him what I've done either? In the end I felt like I was more of a hypocrite than he was."

Instead of that strong on-air personality Vanessa was used to seeing on television, she was seeing a more vulnerable little girl. Vanessa closed her eyes temporarily and whispered a brief prayer that God would heal Alexis's heart.

"That was why I hated the nickname Milky so much," Alexis said.

"Milky?" Vanessa questioned.

"That's what the crew calls me — another long story," Alexis dismissed.

"You've got to tell me."

She inhaled deeply as if she needed a full tank of air to tell this story. "Before I left Kannapolis, a cow at a local town fair doused me with milk on-air, for the whole world to see." She hunched her shoulders as if to question her dumb luck. "I was that cow, plump and just a manufacturing plant for that baby I carried and tried to hide from everyone. We are designed for this one great purpose, which is to sacrifice everything, our bodies, our time, and our resources to bring this life into the world, but I chose to sacrifice that life for my career. It's nothing worse than living with regret, you know?" Her last words were a pitiful squeak.

Vanessa had never been the most compassionate person. She knew the importance of empathy when counseling members about their problems, but today her heart cracked like an egg, and sympathy poured out. She wept with Alexis, not entirely because of the shame of Alexis's situation, but also for her own.

"Stop, you're not supposed to be getting upset like this. You're blessed, Pastor Vanessa, especially since your older, but wiser. This just means I'm going to be overprotective of you and your little one. Let's prop your feet up. What do you need done while I'm waiting?" Alexis asked, looking around for a way to be helpful. "Here, let's take your blood pressure."

"Give me that, girl," Vanessa insisted. "Although I better take it before my Triage nurse-slash-husband comes back."

Vanessa pulled one arm out of her robe and fit the cuff around her arm. She powered the digital reader on and pushed start. When the machine beeped, she stared at the monitor. It read 140 over100. She turned it toward Alexis to view.

"Is that high?"

"I think so," Vanessa said. "I'm supposed to call my doctor if it's high. Normal is around 120 over 80."

"Oh my goodness," Alexis panicked. "Give me the number and let me call her."

"Wait," Vanessa said, glued in place. She looked at her watch, and then toward the door. Where was Willie? "Let's do another reading."

Vanessa peeled out of her robe, giving Alexis a more pronounced view of her expectant body under the silk camisole top and lounging pants. She adjusted the cuff and restarted the machine. This time she hesitated before looking. The reading was consistent with before.

"What's your doctor's number? I'm going to call." Alexis took charge.

Vanessa rattled off the number and listened while Alexis

relayed her dilemma to the receptionist. Alexis tried to give Vanessa a try-not-to-worry smile as she waited. Vanessa restarted the machine a third time, hoping her numbers had gone down and she could tell them all it had been a false alarm. She never got a chance to look at the numbers, because Alexis had hung up the phone and turned to her.

"What did they say?" Vanessa asked.

"She said for you to come in, but if your pressure doesn't come down by time you get to the office, you need to be prepared to be admitted to the hospital." Her face showed grave concern as she dispatched the information. "Oh my goodness, Pastor Vanessa, what do you need me to do?"

"Go with me."

Chapter 20

Not so Wise Counsel

"Counseling isn't where you hash out your wedding day agenda, but rather where you hash out your life," Willie said to his sister-in-law who consumed the first fifteen minutes of her pre-marital counseling session with new wedding details and directives. Tuxedos were the topic. "How do we go from our counseling overview to looking through bridal magazines? You're doing a lot of planning for a hypothetical wedding with no definite date. You've got a good man, here. Geez, can't the man pick out his own tuxedo?"

"You need to mind your business, Willie Green," Keisha said, folding over a binder where she kept clippings from various bridal magazines encased in their own sheet protectors.

Today was not the day, Willie thought to himself. If it weren't for this session with Keisha and Paul and his desire to get them down the aisle as soon as possible, he wouldn't have even graced the church today. He had been with Roy all morning preparing, shopping, and meeting with his lawyer. He had put in his time. "Anything discussed in my office is my business, and that's Pastor Green to you."

"Hold up, time out, this is not going to work. Where is Luella? We need to get switched to Vanessa's calendar after all," Keisha said, standing.

"Luella's gone home. That is why Roy is out there now

manning the front desk. Anyway, you and your sister aren't really speaking, remember?" Willie smirked. "So sit. I hope you all are ready to begin. I like to keep my sessions between forty-five minutes to an hour."

Keisha reluctantly took her seat. Willie plowed through the remainder of the *Preparing for Marriage* counseling folder that outlined expectations, topics, and selective readings for the duration of their sessions. The overview usually cut the initial meeting to half the time.

"How do you see yourselves?" Willie asked.

"That's simple - married with kids," Keisha chimed in. She looked at Paul, and then back at him as if to say her answer was sufficient for the both of them.

This brother better find his voice box before he forgets to speak altogether, Willie thought. "I mean beyond your relationship with Paul and beyond his relationship with you. There have been others before him, and he has had other relationships before you, starting with the one with your parents. I am asking, how has that shaped you as individuals? The first couple of sessions are about each of you separately. It's called what do *you* bring to the table?" Willie tried again, clarifying his approach. He was skipping a few basics on love and God's design of marriage that he usually started with. He knew the destination, but he was launching from a different place with these two. "Are you bringing excess baggage? Are you so stuck in your ways that sacrifice and compromise are out of the question? How do you see yourself in the Lord now, and how will the Lord use the two of you together?"

Paul and Keisha looked at each other again. This time they had no immediate joint answer or spokesperson.

"I am, as you know, a PK, or preacher's kid, who hasn't always followed the rules of both my earthly father and my heavenly Father, but like us all, I have been forgiven," Keisha said. "I'm on a leave of absence so to speak from fifteen years of being everything from administrative assistant to project manager. In this stage in my life I am a ministerial student."

"See, you all have an interesting dynamic going on. Although you are marrying a ministerial student, you should never fail to go to God for direction on how to lead your household," Willie said to Paul, and then turned to Keisha, "and how to submit to your husband."

Willie felt his teeth grind on the word submit as he thought about his own marital stalemate. Vanessa wasn't submitting to anything but her own hormones and stubbornness.

"Oh, I see where this is going." Keisha said.

"Do you, really?" *Little Ms. Know-it-all,* Willie thought. Had she always behaved just like his wife? "You think you know what marriage is all about, Minister Morton? Who is going to cook and clean if and when you start taking a full course load at Bible college? How long do you wait to have the kids you mentioned earlier? What happens when the kids come and you need a bigger house on one income? What if Paul decides one day that he doesn't want a woman who ministers all across the city, state, and country?"

"Well, you and Sister Pastor have written the book on being a ministry couple," Paul said.

"Yeah, and if Vanessa can submit to you, I know I can submit to Paul," Keisha said.

It seemed that Willie wasn't the only one who couldn't take the angst out of his voice. It was usually a game of his and his sister-in-law to grind each other's peppercorn. He was seriously thinking of any of his friends in the ministry that his sister-in-law hadn't dated that could counsel the two of them for that reason.

"Are either of you the least bit concerned that your marriage will interfere with the other's call to God?"

Keisha shook her head while Paul nodded. Keisha could have given herself whiplash, cutting her eyes at Paul when she noticed they weren't in agreement.

This made Willie scoot to the edge of his seat. "Expound."

"Keisha has shared with me a little about being the baby in this ministry-driven family and her need to find her niche. She is not Sister Pastor, and sometimes she doesn't feel like she's being taken seriously. She is committed to her studies and nothing is more important to her now." He turned in his seat, inviting her into the conversation. She looked at him as if he were sharing one of her sacred secrets, and breaking her heart in the process. He placed his hand on her knee cap and wiggled it until she cracked a smile. They had a nonverbal communication far beyond a couple engaged for such a short time. "I don't want to interfere with that."

"I can see us teaching together or starting a ministry for married couples at Pleasant Harvest like they have at other churches," Keisha said, surprisingly subdued.

Once again, Paul nodded his agreement. "I've thought about that too."

"You have?" Willie and Keisha said, almost in unison. Paul nodded again.

"You've got a good man here," Willie reiterated to his sister-in-law.

"I get that. Paul is a good catch. You've said that twice already, almost as if you don't think I am. Yes, he is too good for me some days, and some days I'm too good for him. This is the weirdest session ever. Do you normally start every couple's session like this?" Keisha's anger showed on her face, and there was a hint of something else. "Is everything all right?"

"No disrespect, Pastor, but I'm with Keisha. Is it important to have our whole life figured out now? We're trusting and believing that God will lead Keisha to the perfect job and direct us to our ministry. I'm thinking you and Sister Pastor can help facilitate that growth. We're family, right? With marriage under our belt, hopefully we will become surer of our joint purpose."

Willie didn't know if that last statement rang true for him and Vanessa, although he was nearing his one year wedding anniversary. What he knew for sure was whether Paul had to prop or bend, he was going to figure out a way to support his wife-to-be. Had he tried to lift Vanessa up through all of this? He thought that he should be taking counseling from them.

"I apologize," Willie said, using his hand to gesture toward the many factors that were unseen, yet eating at him. "I'm off my script."

He grabbed his desktop Bible and flipped to a familiar passage, prompting Keisha to go for the pocket version in her purse, and Paul to reach for his satchel. "First Corinthians, chapter thirteen, verse four states *love is patient and love is kind. It does not envy or is it puffed up.* And well, you know the scripture. It ends with love never fails. A marriage built on love, like I believe yours will be, and a faith in God should not fail."

Willie's cell phone, set on vibrate, buzzed and fluttered around on his desk like a primitive insect. He recognized the number as Vanessa's and figured he had wasted too much of Keisha and Paul's time already to take a personal call.

"God likened the marriage between a man and a woman to Christ's relationship with His church," Willie continued.

"Aren't you going to answer that?" Keisha asked after the phone stopped its dance on the desktop and started again.

"It's Vanessa," Willie said, checking the display. "She probably just wants me to bring her something on the way home," Willie dismissed.

Keisha grabbed the phone. "Vanessa, girl, I was going to call when I got home to ask you to save me from this man you call husband and this interrogation you call pre-marital . . . What? Where?" Her smile was suddenly drawn in tight like the opening to a duffle bag. "Oh my God, my sister is in the hospital."

It took them less than thirty minutes to get to Washington Hospital Center in their caravan of cars. Vanessa's doctor was not available when they reached the hospital, but Alexis filled them in as to the sequence of events with Vanessa's elevated blood pressure, which led her doctor to admit her as a preventive measure. Willie was thankful she was sensitive not to divulge anything about the pregnancy in front of Keisha, Paul, and Roy. They all seemed relieved.

"Let me go in to see her first," Willie announced before taking off to find the room assigned to his wife.

Willie felt his organs had lurched forward in his chest when Keisha relayed the message and had not yet returned to their normal place. His heart led the way into the room where his wife lay awake on her back watching a crime show on television. She was tethered to an IV pole, and her hair formed a nest beneath her head. He plopped in the seat next to her bed as if he had been there all along and had just returned from the vending machine.

"Aren't you going to say something?" Vanessa asked.

"What can I say, Vanessa? I don't know what you are willing to hear these days." Willie said, bending at the waist to loosen the laces on his shoes before sitting upright and doing the same with his necktie. "I'm camping out until I hear from the doctor."

"I've talked to the doctor." She paused. "She thinks my blood pressure is an indication of preeclampsia. She's putting me on bed rest, maybe for the duration of the pregnancy. She says how I take care of myself will determine whether I do the bed rest here or at home. Once they get my blood pressure under control, I can go home."

Willie let out a puff of air and he turned to look at her for the first time since entering the room. He let his hands rest on the bed and fought the urge to inch them forward and touch her in a way he knew she preferred not to be touched. "It's as if my body is not my own. People wouldn't normally be rubbing my stomach, and I surely don't go around rubbing their tummies," she had said.

She surprised him by finding his hand with hers and scaling the mount of her expectant abdomen with them. Her belly was warm and complete in its curvature, and he fought back emotions in the acceptance he felt in that gesture. "I've been trying to tell you—" he started.

"I've been trying to tell you that I love you and this baby, our baby . . ." She inhaled sharply, sucking back every tear trying to preempt her breakthrough. ". . . and I'm sorry it came out as anger, selfishness, or any other cursed disposition. I come against it all now."

"Shhhhhhhh." He pecked her lips.

"I've been stuck in thinking what if something is wrong. Believing that it was and the doctors weren't telling me. Now I've probably brought this condition on myself. Along with increased visits to the doctor and bed rest, the doctors say they must keep in the back of their mind a strategy in case the baby has to be delivered early." There was panic in her voice. "Which just confirms my fear that I can't—"

"You can do all things through Christ." Willie stood, still holding her hand, still beholding her natural beauty. "We'll pray it away, Vanessa. No more fear, you understand me? We are not a people without hope. Your job now is to rest, so I can take you home."

Their foreheads touched as their hands clasped together and the tears flowed. When they looked up, her sister and the rest of the gang were in the doorway looking as if they just sneaked a look at a peep show.

"She's having my baby, y'all," Willie announced.

Celebration erupted among the six of them as if they all were just finding out the news. Willie noticed Keisha set her wedding book down on Vanessa's tray table. He hunched his wife as her sister extracted a picture of a fitted coral brides-maids dress and a few others. She began to rip it to shreds, letting the pieces rain down over Vanessa's hospital bed. It was the perfect confetti.

Chapter 21
Her Epiphany

Vanessa approached the sacred desk at Pleasant Harvest Baptist Church a little after twelve during Sunday morning service, armed with three truths; her Word, her secret, and the knowledge that this would be her last time preaching for a while. The deal she made with her husband was that she would preach, they would tell their congregation their little secret, and she would go directly to bed. She had been in prayer and meditation since leaving the hospital, as pastors often did. She could not get past the events of the past month and her own personal epiphany. That, she knew, was the revelation the Lord wanted her to share.

"There are over five hundred references to fear in the Bible; five *hundred*. That's a lot, y'all. God hasn't given us a spirit of fear. The Lord is my light and my salvation, whom shall I fear? That's just one of the references found in scripture. That's not counting all the times the Lord suggests to us to be of good courage or to take heart, alluding to our fear." Vanessa stood robed ready to stand and deliver.

Even as she spoke, Vanessa was warring against fear. She was wondering what was behind the stares of her congregants and how much ground and position and respect she stood to lose carrying out God's plan and admitting what had been crippling her. She knew now she only had one choice. She prayed for that blind faith that allowed Peter to get his feet wet and nothing else.

"That many scriptures, that many warnings, but no," Vanessa shook her head and puffed her chest out, "this was me, y'all; the great Vanessa Morton Green will not fall prey to fear. I am a co-pastor to an ever-increasing ministry that just celebrated fifty years, and I sit on the board to what will become one of the largest and surely the greatest coalition and conference of pastors. I am one of only three women to serve on the executive committee of a major religious conference."

Vanessa invited their applause on that achievement. She looked back toward her husband with a knowing look. Another part of their deal was that he would attend the Trinity Conference meetings in her absence and choose a committee to serve on for the upcoming conference thus preserving this spot of recognition for her.

She took a wide stance to help her shift her weight from side to side. "I thought that since I preach and teach about fear that I would counteract this particular devilish plot in my own life. Fear sneaks up behind you and puts his hands over your eyes, blinding you. Fear will have you paranoid, irrational, self-sabotaging. Fear is one of the biggest manipulators out there.

"I don't care who you are, we have to guard ourselves against fear." She pounded her fist with each syllable and stepped back to gauge the crowd. There were those who stood, some hollered out, and others rocked side to side in their seats.

"I don't plan to be before you long. Can I tell my truth and then sit down?" She felt like James Brown prepared to hit it and quit it. His finale song was always the most dramatic. Just like watching him in concert, Vanessa felt physically tired, but emotionally charged at the same time. She didn't need a cape thrown over her to get her second wind though. "You might be wondering where I am going with all this. Sister Pastor must be tripping, taking the subject, The Epiphany, but taking her text from the first part of God's gospel according to Matthew. The Epiphany here in the text is the commonly known time or time period when the wise men got to Jesus's side to witness the miracle of his birth. They journeyed long, some say it took over two years."

She turned her outline over because she felt the help of the Holy Spirit and didn't want anything in her hands to hinder His flight. "The miracle had already happened. It was their job to worship God for their gift. See, fear comes when you forget the gift."

She unhooked the microphone and trotted over to the right side of the podium, playing to that side of the house. "Just being here is the miracle. Some of us are in our right mind. Notice, I said some of us." She ran over to the other side to do the same. "Some of us are in one piece, like I said before, some."

This time she returned to the middle." But we are all here, bad knee, false teeth, wig on, wig off. One dollar offering, ten dollar offering, tithes and offering, we are all here! That's a miracle in itself, y'all. I should have been dead and gone, but for the miracle, I received grace. We can't forget the miracle. We should be worshipping Him, and worship cuts down fear at the root."

She heard Willie yell out like the co-signers in JB's band and she smiled, thanking God for back-up while she wiped her sweat soaked forehead. "King Herod plotted to use the wise men to exact the location of Jesus. He told them that when they returned that he would like to know where they found our Lord so he, too, could go worship Him—code word for kill Him. Yes, there was a hater plotting to kill Jesus before Judas. The devil is a lie. Y'all know me, I would have been thinking, if the Lord is your light and salvation, does not the same star we plan to follow not shine bright for you as well? But these were wise men, not Vanessa from North Forestville. They followed the star, worshipped the King, and listened to the Lord when He told them to not to go back the same way they came. The lesson here is you can't tell everyone about your miracle.

"Oh, I just said something." The revelation of the Word was so sweet to her. It dissolved her fear and sweetened her disposition. "I said, you can't tell everyone about your miracle, but . . ." Vanessa teased.

"But," Some of her congregants instinctively reiterated with anticipation. Her sister was the loudest.

"But . . ." She let several more painstaking moments pass by. "But you're my members. Family, can I clue you in on my miracle and trust you to help me worship the Lord our God for the gift? Come here, honey. Walk this thing with me." She beckoned to Willie, and he eagerly joined her side. She unzipped the front of her robe, revealing a pale purple sheath silhouetting the pure plumpness and miracle of her pregnancy. With Willie's help she stepped out of the robe and crossed in front of the pulpit podium. She cupped her tummy for those in the back who couldn't see her bump. "We are going to be welcoming a new member to the Pleasant Harvest family in a few short months."

The congregation erupted in a mixture of celebration and surprise. Again, she felt like a rock star. She had struck a harmonious chord. "Heaven help us. Brother Pastor will tell you I was so fearful at first that I forgot to praise and worship God. I saw it as a curse to my future rather than a blessing. This baby will change our lives, and we can't go back the way we came. Hey!" That last statement gave her reason to dance.

The musicians backed her up, and once again she was JB

conducting a jam session. Willie backed up to give her room for her happy dance, forcing the podium back for added space. He just shook his head as if he wished he were gifted in that way. Others expressed similar giftedness in the aisles. It was not like she could stop herself if she wanted to, but she knew the Holy Spirit in her wouldn't allow her to harm herself or her unborn child while she was in praise.

Vanessa put her hand up and the musicians hit a break. "I'm in no way comparing this child to Christ, and in no way am I suggesting we were found worthy like the earthly parents of Christ, but Brother Pastor and I will need your gifts like the wise men brought. We will need advice. Do we have any wise men and women? We will need home remedies and a few home-cooked meals. We need armor bearers and Sunday School teachers and well wishers and prayer warriors to help us with our child. Although Brother Pastor will serve as your Senior Pastor, if you will, please do me a favor and let my husband, Big Daddy here, come home sometimes and tend to his family the way you tend to yours."

Vanessa winked at Alexis, sitting in her usual seat since joining their ministry at the end of the fourth pew. She was jotting down notes as if she were on assignment. "It takes a whole village to raise a child, and the Daddy should be found among it. Hallelujah!"

Just when Vanessa felt she had done and said enough, she felt another surge of the Holy Spirit. She figured since this was her last sermon for a while, she might as well have an all out praise party. She brought the musicians back in.

"I see some Herods out there. Don't hate because I'm a bad mama jamma," Vanessa said over the music jubilation. She remembered the service was being recorded and couldn't wait to order two copies. One was for her best friend, Pat, and the other she would put in a time capsule for little baby Green.

Chapter 22

Bent on Intent

Alexis's mouth was working overtime finding the air pockets in her chewing gum so she could make it pop loudly like she used to do when she was younger and about to get into a fight. She was behind the scenes watching Lizzy London carelessly cover her Harvest Baptist Church fire story before it was her turn to introduce her own story for the evening.

"Without Mr. Thompson's confession, the state is hoping they have enough evidence to get a conviction in court. A trial date has been set for late next month," Lizzy concluded.

Alexis thought Lizzy's oyster shell headband held back her obnoxiously bouncy curls from her smug face the same way her Botox injections held back her frown lines. Her enhanced breasts provided a camera marker for her headshot. She all but winked at the viewing audience.

Alexis thought she would be ill. Lizzy was too busy stitching seams, trying to hem up the series and Alexis's time on what she deemed was her show that she failed to see it through, to be probing, to be a reporter. The whole thing was bound to fall apart under the weight of unanswered questions. What could have been Charley Thompson's motivation? She was salivating, thinking about how she would have loved to put Captain Rich on the hot seat. Was there even enough probable cause to extradite him, or was the dramatic convoy Lizzy described in her piece more of the captain's strong arming?

Why would Charley Thompson be refusing to speak at the most critical time in his life? Could he be innocent?

Alexis was by no means a fan of Charley Thompson, but she was fiending to once again call the justice system to question. She couldn't believe she was about to introduce her second piece about a man who never got a trial, but rather was sentenced at his arraignment. The only hope he had of reducing his six month sentence was to come to a mutually agreed upon plea bargain with his four co-defendants.

The light came on to indicate the live show was gone to commercial. That gave Alexis time to get settled in her chair opposite Lizzy and mic'd for her introduction. She blew one last bubble with her gum hoping to suspend her frustration in the airy glucose before taking the wad from her mouth and dropping it in the ditch bin just outside the set. She sat knee cap to knee cap with Lizzy, but didn't acknowledge her until the countdown to air.

"We welcome again special reporter, Alexis Montgomery, to the *Inside 7* report tonight as she brings us part two of her story, The Righteous Renegade, and finally concludes her series on The Church Fire Inferno. I tell you, Alexis, you sure had us all held hostage on this series, but now that they have the arsonist behind bars I, guess we'll soon be bidding you goodbye." Her smile was about as fake as a glass of false teeth as she volleyed the ball into Alexis's court.

Not so fast, Lizzy. Alexis chuckled. She had gotten the overt hint, but couldn't sacrifice any of her time sparing with Lizzie. "You know when I started this series I had no idea it would branch out the way it has and touch so many viewers. It proves that it is not that which has been burned, broken, or stolen that makes a good story, but rather what lies in the hearts of men — their intent. Roy Jones, the homeless street preacher, serving up his brand of ministry on the very streets that both

destroyed and re-made him, had great intentions; to get people off drugs and off the streets. He never imagined after being clean and sober for nine months he would find himself in
prison for drug possession and distribution. I talked with Roy
Jones shortly before his arraignment and later at the county
jail about an ordeal that he feels was initiated by the area drug
task force, but ultimately orchestrated by God."

Alexis paused until the countdown to clear. She couldn't
bear to be tethered to her mic and chair any longer. Lizzy
must have felt the same because she popped up and her assistant hurried to her side with a cup of coffee waiting for her.
Alexis was anxious to get to the editing room. She had an idea
about how the rest of her interview should flow. Usually she
had to rush to an assignment and didn't know how the final
story format would play out until it aired. She hadn't been on
assignment since she started researching and tracking down
leads for this broadcast. If Lizzy was correct about her time
left on the news magazine, she would have to get readjusted
to the beat.

"This story is running to the last station break. Let's get the
wrap-up now. Two minutes, Lizzy. Alexis, are you staying in
the shot to close the show?" the crew assistant asked.

Alexis and Lizzy both looked at one another and shook
their heads. Lizzy's was a little too emphatic. Alexis remembered a time when she would not pass up an opportunity to
be on camera. She would have sat back down to spite Lizzy
and chime in on her sign-off, but she had more important
things to do. Leave Lizzy with her on-air façade; she was more
concerned with impacting her story's delivery.

The production team was already assembled in one of the
editing rooms when Alexis slipped into the back. They had a
tip sheet for each remote interview she had shot before them
and were trying to decide in what order to piece them together. Alexis cleared her throat in an attempt to interject.

"If I may," Alexis finally said.

All eyes turned to her. Mark Shaw spoke. "Yes, Alexis, if you have a suggestion, then by all means share it."

They yielded the way to the front of the editing desk where both tapes were loaded. Alexis stood to the side of the editing desk as if she were doing an oral presentation in front of a classroom.

"Well, I tried to come from an angle of intent and purposes," Alexis explained. "What was Mr. Jones's intent on the street, as well as what was the intent of the area task force? Why were they concentrated in this area at this time? Is there any rhyme or reason to these sweeps? Are they even legal? I get both perspectives. The questions I asked Mr. Jones, I turned around and posed similar ones to Mr. Quino, who is the representative, something or the other from the Office of the PG County Drug Czar. It was the best I could do, but apparently he handles the media for the task force from time to time. I was hoping to flip-flop back and forth between interviews. I think it may take a little more effort in editing, but it will flow more fluidly for the audience," *who will ultimately judge and may be moved to action.*

There was a hush. Alexis looked for a hint of approval. Some avoided her eyes as if it were more work than they bargained for. They all waited for Mark who was contemplating the job in his pondering stance with his hand covering his mouth.

"Sometimes the more you cut away the more you lose, like the setting. What are we talking here? We want the viewers to get a sense of where you are," Mark said.

"One or two cuts at the most. You'll still have your jailhouse on the one end where I ask about the details and fairness of his sentence, and your authoritative shield of the police station on the other where they try to explain how an innocent man could get so tangled up in the system." She held her breath.

"No delegate and go," Mark said, sifting through his Blackberry. Alexis understood that was his job. "And you'll work with the team here until it's through?"

"Yes, sir," Alexis agreed.

"Get it down to fifteen, I need to see it in sixty." He wrapped his knuckles twice on the monitor with that order before turning on his heels to leave. Two assistants went with him.

"Looks like she is trying to get a production credit," called out one of his assistants as they were leaving.

"That's okay, she's hardworking and always thinking. I like that," came Mark's seal of approval.

Thank you God, Alexis thought.

The editing tech started playing the first reel, waiting for her to indicate where to make the first incision. All of a sudden it had become a horror film that she couldn't bare to look at. The beginning of the tape was when Roy was out on bail and walking her through the neighborhood. Then the tape abruptly shifted. Roy was in an orange prison-issued jumpsuit talking about how he remembered someone snapping pictures up and down Lincoln Avenue about a month previous to his arrest. He was surprisingly well-groomed and his voice was upbeat.

"Rewind, we need to get all of this part in jail. Go back to the top question." Alexis directed as if she had been working in editing all her life.

The tech did as he was told and they re-watched the footage from her starting point. From there the markers were set. *From his lips to the camera's lens*, Alexis reminded herself.

"I had a couple of people waiting for me, you know, who were going to try and make it down to the clinic. So when I got off the shelter van headed for the terrace, the cops had a couple kids in handcuffs and were chasing some others. They literally picked me off like a sitting duck. I knew they were from the task force because they had the brown jackets over plain clothes. One asked was I in the book. His partner started looking through photos and there I was in the back," Roy said from a conference room holding cell where inmates met with their lawyers.

"So it appeared you were set up?" Alexis questioned.

"Yeah, I got to praying immediately, because I didn't see any mid-range dealers in the book or the van. It's like they knew what days to be present and what days to be absent. Like I said, there were mostly kids, junkies and low ball hustlers in the van. I started praying for them all. Didn't know they would all become my co-defendants. We were given a panel judge to represent all of us. I knew they were sweeping the streets, but I wasn't dealing. I never knew they could lump people's cases together like that," he continued.

"Stop . . . stop," Alexis ordered. "I'll lay down a track about his sentencing later. I was there, poor Roy, they gave him six months. My part will be short and sweet, but it will segue nicely into the general reply from the guy over at the task force." Alexis's hand was already on the button panel that she knew how to control by watching the tech. He nodded the go ahead to stop one reel and start the other while he carefully recorded the stopping point on Roy's interview. She used the fast forward to skim past the set up markers, not realizing how fast the reel would move.

She stopped at the beginning of her interview with Mr. Quino. ". . . and in Mr. Jones's case? Is it customary that the folks that you pick up in these sweeps don't have a chance to prepare a case and defend themselves?"

"Mr. Jones was charged with possession with intent to distribute. It was a sealed indictment, which means a grand jury made a decision before the arraignment that Mr. Jones and his co-defendants committed the crime."

"And his only hope is to take a plea?" Alexis asked. Her demand for an explanation was evident.

"This just speaks to the commitment to cleaning up our neighborhood streets. These drug sweeps are also designed to clean up those addicts that drive up demand for illicit drugs sold on the streets as well as the dealers. Our program has been proven effective."

With her arms propped on the desk, Alexis bridged her head between her hands as the footage continued to roll on. She tore into Mr. Quino for another several minutes, hoping to shame him into Roy's shoes. Instead of his comfortable existence in a cushy civil service job, she wanted him to see the irony of being a middle-aged homeless man who was strong enough to knock a drug habit on his own, but was thrown in jail on trumped up charges. The tech guy kept his fingers poised above the stop button, looking like he wanted to stop several times and bring an end to the cruelty. Alexis remembered being harried and on the kill. She was anything but professional, anything but objective.

"Ms. Montgomery, methadone is a controlled dangerous substance sold on the streets in various forms. Even the prescribed doses can be addictive without being under the direct supervision of a doctor." Mr. Quino tried to remain calm and collected as the interview intensified although a thin layer of perspiration rested on his brow and above his mouth, dampening his thick moustache.

"He was giving it away, and not given a chance to prove that." Alexis practically screamed.

"Maybe you aren't privy to the information we've compiled." He remained smug.

"I think maybe you all know exactly what he was doing, but just didn't care as long as you can pad your files with your bogus arrests of every misguided kid, junkie, and homeless person out there to justify funding for your program," she snapped.

This time Mr. Quino just laughed. "I think you're upset because it was your little exposé that helped shed light on Mr. Jones's improprieties and just how complex this war on drugs really is. She remembered him promptly standing and taking his mic off his lapel before walking out of a secluded room in the station used as a makeshift set. The truth of the matter was Mr. Quino was right. She should have covered Roy's story from a different angle or not at all. She had sacrificed Roy's efforts for the sake of a story. If anything, now, she just wanted Roy's punishment to fit the crime.

"Ouch," the technician remarked. "I guess it was a good thing Mark let you edit your own film."

"Yeah," Alexis said with nervous laughter. She needed a patch kit. "I guess we can cut that last remark, you know, for the sake of time."

"Good one," the tech guy shot back.

She winked at him. "I'll smooth it over with another track and end with Mr. Jones's resolution."

Except it was anything but a resolution to Alexis. Roy had accepted his fate, she hadn't. She found out that even when his lawyer presented a plea to a lesser sentence. It was one of those deals that they all had to accept or none at all. Roy held out and refused. She didn't ask him why when the camera was rolling, but demanded an answer afterward. *"Because my co-defendants are guilty. I watched them out there every day substituting dope for hope and passing it to others with no consequence."* To Alexis, piecing an acceptable story together, then going home to a messy house with no food was an inevitable reality, not the choice Roy was making.

"Here." Alexis signaled. They had been watching the conclusion of Roy's interview in fast forward mode while the techie digitally cut her rant off the end of the Quino interview. He set the Roy footage to play in real time.

"How do you come to terms with the fate of your sentencing?" Alexis asked more so like a friend rather than a reporter.

Roy crossed his legs to reveal his socks. "I look at it like this; I've been in worse conditions and situations. This is one step closer to getting up. I just know God's allowed me to be set up to set someone free inside."

Alexis thought maybe she could have gotten Pastor Willie to convince him to accept the plea or she could have caused more of a stir with her story, but something about the orange bands across the top of Roy's tube socks helped her come to terms with his reality.

Chapter 23

A Mutual Agreement

Capitol Town Pawn Shop was home to Abe who worked, slept, and ate there. It had become his sanctuary and office for the past month and a half since the Ministry of Support Sunday when he started hearing from the Lord again and started receiving God's overflow. He wished he had some hired help to tend to the occasional customer so he could commune, study, and write lessons and sermons that the Lord was giving him. He thought about giving up his apartment since he wasn't hearing from the Lord there, but mostly the collection of stuff including the tapes, CD's and DVD's of sermons he had come to rely on to feed his flock.

God was sending fresh Word and manna from heaven to support his ministry. The participating churches Blanche rallied together for the Ministry of Support Sunday helped raise close to 100,000 dollars. Abe hired the accounting firm that Blanche also recommended to handle that and the 535,000 dollars recently released from the insurance company after finally placing a claim. He was almost afraid to touch it.

Everything was in place for rebuilding the church. Abe got off the phone with the general contractor who assured him the yellow boundary tape had been removed and the foundation was sound enough to meet together with the architects in the next couple days for the preliminary planning. He tried to think of a few members he could appoint to represent the congregation on the planning committee. Each list he drafted was incomplete without Blanche.

He hadn't talked to her in several weeks although he'd thought about her daily. After their encounter at his apartment about a month ago, he and Blanche maintained a professional relationship. She'd leave toward the end of the service, in his mind, to avoid being alone with him or even getting close enough to have a conversation. He felt he shouldn't even try to call her. After the Ministry of Hope Sunday her attendance declined like the other amateur sleuths who stopped coming after *Inside 7* concluded their series of stories on the church fire.

Ironically, they had spent time dreaming about a newly refurbished Harvest Baptist Church the way a couple would their home. Abe flipped the 'open' sign in front of the shop to 'closed' in order to take his lunch break in the back. He picked up the phone to call her. He hadn't contemplated what he would say when she picked up on the third ring.

"Blanche, this is Abe. I haven't seen you in awhile," he said.

"Well, it was nice of you to call, Pastor. I've been out of town and seemed to have come back with a bug. I've just recently gone back to work. Don't worry though, I'll send my offering in the mail."

"Right, your offering," Abe said, scratching the nape of his neck. She was a puzzle that was hard to figure out.

"Don't want to block my blessings anymore than I have. I know you can't buy your way into heaven, but maybe it will keep me out of hell."

"Look, let's put that night in my apartment behind us. God is a forgiving God. I've done a lot of praying, mostly for forgiveness of my own past, purging myself so I can free myself up. I hope that you've done the same."

Abe looked up at the ceiling as if seeking approval from the Lord. Was it wrong to want this woman? He knew the Lord's position: *Seek ye first the kingdom of heaven.* The Holy Spirit continued to reiterate that point during their ongoing debates about how he could curb his strong desire for her and reshape it into something more acceptable.

Abe cleared his throat. "I called to say the insurance company released the check for the church. I'm supposed to meet with a team to start rebuilding the church. As much as we talked about what Harvest could be I-I need you there with me and in my corner."

"Really?" she asked.

"Well, yeah," Abe replied.

"Then I'd love to. I do like to see a project to the end. No matter what anyone says, I still care about the church and want to make good on my original commitment."

His smile preceded his admission. "That's great, Blanche. I'm looking forward to working with you."

Abe tried desperately to think of something else to say to keep her on the phone. He had fallen into the trance of listening for her breaths through the silence.

"Abe," she said, startling him. "Is it possible we could meet for lunch before then?"

I thought you'd never ask. "Sure," Abe said, "when and where?"

Abe was already there when Blanche walked in to the Peruvian chicken café. She acknowledged his presence with a shy smile. He stood while she was seated, taking notice of her casual but chic attire. His compliments were automatic.

"You look amazing to have been sick. I've never been to this place. What do you recommend?" Abe asked.

"The fajitas are good," Blanche said, forcing herself closer in the circular booth to point out the selection on his menu. "Usually, I get the quarter-dark, with red beans and rice."

The waitress came and they ordered two of Blanche's favorites. She was much more reserved, almost reluctant to speak, and Abe began to wonder what she had in mind to say when she suggested they meet there. He began reading something into her every movement. He started to speak on several occasions. He knew what he wanted and the conditions he had to follow to obtain it.

"I miss our outings and spending time with you. I've never been to so many swank and trendy eating places in my life. I can't say that my pockets aren't happy, but my stomach sure misses it," Abe said. Her smile gave him hope. "I don't think we have to stop going out because of what happened. I just fear if we are not careful, we will end up in the same predicament."

"Fear, huh? I can't say I've ever had that type of effect on a man." Blanche shifted in her seat and sighed loudly. "You know the question you asked that night in your apartment kept haunting me. No one has ever asked me who I really am. I guess no one cared to know. I gave it a lot of thought. I figured you deserve an answer."

She studied her napkin before beginning. "Growing up, my parents struggled to feed me and my brothers. I was the youngest and learned early that the education fund didn't extend to me even though I liked to believe I was pretty smart. Even won $500 for an essay contest that my parents ended up using to send my older brother, Pete, to Chicago. Momma trained me to use what I got, so to speak. She thought the best that I could hope for was to be taken care of by some man."

Blanche dropped her head and shook it from side to side as if she couldn't believe she was speaking her truth. Abe felt he should offer her some sort of comfort, so he put his arms around her shoulder. She sighed heavily, "But men have always taken from me. In the corporate world, in relationships, it's all the same. They take what I have to offer and leave me with nothing."

"Could it be that you've bought into your mother's theory? You've done pretty well for yourself. You've worked in finances and now have started your own PR firm. You're a prize. You certainly don't need a man to take care of you. As far as relationships go, you have to ask yourself what it is that you are looking for."

Their waitress returned surprisingly quick with a pan of sizzling hot chicken mixed with onions and peppers, fajita shells and bowls of red beans and rice. They both stared at the pan as if they didn't know where to begin. Abe blessed the table and encouraged her to continue.

"I guess I want what other women want in a relationship, something real, but I also want to be a part of something big. I want to retire from the grind. Heck, I do want to be taken care of," she admitted.

"And with Willie Green?" Abe wanted to silence his conscience that reminded him that once again he played second fiddle to the former pastor of his church. "What was your relationship with him about?"

"The same," Blanche admitted, swallowing back a bite of fajita, obviously caught off guard by his inquiry.

Abe stopped preparing his fajita. "I guess you have a thing for Harvest Baptist Church and the guys who pastor there."

She dabbed the corner of her mouth before giving him a weak smile. "To be honest, I was tired of dating the pompous jerks that I encountered. You and Willie are what I consider the good guys. I just wanted to find one."

He digested what he considered her truth. "I want you to know that I'd be honored if you were my lady. I want the relationship to be right, though, and not just a temporary thing that God ends up taking away from us because we're fooling around. You know what I mean?"

He took it that she understood the way she cleared her

throat and looked away. "I feel in many ways that I am just coming into my manhood, and as a man you've got to trust me enough to pursue you the right way and treat you right."

She left him hanging while she took a long swig of her iced tea. His food went untouched. Her eyelashes batted at him from above what he hoped were sincere eyes. "I'm flattered. It's been a long time since someone has made *me* blush, and I sorta like it."

"I aim to please," Abe proclaimed, feeling free to take his first bite and even flirt a bit.

"So can I expect an immediate public acknowledgement in church and a weekly bouquet of flowers?" Blanche asked.

"I think I can swing that." Abe grabbed her hand. "Up until now it's been all about the church, but I need you to have my back no matter what's going on at Harvest."

Her face formed a question mark. "Is everything all right? It's your aunt and uncle, isn't it? I hope they are not planning to release that man."

"No no. Aunt Elaine is fine. She's getting adjusted to living on her own. Uncle Charley has been charged with arson and his trial is set to begin soon, and since he's still not speaking to anyone, she feels it really doesn't make any sense for any of us to go up there to try and see him," Abe said, "but what I was saying is membership has gone back down at Harvest. I don't know if it's because the hype is dying down or because I've radically changed my preaching style, but I've got to stay authentic. It feels so good being true to myself."

"Don't worry about the people. They'll come flooding back, you'll see. I got some things in mind," Blanche said, "but first my man needs a total lifestyle makeover, starting with that apartment of yours. You better be glad you're so adorable, because I usually charge for image consulting."

They both laughed. She had him thinking ahead to wedding bells ringing in a sanctuary that they would design together. He tilted her chin and kissed her. Although the kiss didn't burn hot like that night in his apartment, it smoldered with a new passion. He looked into her eyes and wanted to believe he was responsible for the spark he saw there.

"So?" Blanche said, clearing her throat. "I guess that sealed the deal."

"I think it did," Abe said.

Chapter 24
The Man Cave

Willie took the trek down the hallway to his office with his call back list, courtesy of Luella, and the day's paper. He needed a timeout. It was a conspiracy that most of the things on his agenda these days were penciled in by his bedridden wife and her assistant, in the exact order that they wanted it done. Luella served as both enforcer and informant.

He had his choice of space now and could easily move all his resources and aids down to take over the large central office where he spent most of the day budgeting, counseling, negotiating, and troubleshooting. But he preferred his own space. That is where he could think and commune. He closed the door behind him when he entered and sat to finish the article he had started titled, *Muted Defendant faces Felony Arson Charges.*

Willie read how his old friend and deacon was arrested, charged, and indicted all while refusing to speak. Two separate attorneys had taken the case and had since requested to withdraw from defending him. *What was he doing?* He couldn't presume to know anymore. He had to admit he thought about visiting Charley's wife to see how she was fairing throughout all this, but with increased duties at work and Vanessa on bed rest at home he really had no time for his own personal agenda. Willie thought how ironic it was that Charley and Roy would end up at the same jail. Irony is God's intervention, Willie thought. His thoughts were interrupted by Luella who buzzed in to tell him she was putting a call through from Syllas Kennedy who served on the executive board of the Trinity Conference with Vanessa.

Pastor Kennedy was on the top of Willie's call back list, and he felt a little bit guilty that he hadn't gotten to him first.

"Hello," Willie said.

"Dr. Green," the man responded, "I'm glad I finally got you on the phone."

"Pastor, it's just Pastor," Willie clarified.

"I wanted to cover my bases. I wasn't sure. Some people get offended if you mess up their title."

"Well, you'll find I don't offend easily, nor do I think of myself more highly than I ought," Willie said, raring back in his leather office chair. "You must be Dr. Syllas Kennedy."

"Yes, that is my résumé title. I guess since I did the time in training and study, I should be proud of it, but I prefer plain ole' Reverend. My daddy was a reverend, and if it is good for my daddy, it's good enough for me."

"I remember we all used to be reverends," Willie added.

"Or ministers, ministers of the gospel," Reverend Kennedy declared as if it were a dying breed. "Titles can either further distinguish us or divide us. Prayerfully, we're all doing the same thing."

"D-r-, R-e-v, or M-i-n, it's all the same and cannot possibly compare to G-O-D."

"You've got that right," the man said with a half cough, half chuckle. "Vanessa said we would hit it off famously. I hope I am not bothering you."

"No, sir; actually, you caught me in my cave," Willie said.

"Cave?"

"I converted the former first lady's lounge into a man zone,"

Willie said so amused he set his trapeze of stainless steel meditation balls on his desk in motion. "Our poor administrative assistant is so vexed when I come down here rather than being at her beck and call in the main office suites. She feels when I am down here, I am in this sacred clubhouse she can't enter without a password, and I let her believe it."

"Sounds like a sweet set up," he said on the tail end of a good cough. "The two that work with me around here know to approach me in a whole different way when I've loosened my necktie. Then I want to deal with emergencies only, other than that they know to leave me alone."

"I hear ya," Willie said.

"Pastor Carlton Cartwright, the founder, and some others of us on the board of the Trinity Conference received a letter or phone call from your wife. Congratulations are in order."

"Thank you, sir. We'll need your prayers, Reverend. It had to take Vanessa going in and out of the hospital for her to realize she needs to slow down. Call us seasoned newbies over here."

"Wasn't Elisabeth and Zacharius the same?"

"Please don't make that analogy around my wife."

They both laughed. Age was still a sore spot with Vanessa and making mention of others who were much older who have given birth, even biblical examples, did not help.

"Speaking about your wife, she asked us to receive you with open arms," Reverend Kennedy said. "I got to say I look forward to meeting you."

"Same here, but I must be honest. I haven't been exactly supportive of these religious conferences in the past. My involvement with the Trinity Conference is to hold my wife's spot, and while I'm at it, make sure it is a worthwhile venture for Mt. Pleasant to become involved in."

"I'd say if we are successful in our endeavors, then the

Trinity Conference will be one of a kind. We study ministry models, fund ministry projects, and address the needs of our community. I can't say that I've seen another conference that can boast that mission statement."

Willie stretched his legs out in front of him as he thought about it, but he still wasn't convinced. "Vanessa sees this as a way to gain notoriety, or I guess, lend credibility to her own personal mission as a female pastor. Like you said before, we're all ministers, and you know how the brethren can be. Honestly, is there a real role for her?"

"I guess you'll see when you assume her duties."

"Come on, Reverend, this is my wife we're talking about. I just as soon walk before I let you all placate her."

Reverend Kennedy sent a lungful of air through the phone. "Some of our colleagues definitely saw our female counterparts in a particular role, but—"

"But?" Willie sat straight up in his chair prepared to be outraged.

"Vanessa was one of the first at the table with her assessments, and more than that, she came with her ideas—good ones. No one can deny her that. Of course you know this, but she can be demanding, yet democratic in her approach. She knows how to get things passed. Surely you know your wife is not one to be mollified."

Willie knew that to be true. He secretly wanted to see his wife's naysayers. "So what am I getting myself into?"

"All the board members assumed leadership of one of the planning committees. I think Vanessa was looking at Budget and Finance."

"Naturally," Willie said, shaking his head as if the reverend could see him. "Rev., man, I am not the one. That's my wife's job at church and at home."

Reverend Kennedy let out a lighthearted chuckle at Willie's admission. "Well, since you're new, you can just join one of the existing committees, but I called to set up a date when I can come out and spend the day visiting your ministry."

Willie was taken aback. *Here's where the hazing begins*, he thought. He should have known it wouldn't be that easy to join the club.

"I'd like to see your church as well," Willie said, flipping the script.

"There is not much to see. My building is no more than twice the size of a mobile home, and it almost would be better if it were mobile. It's probably no bigger than your cave over there at Mt. Pleasant. We are on the corner of Jefferson and Patterson Streets in the District. It's mostly classroom space to train and fortify my congregation of about sixty-five traveling missionaries. Anytime you want to come by and see us when we are not out of the country, you're certainly welcome."

"Wow, I don't think I've ever heard of a church of missionaries." His skepticism squelched. He wondered how a congregation so small could come up with the start-up dues for the conference.

"I got tired of the day to day struggles of running a traditional church. I guess it comes down to your congregation's definition of ministry. To me, it's meeting the needs of people and spreading the gospel throughout the world. I'm getting older and can't travel as frequently, but church is like our headquarters. You learn about all different types of ministries through the conference. I'm hoping Trinity will help fund some projects we want to do in West Africa."

Willie heard Luella knock on the door like a parent warning him it was time to wrap up his call. She had found him. Willie knew he had a few other tasks he couldn't go home without completing, but he felt he could talk to the reverend all day.

"Look, Reverend, I've got to run. How'd you like to visit the cave early next week?" Willie asked.

Chapter 25

The Bedside Clinician and

the Heavenly Prescription

Vanessa didn't realize when the doctors put her on bed rest that they actually meant spend the majority of her waking hours reclined in bed. She figured since she was home she could catch up with her housework and could potentially have the guest room cleared for the nursery. Her assumptions landed her back in the hospital two weeks after she preached her last sermon to stabilize her blood pressure and to fortify the baby in the event she was forced to deliver early.

With all the talk about late maternal age, Vanessa just assumed that it was her maturity that caused the baby difficulties. It wasn't that she wasn't being educated about her current state; she just wasn't a good listener. One nurse made it clear to her when she said, "In cases like yours our goal is to deliver you both alive and healthy as close to the baby's due date as possible." Vanessa was forced to remove her cape. She realized she was just as fragile as the baby.

Around the same time, Vanessa gave up the notion of waiting until the day she delivered to find out the sex of their child. She didn't tell Willie immediately, baiting him into a guessing game when he came to pick her up.

"So what will we be raising, a young man or young lady?"

he asked, staring down at her in her hospital bed the same day she found out.

"Wouldn't you like to know?" she teased.

"Okay, I see how this is going to go. In the bathroom, will the baby sit or stand?"

"It's a baby, Willie. You'll have to change its diapers," she said, "and don't we all sit eventually?"

"Okay, okay inside the diaper, will the baby have an innie or outie?"

"It depends on how they cut the umbilical cord."

Time went by and she thought they were done with the game, then Willie asked out the blue, "On prom night, will I be throwing our child the car keys or shaking down a date?"

"I guess it all depends on whether or not our child lands a date," she said.

"At our child's wedding, will I be standing at the front of the church or walking down the aisle?"

"Are you assuming you will be officiating?" Vanessa asked.

That seemed to be the straw that broke the camel's back, because he sat in the chair next to her bed and positioned himself so he could lay his head beside her to rest while they waited for Vanessa to be discharged.

"Will our child follow in your footsteps or mine?" he murmured.

"We're both preachers, honey."

He sat up suddenly as if he were possessed. "You can end this, you know."

"You can too, by asking the right question," she said, shoving him to let him know she was having too much fun torturing him.

"What would be a good name for our child?" Willie asked, relaxing his head back down as if he expected her to think of a unisex name like Terrie to keep up the mystery.

"Elijah," she whispered, stroking the back of her husband's head as he kissed the sheets of her hospital bed with his smile, "because he will be a prophet like his daddy."

Vanessa wished the joy of the guessing game and the possibility of their child's future could last throughout the duration. Six months of pregnancy had her nose spread across her face with strange dots, marks and moles appearing over her body that wasn't a good look to anyone but her husband. She was home once again, and her husband brought in a specially trained watchdog, Keisha, to check up on her when she wasn't in class. He didn't know Vanessa would be allergic to her sister's dander.

As much as she couldn't stand being treated with pet gloves and not allowed to do anything for herself when Willie was home, she almost had to remind Keisha why she was there. She didn't follow orders, and to Vanessa, she was too self-absorbed to be attentive. It felt like they were twelve and thirteen again, a time when Keisha would come into her bedroom and brag about having privileges when Vanessa was punished. She talked incessantly about the things she's done or places she's visited recently when Vanessa could only imagine what the hot August air felt like. It left her wondering what her mind was supposed to be doing while her body was at rest.

Just when it seemed like her sedentary state settled into a full blown sadness, Willie came up with the bright idea of having a Sister Circle one Sunday after church. It was a combination baby shower and Sunday dinner with her close sister-mother-friends from church. Pat even made the drive up. That and the fact that Willie had the affair catered and got a few of the guys together to serve her guests made the entire event bearable.

Vanessa wiggled into the nicest maternity tunic she owned and maternity jeans and joined her guests downstairs in the dining room. Pat, Mother Thomlin, Luella, and Alexis were all getting acquainted. A new glider with matching ottoman pulled up to the head of the table marked her place of distinction. Savory aromas came from chafing dishes set up on their wall buffet.

Willie came in with a pitcher of iced tea. Alexis went to grab it from him.

"Let me get that for you, Pastor," she said.

"No, Alexis, it's my party and the men are serving today," Vanessa said, winking at her husband to show her appreciation for his efforts. The women all applauded the day off.

"That's right. Just call me Jeeves," Willie said, pouring a glass for each table setting. He reached for the bottle of cranberry juice left on the edge of the buffet to make a special drink for his wife that was more juice and less tea before leaving the room. He returned with a few men from the church to serve salad plates for the first course, and then they retired to the kitchen.

The attention turned to Vanessa and talk about everything from her swollen ankles to her roly-poly figure ensued. "I don't want to spend all afternoon discussing me. Shoot, I am home twenty-four seven with myself. Tell me about church and what all of you are doing. Please, I beg of you."

Vanessa devoured every tidbit. Of course she talked to Pat and Luella almost every day, so there was not much to catch up on, but the minute details of Sister Thomlin's large family and Alexis's job were fascinating. Alexis shared that it was rumored around the station that her series of stories on Harvest Baptist Church would be nominated for a local news award for outstanding investigative news reporting. Her producers had also made mention of her becoming a full time anchor and co-host of the expanded hour version of *Inside 7* segment in the fall, leaving her with a lot to think about and just plain thankful to God.

Keisha finally arrived with her fiancé and future mother-in-law in tow. She carried two large gift bags for Vanessa and the baby, filled to capacity, which showed how else she had spent her time since quitting her job.

"Sorry we're late, Sister Pastor. The two of them got to talking so much after church like they couldn't bear to part from one another until we told him to just come with us," Thelma Grant said.

"To the left, to the left," Pat started, pointing back and forth in a steady rhythm from where Paul was standing to the direction he needed to move into to leave the ladies-only gathering. All the ladies joined in with similar hand motions until Paul got the message and joined the other butlers in the kitchen.

"Do we dare ask her what's new in the land of wedding planning?" Vanessa polled her guest. "She's been surprisingly hushed mouth about it."

"That's because you've thrown a major monkey wrench in my plans," Keisha explained dropping off the gift bags at the foot of Vanessa's throne. She took off her sunshades and folded the arm over the bib of her sundress to let it hang for safekeeping.

"Don't blame it on me," Vanessa said with her hands up in protest.

"No, I blame it on the man that knocked you up," Keisha said, raising her voice with no shame. "Y'all excuse me. You know after church it's no more pastor stuff. My brother-in-law and I love to go at it. I love him to death, but y'all know we were looking toward October for the wedding, but now that our guest of honor here is due and darn near out of commission until then, October is out."

"That's why if we had planned it for the family reunion, you'd be getting married next week," Thelma said. The future mother and daughter-in-law smiled at one another to remind each other this was an area that they would agree to disagree.

"I want to just push it back into next year now, but Mr. Grant is suddenly so adamant that we will be married before the year is out," Keisha said, whispering this time.

"The man has spoken," Mother Thomlin said.

"That's right, you can't make that man wait," Pat said.

"What? Why not? What about my dream wedding?" Keisha looked around the table.

"Girl, please," was all Pat could say.

"Take it easy on her, she's young," Mother Thomlin pleaded.

"Let me take this one, y'all. I might be on bed rest, but I can still write prescriptions," Vanessa said, referring to her sermon footnotes that usually ended with a Bible verse or two to study. She forced her bulge forward to keep their conversation from wafting into the kitchen. "Did not Paul, the apostle, not your fiancé, say it's better a man marry than burn in his lust? Paul, your fiancé, not the apostle, is a hot, red-blooded, American male, and I don't mean because he spends time outside in the August heat. The man is tired of waiting and could care less about a corsage, bouquet, or color scheme."

"I wish I had that predicament," Luella said, slapping an awaiting five with Alexis who felt the same way.

"I know I got a good looking son. Don't be surprised when your natural instincts kick in when you're wedding planning over at his house or he's over at yours when I call late at night. Ain't that what you call it?" Thelma Grant said with raised brows.

"Uh-huh, I think Minister Morton needs a complete prescription; 'cause she's playing with fire. Too much can happen in a year," Vanessa said.

"I can't tell you how many people Ben and I counsel that

end up like Vanessa in between getting the ring and walking down the aisle," Pat said.

They could barely contain themselves when the men appeared with their entrees, thinly sliced roast beef apparently carved in the kitchen. They each waited in line to add asparagus and a twice baked potato or rice to each plate before serving the women.

"That's right, Paul, serve your fiancée first," Miss Thelma said.

"She was just saying she wondered if you had some *hot* buttered buns in there to serve up," Pat added.

They lost it. Keisha was left red-faced and about to choke on a piece of ice as everyone else around the table laughed shamelessly.

"I'll check?" Paul questioned, not knowing what he walked into.

Willie grabbed his shoulder and whispered, "Run," into Paul's ear.

When the coast was clear, Keisha had her own admission to whisper. "Why do you think I work out so much now? I got to do something with that pent up energy."

"So that leaves the month of November and December in the year and some serious planning," Alexis said.

"Paul's father and I were married on November fifteenth. It would have been twelve years if he didn't get killed out there in Vietnam." Miss Thelma hugged herself.

"Daddy and Momma were also married in November, the twenty-third. They shared thirty-six years before he died," Vanessa reminded.

"That's close to fifty years between those two dates," Luella said.

"Who's got a calendar?" Keisha asked.

Luella handed her the pocket version from her purse. Keisha flipped quickly to the desired month and skimmed her finger to find the weekend that fit between the two dates. "November eighteenth," Keisha declared with a smile. "I'm getting married on November eighteenth."

"Good, now we can eat," Miss Thelma said as if that was what was really holding them back from eating.

Cutting, slurping, and lip-smacking was all that could be heard among the women in the Sister Circle as they satisfied their basic need. Vanessa surveyed the women in the room and was thankful she got her mind off her mundane weekly existence for a little while.

"You know, Sister Pastor, I sure miss your weekly prescriptions. I still have that one about forgiveness you wrote me at the time I was going through with my sister and her family when they came to live with me that summer and nearly turned my household upside down. Matthew 5:44: *pray for them that despitefully use you.* Yes, Lord, you should write a book," Mother Thomlin said between bites.

"That's a good idea," Keisha added.

"Prescriptions—" Pat started, painting a picture with her right hand of how it would look and sound as a book title.

"For an ailing world," rolled off Vanessa's tongue as if it were planted there. She was in a vacuum where all she could hear was her thoughts. She contemplated the many tough issues brought to her in counseling that she tried to tie up simply with a prescription. Then she thought about the countless sermons that ended with a course outline of study that she issued out in prescriptions.

"Willie," she hollered with grave desperation.

He bound from the kitchen with the others afoot. "Yes, baby, what's wrong?"

"I'm going to write a book," she declared, "while I'm on bed rest."

"*Prescriptions for an Ailing World*," Keisha couldn't resist. "And I'm getting married November eighteenth." Keisha winked at her fiancé standing in the doorway. The other men were so shocked and amazed by all the revelations of the evening that they were afraid fully to enter the room.

"I'm gonna need my laptop and the files from my office computer copied to a drive, and—" Vanessa said, her thoughts as free-flowing as her words.

"All right, calm down. I see you're serious about this. Luella will help compile all that you need," Willie said.

"Luella," Vanessa reached out for her like Celie did Nettie in *The Color Purple* when Mister threw her sister off their farm. "I need—Luella."

Silence abounded at the audacity of her request to take the only administrative assistant away from their active ministry, but Vanessa knew she couldn't do it without her trusty sidekick.

"Hold up, I think I got the remedy," Willie said, raising his arm in the air as if he were a superhero there to save the day. He crossed over his wife and dropped to one knee in front of her sister. "Will you be my administrative assistant and help me run the mother ship called the Pleasant Harvest Baptist Church? We'll have to work out the pay with the joint board, but you can have the joint study."

Willie got off his knee and took a bow for his idea and dramatic presentation. It just made sense. Luella was hand chosen by Vanessa and better suited for her leadership style. Keisha was working Vanessa's nerve just looking in on her a couple times a week. Willie was almost certain if she were assigned to assist Vanessa with her book project, he'd come to find their family ties permanently severed.

"Yes, yes, yes," Keisha said, taking the Academy Award for her acceptance. She stood as she hugged her brother-in-law and was surprised that Paul joined in on the group hug.

"Now we can have the extra money to get the horse drawn carriage for the wedding," Keisha said. They all chuckled as they held on to one another, knowing full well she was serious.

"Good, now we can have dessert," Miss Thelma added.

Chapter 26
Motion of Discovery

The day that Reverend Kennedy came to visit Willie, Pleasant Harvest was in transition. Luella was moving out and Keisha was moving in as the church's administrative assistant. The phones were ringing off the hook, and admittedly, Willie hadn't given the Trinity Conference a second thought.

He was so distracted watching the ever-professional Luella trying to show the ropes to the hopelessly distracted Keisha that he hadn't t seen the odd looking man come into the waiting area. The reverend was a lot shorter than he expected, capping off at a little past five feet. Every follicle of his hair had turned grey and stood straight up from his scalp. His height coupled with his extremely long and thick patches of brows gave the man an elf-like quality.

Willie introduced himself and took him on a tour of the church, ending with the cave.

"You've had an adventurous two years," Reverend Kennedy said when they had finally settled in to Willie's office.

Willie noticed that the reverend referenced a page in a portfolio of some sort that made Willie feel like this conversation was more than mere small talk. He began thinking about where he was two years ago compared to now and all that had transpired since then. He had met his wife and married her. Together they had to endure the growing pains of shuffling people around and combining their churches. Now they were having a child and the ministry continued to change.

"I certainly have. I am good and ready for life to slow down a bit," Willie said.

"Are you really? Well let me tell you that will not happen with a baby on the way." Reverend Kennedy smirked.

"No?" Willie shook his head and questioned if this wiser man could possibly be wrong with his assertion.

"Most certainly not, and wait until the baby becomes a roaming toddler, and then a rebellious teenager; Lord have mercy, an independently-minded, but not independently-funded young adult." The Reverend tapped his cane to make his point.

"No slowing down for me, huh?" Willie asked.

"No slowing down for either of you, but I believe the two of you thrive that way. Vanessa's probably at home going crazy. She always brought such energy to our meetings. I am going to miss that."

Willie wondered if his new friend didn't possess a crystal ball inside that portfolio he kept open on his lap, he was so on point. He wanted to tell him he'd see Vanessa soon enough after the baby was born, but didn't want to admit the fact that he hadn't really thought much about the care of the child once their son was born.

"I believe you, sir, have a quality to affect people that most people, even ministers, don't naturally have," Reverend Kennedy continued.

Willie was more than fascinated at the reverend's ability to read people that he wanted to call him on it, but the phone rang down the hall. His extension light flashed, and he ignored it.

"How can you assume that about me? We just met."

"I observe and investigate and the rest I ask God to help

me discern. Case in point, the way you're helping out your sister-in-law. You didn't just say she was in need of a job, you helped her." He looked down at his portfolio that he must have made a note on without Willie seeing. "You said she was a ministerial student and you wanted to mentor her in the things of ministry. I also saw the first part of the news series on a Roy Jones. It was phenomenal. Here we have a homeless man who wants to share the gospel, and he sang your praises for inspiring him to do so."

"I can't claim victory there, Reverend. If you saw the second piece you'll know he's in jail facing real time. Some of those cats they've got him tied to have several offenses. From what I understand, a lot of drugs, guns, and money were confiscated from them collectively. He'll be in there as long as they will because he never got a trial or took a plea bargain for a misdemeanor rather than a felony when he had a chance."

"Do you believe in Roy's ability to change lives?" Reverend Kennedy questioned.

"You never know with Roy. He's got real issues that need to be addressed. I just don't know if it will happen in jail." Willie gave up on gesturing half-way through his statement and let his hands drop to the desktop.

"I thought he was half-crazy, but do you believe in him?" Pastor Kennedy persisted, leaning forward on the hook of his cane.

"Yes." Willie wiped his face with the flat of his hand. "It's funny; he was able to call here, and he told me he was starting a Bible study inside and asked if I could get them some Bibles."

"Will you? Wait a minute, sure you will, 'cause you, my friend, are a true servant and have a heart for God's people."

It took a moment for Willie to digest what was being said and accepted the compliment. "Spoken from the consummate missionary, I guess it takes one to know one. A wise man once said it goes back to your personal definition of ministry."

The flashing light on the phone once again signaled that the main line was ringing up the hall. Willie put a finger up to Reverend Kennedy to halt their conversation while he stepped to the door of his office. He called out to whichever assistant was on duty at the time. He knew both Keisha and Luella could be in the study clearing out anything Vanessa might need to begin her project. He got a reply from his sister-in-law who reported she was still learning their telephone's operating system. She called out like a mother calling a kid in for dinner from a third floor window that if or when the attorney who called earlier should call back, she would give him Willie's cell phone number instead of trying to transfer him again.

Willie came back into the office amused and a little embarrassed. He hoped Keisha was a quick study, because they couldn't continue hollering down the hall every time he got a call.

"Speaking of Roy, my lovely assistant just informed me an attorney would be calling me. I hope you don't mind me taking the call when it comes through."

"No, not at all. I don't need a babysitter, I am here to observe. You can even put me to work."

"Well in that case . . ." Willie said, putting his chair in reverse to retrieve a file.

They talked extensively about foreign missions. They were able to exchange ideas that led to a few connections for the Young Missionaries program he wanted to spearhead at Pleasant Harvest. The conversation soon turned to issues facing their local community like the war on drugs and the church's answer to such societal ills.

"The church needs to do more. Set up community and

drug treatment centers, set up businesses, and food co-ops. I have to be honest, I'd love to spend a couple days a week out in the field, canvassing the needs of the people, but my members got me tied to my desk."

"I thought you like being a cave dweller." The reverend's sense of humor was sarcastic, but endearing nonetheless.

"The cave serves its purpose, but the question is are we?"

"Brilliant. Are you normally this poetic?"

"Will the people perish if I'm not here sometimes? I think not, but you can't tell Vanessa that." Willie ascended his soapbox. "Don't get me wrong, I adore my wife, but it's all about authority, order, and efficiency with her. I think you should get to the point where the church runs itself, the members grow up and help out so you can be about the business of helping other people."

Keisha circumvented his next thought by barging in the door with his cell phone extended in her left hand. "You apparently left your phone up front when you helped Luella with that box earlier. Here, I can't be walking this hallway back and forth. It's that attorney again."

Willie snatched the phone from her and turned his back, not to be rude, but because he didn't know how long she had the man waiting. To Willie's surprise, the young sounding lawyer didn't represent Roy at all, but rather was appointed to defend Charley Thompson. He explained that Charley had a highly irregular case, and despite his despondency, he managed to speak one name—his.

Willie explained to Reverend Kennedy and Keisha, when he got off the phone, that it was a shot in the dark, but his new attorney put credence in his only utterance and really thought that Willie could get Charley to open up. He had not seen Charley since arbitration and tried not to let that be the reason he refused to help. First it was Alexis and her news reports and now this. He just wasn't sure he wanted to get further involved.

"What would you typically do?" Reverend Kennedy asked to help solve his dilemma.

"I would," Willie paused to think, "probably anger my wife by dropping everything I'm doing here to see how I'm needed there."

He looked to his sister-in-law for her opinion and she just shooed him on. Reverend Kennedy agreed to help Keisha familiarize herself with the phone system, and she agreed to play hostess and take him to lunch in the hopes that Willie would be able to join them later.

Once again, Willie donned his superhero costume to try and save the day. Willie was a mix of emotions by the time he reached the correctional facility. He had clearance through Charley's third string defense attorney, Curtis Gibson. The newspaper article said at least two others had dropped the case because Charley refused to talk. Willie wondered if this one was hungry for justice or desperate for a case. The young man and his assistant thanked him for coming as they waited for Charley to be brought in the small conference room from holding.

Charley looked like any other inmate who had been stripped of his identity and made to wear the brand of the state. He made brief eye contact with Willie, but mainly kept his head down. He was un-cuffed and sat at the table with them without prompting.

"All right, Mr. Thompson, as you know your trial is set to begin next Monday. We haven't covered much ground, but I ask you now, like I've done each time in the past, what is your pleasure regarding your plea you want me to submit on your behalf?"

Willie had his own suspense music playing in his head,

because other than that, it was silent. He wondered if Charley had heard the question, because even his face didn't register anything.

"Where is his wife?" Willie whispered as if he didn't know if he could speak directly to Charley or think he could be heard in this deafening silence.

Mr. Gibson put a finger up to halt his inquiries. "A motion of discovery was filed to have access to the evidence the state plans to use against Mr. Thompson. Sarah Rowe will be working on my team. I just got this today." He threw a file toward Ms. Rowe who he deemed his forensics evidence expert. Ms. Rowe, a plain-Jane woman with long stringy hair in an extra plain grey suit shuffled through the mostly printed file.

"What do we have?" Gibson asked, apparently inept from interpreting the evidence himself.

"Not your best detective work, I can tell you. By in large it looked like they were grabbing at straws and came up with coffee stirrers. We have inconclusive phone records from a new pay-as-you go phone used to report the fire; don't have to worry about that. A metal lock box; I'm not sure what that is all about," the aide said dismissively. "We got melted remnants from what they are calling a Molotov cocktail, red bottle top with an indistinguishable serial number they claim is the source of the incendiary ingredient. Sneaky dirt bags listed the active ingredients instead of the name to hide the identity of the mystery substance from us. Di-methyl-ketone, I believe it's another name for acetone. I'll look it up." The aide showed the picture of the partially-dissolved small cap resting in a clear plastic bag.

"So I take it it's not soda," Gibson inferred.

"Something household related, oh yikes!" She wiped her face, leaving them all in suspense. "Someone played a danger-ous game trying to rig their own timing device with a soaked carpet, a cracked window and candles sticking out of the drink like a straw."

"Nothing like a good cocktail," Mr. Gibson said snidely.

"Apparently they were strategically placed between couch cushions and by the drapes. This puppy was lit hours before it ignited. Church had to be going on at the time."

That little tidbit made Willie's blood run cold. They all glanced at Charley, which wasn't a good sign to Willie.

"If I were working for the prosecution, I'd push for increased charges just for the disregard of human life. A whole congregation could have succumbed," Sarah Rowe said.

"This would be a good time to help us out, Mr. Thompson," Mr. Gibson said with a hint of disgust.

This was like a bad episode of *Perry Mason*, *Law and Order* and *CSI* all wrapped up together, Willie thought. He felt as if he would be sick to his stomach.

"Alibi, alibi," Curtis chanted. "Anything else, anything that will stick?"

"An identical cap was found crushed outside the back entrance of the church. Bad thing is, so were faded tire tracks that matched Mr. Thompson's car with depressed treads that they will try to say smashed the said cap. That and the metal lock box are supposed to mark him at the scene of the crime. But so was the entire congregation. Just two witnesses, of course the top of the witness list is the fire marshal," She threw the stack aside as if her part was done.

"Let's start on his cross examination when we get back to the office," Attorney Gibson said, packing up the Discovery file as if he were preparing to leave. "This is going to be sticky."

"Why do you say that?" Willie spoke up. "He's only going to present what you've seen today, right?"

"Because, Mr. Green, an average person can only offer in court what he saw or heard, but a marshal is seen as an expert in the field of fire investigations. That means he can offer his opinion as well. It's hard to anticipate that."

Willie knew full well the opinion of Chief Rich, which was to wrap up the case sooner rather than later. *So what was he there for?*

"It's our job to make the fire marshal look incompetent." This time it was no mistaking their intentions to leave. Ms. Rowe rose, smoothed her skirt, and grabbed her handbag.

"Is that it? When do you talk *to* him?" Willie went off. He pushed back in his rolling chair and stood to his feet as if he were going to charge the two of them.

"That's what we've been doing for the last half an hour. We only get forty-five minutes. That is a short time to get a plea. We've shared with him the newest development in his case. He, on the other hand, hasn't seen fit to share anything with us. We only have five days until this trial. We have major work to do."

"Where do I come in?" Willie asked.

Mr. Gibson sighed heavily, "I thought seeing you would make a difference, but . . ." The impatient attorney said, swinging his arm in Charley's direction after slinging his messenger bag on his shoulder.

Willie pushed past the young attorney as he headed toward the door and did what he came to do. He took the seat nearest Charley and rolled it close to his former deacon. Only then did Willie become aware of the guard outside the door. The sudden movement alerted the burly man to stick his head inside and give them a countdown of ten minutes.

"Charley, help me understand this now. You can't hide from the truth. Why . . . I mean, what happened on Easter? What do you know?" Willie stared desperately into Charley's cold eyes for acknowledgement, then at his lips that did not move. He looked at Mr. Gibson and Ms. Rowe, who were not in as much of a hurry as they originally proclaimed.

"We tested the theory that maybe Mr. Thompson was unfit to stand trial because of his short term memory loss," Mr. Gibson said.

"Memory loss?" *The prosecution wasn't the only one holding on to coffee stirrers,* Willie thought.

"According to his wife, he has short term memory loss," Mr. Gibson said, in a questioning tone that could be interpreted as, 'you didn't know.' "We asked him to name his church and he wrote down Harvest Baptist. Then we asked him who his pastor was. He said you. He spoke your name, then nothing."

"Isn't his wife the second witness for the prosecution?" Ms. Rowe asked.

"Yeah," Mr. Gibson confirmed.

"His wife?" Willie said, craning his upper body to address the pair of lawyers responsible for Charley's fate. "Can they make her testify against her own husband?"

"No one is making her. She waived marital privilege, which could have protected her against having to tell on or testify against Mr. Thompson," Ms. Rowe said.

"What?" Willie asked the duo. Then he turned back to Charley. He demanded to know the truth, not just for himself, but for all his former members Charley persuaded against the move to Mt. Pleasant whose lives could have easily been taken out in an intentionally set blaze. "Did you do it? And if it wasn't you, then why did you flee? Tell these people, Charley 'cause right now the prosecution might have enough to put you behind bars for a long time. You hear me? My goodness, Charley, you of all people know what's done in the dark will come to light. God is a forgiving God. He'll forgive you."

"I'm sorry, Mr. Green," Mr. Gibson said, apologizing like Willie was his client about to face jail time for arson charges. When the guard came to escort Charley back to his cell he continued, "Obviously you haven't been told the full story."

"Obviously I haven't. I could have saved myself the trip and told you over the phone I wasn't a miracle worker or the Messiah. Apparently that is who Mr. Thompson would prefer to confide in on the day of judgment," Willie said, looking down one last time before turning his back on Charley.

"I didn't do it." Charley whispered the words that would make all the difference, "I'm just cursed."

Chapter 27

The Fate of the Fire

Willie's head could not hold all the thoughts swarming through it. He mindlessly drove at a feverish pace to get away from the correctional facility where both Charley and the truth were being held. Mr. Gibson had explained that on top of possible arson charges, Charley would have to face additional charges for abducting his wife and forcibly keeping her against her will. Poor Elaine, Willie thought. She looked so peaceful and in good spirits the last time he saw her. She didn't know her life was about to change so drastically.

Willie called Keisha to tell her that he wouldn't be joining her and Reverend Kennedy. He explained a little of what went on to Reverend Kennedy while he drove. Reverend Kennedy understood that lunch was the last thing on Willie's mind, and that there was only one place he could go to bury the rest of the burdens that were plaguing it.

Willie pulled up in front of his former church home. The brick façade was in place, but the top looked deflated from the street like a spoiled soufflé. The beams that formed a steeple had collapsed. Willie was thankful the place seemed deserted now, although huge dumpsters out front and Gatorade dispensers on the top of the landing let him know a crew had been working to gut the place out. He walked toward the back, running his hand along the side as he thought about the times he would catch Roy sleeping out by the footpath and other times when he and Charley did light maintenance outside the church on Wednesdays. The thoughts pierced his heart.

The wall gave way to a full tarp at the back where most of the damage was evident. He pulled back the draping to step inside. He could see the sanctuary. Each pew was turned upside down and he wondered what dump or salvage yard would be getting these remnants. He clamored over piles of wood and debris to get closer to the altar, but it was completely blocked, so he knelt where he was and began to pray.

"Lord, what am I supposed to get from this?" Willie asked aloud, looking up past the charred roof. "I have to question did I really know the people I ministered to. Did I do my job? I can't save them, Lord. I couldn't save Roy, I can't save Charley. I'm leaving it all here this time. I got Vanessa and the baby. That's all."

Willie thought he heard something. The enthusiastic giggles and whispers of a couple coming from the front of the church were coming his way.

"Somebody's in here," a man said.

"Give me a minute, and I'll be out of your way," Willie said, wiping his eyes and preparing to leave.

The man approached without the woman, who lingered at the door as if he were a true intruder. Willie shielded his eyes as he stood to see just who it was.

"Pastor Green?"

"Just a minute, please." Willie dusted off his pants at the knee.

At the mention of his name, the woman drew nearer. She stood slightly off the shoulder of his successor and present pastor of Harvest church.

"No, you're fine." Abe studied him. "We're due to meet

with the contractor and just trying to imagine how the place will look in twelve to eighteen months."

"Well, it's your church," A mix of anger and something else would not let Willie look up and meet Abe's glance.

"Hello, Willie," the woman said, stepping out of the shadow.

Willie scrunched his eyes although there was no direct sunlight. "Blanche?" He looked back and forth between the two of them as if to size up the situation.

"Blanche is our, uhm, she's my—" Abe stammered.

"We're in love," Blanche blurted out, clinging to Abe possessively.

Willie didn't know if that was supposed to be for his benefit, but it seemed to catch Abe by complete surprise. Willie put up both hands to signal that he had no comment for her declaration. He came there on a whim of emotions and maybe it was a mistake. He thought it best to finally move on.

"What do you think?" Abe asked.

"About what?" Willie asked incredulously. He gathered his wits about him for a second and decided not to be rude. "I'm happy for you; now if you'll excuse me."

Willie didn't get two feet around the long flanks of wood before Abe called out to him. "No, about the church. We're going to expand on the lot out back. We could have a full pantry back there. I'd love to carry out some of the vision you had for this place."

"What is your vision, huh? Pray to the Lord and ask for your anointing," Willie said, turning. "Might I remind you that to whom much is given, much is required."

Willie almost felt sorry for the young minister who appeared to hang his head in shame. Blanche dropped his hand and turned toward the altar with her hand over her mouth as if in her own prayer.

"I've been preaching in your shadow ever since my uncle introduced me to this church. There was many a day I felt like giving up, coming to someone like yourself and being an apprentice of your pulpit. Any given day I just as soon hand the keys back over to you. Preaching is one thing; shepherding is a whole 'nother story. It's serious business." Willie heard the quiver in Abe's voice. "I so don't want to misstep."

In two steps Willie was up in Abe's face like a drill sergeant. "You think you are going to get sympathy from me? I don't want to hear that, Townsend. You sat in arbitration and made like you were ready. You are here for a reason. Don't you dare take your hand off the plow now."

The Holy Spirit brought back to Willie's remembrance a not so private meeting he had had here with Abe's Uncle Charley, where Willie lowered himself and slapped him. Willie turned to walk away before that same urge hit him. He turned on a dime as if he forgot something. "You're busy courting and making plans; when was the last time you've seen your uncle or your aunt? I just left the jail seeing your uncle, your member. He shouldn't have forced your aunt to leave the state, but has Elaine talked to him or been to see him at all?"

"He hits her, Pastor. That's why she hasn't been to see him. My Uncle Charley has been abusing my aunt for years." Abe's words seemed to knock the wind out of the Big Bad Wolf.

Once again, Willie tried to see past the charred roof to catch a glimpse of heaven. Obviously he didn't know the full story. He tried a new approach. Lowering his voice significantly he said, "When do they begin to heal?"

"After he faces the fate of the fire," Abe said.

Willie paced in a mini circle. He should have left when he originally planned to, because the overwhelming desire to help was on him again. "He said he didn't do it. He told me himself. The first words out of his mouth were to me, and he said he didn't do it."

"He was there, Pastor. My aunt showed me a metal lock box discolored from the heat of the fire that my uncle brought home," Abe said, with a raised voice and elevated emotions.

"And he's a batterer," Blanche added from afar.

"Yeah, but that doesn't make him an arsonist." Willie had his hands on his waist. He kicked rubble as he thought aloud. "He deserves to be held accountable for harming his wife, but my compassion lies with the both of them. Everybody's written him off, including his lawyers. I wish I could talk to Elaine, if it's even possible. The last time I saw her was on—"

Willie grabbed his head with both hands as if the sky was falling on top of him. A picture flashed in his mind, the one captured by Alexis's cameraman on Easter Sunday that Chief Rich brought by for them to ID people. Everyone was dressed up, everyone familiar, but now, one was clearly out of place. Willie thought about what Brother Brown had said at Sunday dinner. "Arsonists love to hang around a scene and see their own work." *Why was she really visiting with them at Pleasant Harvest on Easter Sunday?*

The pictures began falling into place like snapshots in a slideshow. Willie bolted for the front door almost knocking over Pastor Kennedy and his sister-in-law who apparently had come to check on him, but he hadn't seen come in. He broke the seal on the door that opened like it was vacuum compressed or warped from extreme heat and took the stairs to Lincoln Avenue. Despite hearing his name being called by all that assembled at Harvest Church that afternoon, he walked between cars, waiting at the light like a crazed man until he reached his destination.

The bell announced Willie's arrival as one of the Brothers Jacques arose from behind the counter perch. Willie's hunch

was not on coffee stirrers, but rather little red caps. Charley
had said he was cursed, and Willie remembered Charley's
lack of fondness for women preachers had led him to use that
term before regarding his wife. The only other people that he
knew regularly used that term were the Jacques Brothers. He
figured now there was more to their voodoo babble.

"Hey, Preacher man," the younger more enthusiastic one
cheered." You can't stay away."

"Awhile ago you said a woman was stirring up something,"
Willie said, demonstrating a stirring motion with an imaginary bowl and spoon. He was shouting as if the brother was
hard of hearing. "Where is it?"

"Ah, I remember, the priestess. Usually so mild, came in
like a storm that day. Was I right?"

"Please, just show me what was it that she bought from
you?"

Jacque's long narrow finger pointed him down the aisle.
"There is one bottle left. We haven't re-ordered, fearing she'll
come back."

Willie searched the aisle like a man ailing in need of the
last bottle of pain reliever. He came to a row lined up with toi-
letries that the brothers sold for their customers' convenience
or emergencies. He saw a void in the display before spotting a
lone bottle of nail polish remover pushed in the back, secured
with a little red cap.

Willie brought the last bottle back to the counter with him
as if he were going to purchase it. "You've known all along.
You've got to tell the chief what the lady bought from your
store, and when. That is critical information in the investigation of the church fire across the street."

They were the exact opposites. Willie felt like a raving luna-
tic while Jacque was careless and unconcerned. "Why do you
care, Preacher? You've moved on."

"Because it's the truth. You've got to tell what you know."

He turned away from Willie as if he couldn't bear to look at him. "Le temps nous dira—"

"In English," Willie demanded before he could finish.

"Time will tell, but I won't. Only a fool interferes with a curse," the brother said, taking leave of the conversation on his perch behind the counter.

Willie thought about going over the counter after him, but didn't. He dropped the bottle of nail polish remover on the counter and carried the weight of knowing out the door.

Willie stumbled out the door like a man with amnesia. He stopped on a patch of grass that rimmed the sidewalk with Jacques's store in the background. He didn't know his name. He didn't know the people encircling him, and he definitely didn't know what to do with the facts he had put together.

"He didn't do it," Willie said, looking at all of them—Blanche, and Abe, Keisha, and Pastor Kennedy. He bent at the waist as if from a sudden pain. "I know—he didn't. It was Elaine Thompson, all along. It was his wife."

"Wait; that can't be," Abe said.

"Are you all right bro? It's gonna be all right. Just sit on the curb here," Keisha said, taking him by the arm and leading him to the solid stability of the ground.

"She bought almost the entire stock of flammable polish remover from the brothers there, did her deed, and came to Pleasant Harvest for the day." Willie said more so for himself. "Why on earth would she come directly over to Harvest with us when we found out about the fire instead of going directly home to check on her husband or anyone else she cared about at her own church? I remember now; pale blue suit, pillbox hat, and a smile to beat the band. All captured in a photo. We were all praising, but she . . . she seemed to be cheering. She wasn't devastated over the loss of her church; she was a spectator."

"This doesn't make any sense. My Aunt Elaine is the sweetest, meekest, most generous woman I know," Abe said, shaking his head as if he could somehow prevent those thoughts from entering his brain.

"Oh my God!" Willie's face lit with the beam of an 'ah-ha' moment, then immediately drooped. He brought his hand to his face to cover it.

"Bro?" Keisha knelt in front of him.

"She had his car," Willie said so loud Keisha had to back away. "It was late and she had parked so far away. I sent Mac to walk her down the street. He commented about the Cadillac Grand. That's his car."

"Why, though? Why would she do something like that?" Abe asked, reeling from his own thoughts.

"Why?" Willie parroted. "You said yourself that she was abused. Who knows what lies in the hearts of the scorned?"

"So what are you going to do now?" Blanche asked from the background. "Oh, you should call your friend the reporter."

Willie shook his head as if he hadn't thought that far. This was not about a story to him; this was a sad reality. He wiped his face with the flat of his hand.

Pastor Kennedy stepped down off the curb in front of Willie, which seemed to take close to a foot off his already small stature. "You're going to do what you do every Sunday, son. You protect the truth and be that lens. Go to the authorities and show them what they couldn't or didn't want to see."

Chapter 28

A Bishop's Worth

The second Sunday in the month of September in the year of the fateful Easter fire, Willie Green preached a message to his congregation from Genesis where Jacob wrestled with the Spirit of the Lord, saying, 'I will not let go until thou bless me.' Willie titled his sermon, *Before, I Let Go*. He had done his own wrestling with the Lord since calling both Chief Rich and Charley's attorney and sharing what he knew. It helped release some of his guilt and hopefully release his guardianship over the Harvest Baptist Church. Then spent four days at home on vacation staring into his wife's wide-nosed face and rubbing her roly-poly belly. It was the first time in the seven months of her pregnancy he got to truly cater to her around the clock.

Around the same time, Elaine Thompson admitted to setting the Harvest Baptist Church on fire. Her guilt did not totally exonerate her husband of his wrongdoings, but it was out of Willie's hand. He gave Alexis the heads up, and she was able to run another chapter of the Easter Sunday Inferno series. The *Inside 7* segment, the show Alexis was officially the new co-host of, was the only coverage he watched. His congregants let him know that there were several snippets of different courtroom analysts on various channels, speculating as to why Elaine Thompson set the blaze. Theories meandered around her wanting to hurt her husband by burning down his beloved church and setting him up for doing it as payback for the abuse in the process. The only quote recorded from her was, "I did it for Charley."

By day five, Vanessa was pushing Willie out of the house to a meeting of the Trinity Conference's Steering Committee and Executive Board. He put on one of his designer suits even though it was a Saturday. He didn't want to look like a slouch in comparison to the small league of pastors he was about to convene with. He looked forward to reconnecting with his new friend, Syllas Kennedy.

Reverend Kennedy suggested they meet outside of the Randolph Baptist Church where the meeting was to be held. Willie thought it was a good idea so that he could go over the ropes of what to expect. The old man was already there when Willie walked up.

"Reverend." Willie extended his hand.

"Pastor, for today," Kennedy said. "You know, for appearances. Wouldn't want the brethren to think you were talking down to me."

"I see," Willie said, taken aback. "Why don't we go inside?"

"It's so nice out, why don't we talk out here? Better enjoy this Indian summer while we can." Kennedy hobbled over to the gated railing. Willie followed, getting concerned about what his friend might share about the conference that he wanted to keep out of earshot.

"You've been mighty scarce these days. I returned your call to say I've been well, and your associate said you were out in the field. Preparing for another mission?" Willie asked, standing on a lower step that made eye level comparable for the two men.

"Preparing for this meeting, and you know, visiting other ministries."

"Well, I feel totally unprepared. I called Pastor Cartwright and told him Budget and Finance might have been right up Vanessa's alley, but it was not a good fit for me. I told him I could help chair another committee. So what do you say? Is there room on your committee for me?" Willie asked.

"I'm sorry, that's not going to be possible."

Willie tried not to be offended. He felt like a kid being rejected by the neighborhood clubhouse. He knew this affiliation was a bad idea. "Is your committee super exclusive or something?"

"Actually it is, but not in the way you think. It's what I want to talk to you about before the meeting. I am on the Bishop Selection committee. Three of us have been interviewing pastors on everything from faith, family, and ministry worldview to come up with our nominees for the opening conference. Each one of us had to come up with one name." Pastor Kennedy gave him time to let it sink in. "I choose you. I'd like to submit your name today as a candidate for bishop of this conference."

"Bishop?" Willie said, bracing himself on the railing to keep himself from falling down the remaining stairs from the shock. "You want me to join the ranks of those with self imposed titles?"

"This is not a self imposed title, but one granted on merit," Kennedy corrected. "Is the title Bishop mentioned in the Bible?"

"Yeah, but interchangeably with pastor or elder," Willie said.

"Faithful, sober, husband of one wife, hospitable, apt to teach, is that not you?" He raised one over-grown eyebrow at his inquiry.

"Or anyone else on the Executive Board." Willie realized he didn't know those people, and they didn't know him. "Probably?"

"I've watched you, Willie Green. The Lord allowed me to visit on one of the most hectic and chaotic days for you, and you still came out smelling like a rose. You were caring and compassionate even when you didn't want to be. You minister everywhere you go. You minister with your heart. You're my man."

Willie stared at the man standing above him as if he were a Jedi Master telling him he was the chosen one. It was humbling and hard to digest.

"Don't I have to accept this nomination?"

"Yes, then there is a six month vetting process. Campaigns can officially begin three months prior to conference. At the conference you will be elected and serve a two year term. Don't worry, the first year you don't even lead, but get a healthy endowment to develop your platform and approve conference-wide ministry projects."

"We're talking three years of my life." Willie did the math.

"Maybe more if we get the right man in. We're hoping to push the term to the limit to set a precedent."

"I have a wife and a child on the way. I can't forge that kind of time," Willie said.

They paused to say hello to a couple of colleagues who also got there early. Kennedy took great care in introducing Willie. He waited until the men were inside before beginning again.

"It's because you have a wife in ministry with you and such a supportive team that you are able to do this. The endowment will help you hire some people to help you keep it all on track. I think Vanessa will be ecstatic. Huh?"

Apparently he didn't know Vanessa either, Willie thought. Trinity was her idea and reaching peaks of leadership was her dream. Ecstatic would not be the right word to express Vanessa's reaction.

Willie shook his head. "You tricked me, old man. All the time you've been spying on me. I invited you into my cave, and you keep a secret like this."

"Caves are tombs, and you can't continue to bury yourself inside one. You've shown and proven you have a broader defi- nition of ministry. C'mon, don't fight me on this." This time it was Pastor Kennedy's turn to act offended. Willie sort of felt like a heel for disagreeing with him.

More and more pastors ascended the steps making it appar- ent that the meeting was about to start and Willie needed to make a decision. He already felt like he was campaigning with his fake smile frozen into place as he was introduced to the stakeholders of the conference.

"This is not something you spring on a man. It's a lot to think about, and you know my personal feelings about those self-aggrandizing hierarchies," Willie whispered as a few oth- ers followed suit and took in the warmth of the day before sitting in the brisk air-conditioning throughout the meeting.

"That is why out of all the people I interviewed, you are the man for the job, because you question the status-quo. I believe in you."

Willie laughed. "This is irony at its finest."

"God's intervention. Maybe it is your destiny to prove a bishop's worth." He turned on unsteady hips to make his way inside. "I can submit your name now or not. It's your call unless you need to talk it over with Vanessa and clear it with her first."

Maybe this was his destiny, Willie thought. Pastor Kennedy had raised many strong arguments. None were as convincing as his last off-handed comment about his wife, and for that reason alone did he say yes to the nomination of Bishop.

Epilogue

Vanessa went along for the ride with her family on a drive-by. Willie, Keisha, and Paul were her accomplices as she once again broke the rules her obstetrician put in place for her bed rest. Typically they would take Vanessa to her bi-weekly, turned weekly, appointments, and then off on some excursion that usually ended at some restaurant.

Vanessa was playing a game with her condition. Each time her doctor would report how pleased she was with Vanessa and the baby's progression, she would also warn her to be diligently well-rested as she neared her due date. She felt like a player in the game of baseball, sneaking off base and hoping not to get caught. One time they drove by the bridal shop so that Vanessa could see her baby sister in her top two choices of bridal gowns. She sat in a chair provided by the boutique the entire time while the guys sat in the car. Another time she met the wedding entertainer, a guy by the name of Phil Harmonic, who could play "Handel's Messiah" and a host of classic love ballads like Billy Preston's, "You Are So Beautiful" on the harmonica. Just last week, they drove past the reception hall for a cake tasting. Most times she was so far off base she slid into home exhausted and barely able to make it up her stairs to bed.

Each time, Willie would forbid another eventful outing, and each time, Vanessa would rationalize that the activity required limited mobility, and that it was okay since they were already out. Plus, her sister's wedding was two months away. Although she was five weeks away from delivery, it was Vanessa's duty, being her closest relative, to celebrate each milestone leading up to her sister's big day.

Today was not the typical joy ride. It was Vanessa and Willie's anniversary, and since she was limited physically by the pregnancy, she figured she was due a special outing. They started off the day at the doctor's. Vanessa didn't know whether it was her fluid samples or if it were because her legs were the size of tree trunks that led her doctor to threaten to induce labor before her due date. The plan was to go with Keisha and Paul to the courthouse so that her sister and soon to be brother-in-law could file for a marriage license. As it stood, any celebration would be limited to driving past the colonel for a bucket of his southern fried hospitality to go.

Vanessa reclined the seat on the passenger side of Willie's car. Baby Green was turning somersaults in her belly. She couldn't get comfortable as she waited with Willie outside the courthouse. She was anxious and eager to get back home, prop her feet up and maybe work on her book before dinner. Her tunnel vision, as it related to working on translating her spiritual advice into a helpful guide for the modern day Christian, gave way to the light. She was seeing the end. Soon she and Luella would have the tedious job of editing the manuscript and making connections in the publishing world. She hoped to birth the completed manuscript around the same time she birthed her son. It appeared he would beat her manuscript to the punch.

"You never told me what committee you ended up joining?" Vanessa said to Willie. She was thinking about how a published book would hallmark her triumphant return to the Trinity Conference leadership in time for the Inaugural session and boost her credibility among her colleagues.

"Huh?" Willie responded.

Vanessa readjusted herself again to sit sideways and address her husband. "Trinity. You told me about Pastor Cartwright's concerns and gave me the notes from the Budget and Finance committee, but you never told me what committee you either joined or are chairing."

"Oh, I'm helping with Public Relations with Pastor Mason from Colonial Beach." Willie waved it off like it was no big deal without as much as a glance in Vanessa's direction.

Vanessa let out a puff of air. "I know you don't appreciate me getting the church, and now, you, personally involved in the conference. You were right; this is my deal. You know if circumstances were different, I would be representing Pleasant Harvest myself."

"I'm in it now." Willie patted her leg although she noticed his focus was still out the front windshield.

"Willie?" Vanessa said to break her husband's apparent trance, her left hand pulling at his forearm. "Look at me, honey."

Vanessa figured he was upset, but was unprepared for Willie to meet her stare with what she could only describe as grave concern. She felt the equivalent of a gail force that sent a chill through her. It remained after he looked away.

"What?" Vanessa asked, rubbing her belly, now in hopes of calming the activity in her womb.

"Nothing, Vanessa. I've got to get you home. As far as I am concerned, all Trinity Conference business and conversations about said business can wait until after my son is born." He huffed. "Where are they?"

"I have no idea. Apparently, a lot of people want to get married." She turned her attention to the front windshield also.

Vanessa sat forward when she saw a couple exit from the front door of the courthouse, thinking it was her M.I.A. sister and fiancé. They had been inside for well over the thirty minutes they said it would take. She sat back against the seat when the elegantly dressed pair proved to be complete strangers. She felt Willie hunch her to take a closer look at the couple that she had dismissed. The man was in a tasteful black pinstripe suit with a thin red tie. The woman was in a meticulously tailored, yet delicately detailed off white suite. Her skirt barely concealed a pale blue garter she wore on her right thigh. They were headed toward a Toyota Avalon parked not too far from them with a sign that read *Just Married* in the back window.

This made Vanessa sit as far forward as her stomach would allow. The man was Abe Townsend, the pastor who took Willie's place. The woman was Blanche Seward, Vanessa's nemesis who had dated Willie before her and maliciously blabbed Vanessa's financial blunders to Willie's entire congregation before their churches combined.

"Townsend and Blanche?" Vanessa exclaimed.

"And the preacher says, 'Judge not,'" Willie said. "Besides, I told you that they were together."

Vanessa watched Willie slouch down in his seat so not to be seen. Vanessa did the same until she realized it was ridiculous to do so. "Yeah, but I didn't know you meant together, together."

Willie and Vanessa watched the couple almost eye level to the dashboard. Abe opened the door for his new bride who clutched a small mini bouquet of off-white lilies. He brought her forward in an embrace that ended in a passionate kiss before assisting her into her seat. Abe jogged around to the driver's side as if he couldn't wait to whisk his bride away. They watched Pastor and First Lady Townsend until they pulled off and the sign was no longer readable from their windshield view.

"Like boiled eggs and peanut butter; a weird combination." Willie said, using his forearm to push himself up.

"What's that, preacher? Did I hear, 'Judge not,'" Vanessa said, although she wanted in on this game too. "I think they're more like pot roast and pancakes."

Vanesssa noticed her husband of exactly one year soberly staring at her before saying, "September twenty-second."

The smile that crossed Vanessa's face quickly got compacted into a scowl. "That harlot stole my wedding day."

He reached out and stroked the cheek of her outraged face. "But she didn't steal your man."

They kissed like two teenagers on a date. Vanessa squirmed against the armrest, cup holders and even her own belly that did not allow her to get as close to her husband as she wanted. She was both chilled and on fire. They were startled by a slam on the driver's side window. Keisha and Paul had returned and her sister had slapped the official document up against the glass for them to see.

Vanessa was jostled. Her heart rate seemed to escalate. Keisha opened the door to the backseat and was talking a mile a minute. She'd asked Willie to get out and take a picture of her, Paul, and the license for her memory book. Everyone seemed to be moving so quickly. The door was ajar and Vanessa felt a rush of wind that didn't exist. She pulled her jacket around her as best she could and held it. She wanted someone to close the door. She wanted someone to tell her why her head was suddenly spinning.

"Did you see Minister Townsend and Blanche Seward?" Paul asked from directly behind her as he entered the car first after the photo shoot.

"Now you know I am too through," Keisha said, poking her head into the backseat and into their conversation before sitting down. "How dare they get married before me?"

How dare she get married on my day, Vanessa wanted to chime in, but she couldn't speak. She was attuned to chaos, noise, and how weak she was feeling. Vanessa felt the jolt of each car door as it slammed shut; one, two, three. She wished they'd stop slamming doors. She wished they'd stop talking. Something was wrong.

"Guys, guys, I think I am going to be sick, or I'm already sick," Vanessa said, clutching her head with one hand and her belly with another.

"Huh? What?" came the peanut gallery in the backseat.

Vanessa looked down at her stomach and held her belly as she rode a wave of either nausea or a sinking feeling of dread. All she wanted to do was go lie down. She thought about what her obstetrician had said about delivering early. Her face must have given it away, because Willie began to look around frantically as if the courthouse somehow had a medical wing.

"Sick as in put in a call to Dr. Ryan, sick, or sick as in get you to the hospital?" Willie asked.

"Both," Vanessa replied.

Her announcement caused a wave of hysteria among her fellow passengers.

Vanessa could feel that her sister had moved over right behind her left shoulder, "Oh my goodness, sis. Is it you? Is it the baby? Is it labor? What's the doctor's number?" Keisha asked, pulling out her phone.

"I got it," Willie cried out. But he didn't. He looked around as if the number fell from the sky onto the ground. Twice he reached for his wallet in his back pocket, but never retrieved anything.

"It's . . ." Vanessa began, but no one was listening.

Paul was busying himself with the touch screen and GPS on his phone, "The nearest hospitals are in Cheverly or Greenbelt."

"Don't you dare. Willie, I want to go to DC, Washington Hospital Center, where my doctor does her deliveries. We can make it. They will more than likely have to induce my labor if it is serious," Vanessa said more adamantly than she wanted due to an unexpected cramp. "I want my luxury birthing suite!"

"You think the baby may come — today?" Willie asked.

"Oh my God," Paul said as if Vanessa were delivering right there, right now, in the car.

"If this baby shows off and comes this early, he's getting put in the wedding party, even if someone has to roll him down the aisle in a wagon." Keisha was serious.

"Not now, Keisha," Willie shouted over his shoulder.

Vanessa imagined this was how it felt to be on the ship with Apostle Paul to Malta when the tides suddenly changed and shipwreck was imminent. People panicked. Vanessa remembered preaching in her sermon that everything would be all right, and that God would deliver the crew safely on shore. That's what Vanessa chose to believe. She had done her own battling with fear during the entire pregnancy. She believed whatever was going on inside her belly would be okay. It had to be. Fear would not win.

"Willie, honey, I need you to snap out of it and drive. Paul, put the GPS away and pray. And Keisha, stop thinking about only yourself and that doggone wedding of yours and hold my hand," Vanessa ordered with a quiet strength.

The foursome arrived like a mass tidal wave in the emergency room of Washington Hospital Center along with Luella and Mrs. Grant who were called by Paul at the onslaught of the frenzy. Willie and Vanessa were removed from the crowd, triaged, and moved to the Labor and Delivery floor. Vanessa tried to ignore the prodding, the tests, and the monitors. Willie, on the other hand, paced the floor. Vanessa wondered *If*

Willie was this nervous now, how would he manage when the baby got here?

The nurses attending to Vanessa had little to say as they carried out the orders of Dr. Ryan. When Dr. Ryan had arrived, she scanned Vanessa's chart and monitor tape before talking to the parents to be. "Remember we talked about the possibility of delivering early? We calculate the baby to be about four pounds, which is small, but a good weight as far as preemies go. Don't worry about the baby. I've seen a four pound baby nursed, monitored, and ready to go home in a week's time. But it is just too dangerous with your rising pressure to continue the pregnancy until you deliver naturally. We'll have to induce labor."

Dr. Ryan must have seen the look of concern on both of their faces, so she assured them, "We'll start an IV of a drug that will send you into active labor. It's like kicking the little tike out early. I hope you've made room for him at home."

"He's sending us a message that he can't stay in there. He must be about his Father's business," Willie added, moving to Vanessa's side to hold her hand.

"Well, the blessing is beyond just being on the way. He's practically here. He'll be here within a few hours," Dr. Ryan said, bidding them farewell.

Vanessa and Willie Green spent the remainder of their anniversary engaging in family ministry of another sort in a luxury suite on the fifth floor maternity wing. Elijah Moses Green decided to show off and show up six hours later to help them celebrate. Neither Vanessa nor Willie could think of a better anniversary gift. And Keisha couldn't think of a better addition to her wedding party.

Reader's Guide Questions

1. Vanessa predicted there would be a change in winds and tides. How was her sermon, "Battin' Down the Hatches," a precursor to the events that followed? Was she correct in her assessment that in the end all would be in a new location, but would fair well?

2. Why did Willie find it so hard to work with Luella as his administrative assistant? What made Keisha a better fit for him?

3. How do the brothers' beliefs prevent them from helping authorities like Chief Rich solve the case?

4. What purpose does Willie's cave serve?

5. Roy's mental stability is again questioned in *Soon After*. Discuss your opinion of his Tube Sock Theology.

6. What relationship lessons can Willie and Vanessa learn from Paul and Keisha?

7. Discuss Pat's decision to leave the anniversary celebration, urging Vanessa to 'get it straight' before getting in the pulpit.

8. Do you think it is necessary and always plausible for a pastor to work out his or her issues before leading a congregation?

9. Do Blanche and Abe want the same thing in a relationship?

10. Can their relationship survive without similar expectations?

11. Willie made reference to not understanding the mind of an arsonist. What was the intent and motivation behind setting the Harvest Baptist Church on fire? What was meant by, "I did it for Charley?"

12. What makes Willie a likely candidate for Bishop? What obstacles can you foresee for him, his family, and his church after accepting the nomination?

Urban Christian His Glory Book Club!

Established January 2007, UC His Glory Book Club is another way by which to introduce to the literary world, Urban Book's much-anticipated new imprint, **Urban Christian** and its authors. We are an online book club supporting Urban Christian authors by purchasing, reading, and providing written reviews of the authors' books that are read. *UC His Glory* welcomes both men and women of the literary world who have a passion for reading Christian-based fiction.

UC His Glory is the brainchild of Joylynn Jossel, author and executive editor of Urban Christian and Kendra Norman-Bellamy, author and copy editor for Urban Christian. The book club will provide support, positive feedback, encouragement, and a forum whereby members can openly discuss and review the literary works of Urban Christian authors. In the future, we anticipate broadening our spectrum of services to include: online author chats, author spotlights, interviews with your favorite Urban Christian author(s), special online groups for *UC Book Club* members, ability to post reviews on the website and amazon.com, membership ID cards, *UC His Glory* Yahoo Group and much more.

Even though there will be no membership fees attached to becoming a member of *UC His Glory Book Club*, we do expect our members to be active, committed and to follow the guidelines of the Book Club.

UC His Glory members pledge to:

- Follow the guidelines of *UC His Glory Book Club*.
- Provide input, opinions, and reviews that build up, rather than tear down.
- Commit to purchasing, reading and discussing featured book(s) of the month.
- Respect the Christian beliefs of *UC His Glory Book Club*.
- Believe that Jesus is the Christ, Son of the Living God

We look forward to the online fellowship.

Many Blessings to You!
Shelia E. Lipsey
President
UC His Glory Book Club

Visit the official Urban Christian Book Club website at <u>www.uchisglorybookclub.net.**</u>

Notes

Notes